FAR FROM YELLOWSTONE

I darted into one of the boarded divisions in the hold of the ship, and pulled the half-dozen planks nailed together as a door in behind me. A few seconds later, I heard a heavy slam as something thudded against it, but it did not open.

Carefully I made my way to the outside wall, the only barrier between me and deep water, leaned on it and listened, but I could not hear much, certainly not enough to tell if we were on our way yet. Then a sudden chugging shook me off the wall as if it were a wild animal. I sat down abruptly on the floor, and shook to my very bones. The sloshing outside turned to churning, pounding against the hull as if it wanted in, a tenor counterpoint to the bass of the ship.

Over it all, completely out of place, a chorus of "baa"s pitched themselves to be heard by the deaf. Both sound and motion were unmistakable. I was stuck in the hold of a steamship with umpteen crates and a herd of – something. Sheep? Goats? My back against a crate, my ears full of bleating animals, the ship pounding beneath me, I laughed till I cried.

I was on my way to the Klondike.

Books by M.M. Justus

Much Ado in Montana

*Cross-Country: Adventures Alone Across
America and Back*

Unearthly Northwest

Sojourn

Time in Yellowstone

Repeating History
True Gold
"Homesick"
Finding Home

TRUE GOLD

A TIME IN YELLOWSTONE NOVEL

M.M. JUSTUS

Carbon
River
Press

True Gold

First print edition published by 2013 Carbon River Press
Copyright © 2012 M.M. Justus
All rights reserved.
Cover design copyright © 2014 by M.M. Justus
Cover art copyright © Can Stock Photo Inc. / Paha_L
978-1492363590
Carbon River Press
http://carbonriverpress.com

ACKNOWLEDGEMENTS

Thanks to the staff of the many sources of Klondike research available in the city of Seattle, including the University of Washington and Seattle Public Library.

And thanks again to Mary Downs, for her excellent cheerleading, brainstorming, and proofreading.

To my parents. The three of us drove the Alaska Highway when I was fourteen and it was 1200 miles of gravel, an adventure I will never forget.

TRUE GOLD

CHAPTER 1

I will always remember July 15, 1897. I, like the rest of the hundreds of people crowded on every bluff and pier, stood and watched the *Portland* steam towards the Seattle docks. I left Miss Alice in the lurch at the Macombers' and at the mercy of Mrs. Macomber's wrath over her daughter's wedding dress, but after reading the newspaper Father brought home last night I could no more have stayed away than I could have flown.

A ton of *gold*. A *ton* of gold. I could not imagine such a thing. Surely the battered little ship should have sunk before it left its Alaskan port with a load that heavy. And that was just the gold. Passengers packed the space at the railing, staring back up at the crowds gazing down at them.

So far as I could tell, the whole world went into a frenzy when the *Excelsior* docked in San Francisco a few days ago and the stories flew as fast as the telegraph wires could carry them. A reporter from the *Post-Intelligencer* had paid an extravagant sum two days ago to be ferried out to the *Portland* and back on a tug just to get the story ahead of his competitors. To get his 'scoop' as the ship threaded its way through the Strait and down the Sound past Ports Angeles and Townsend, along Whidbey Island, past Mukilteo and then Ballard, where I stood shoulder to shoulder with jostling men, women, and children alike above Shilshole Bay, to the port of Seattle where doubtless an even larger mob anxiously awaited its arrival.

When it steamed out of sight past us the entire crowd let out a sigh and streamed back down the hill towards town. The only word I could hear out of the babble was "gold! gold! gold!" until another, one I had first read in that newspaper last night after Father threw it down took over its place. "Klondike! Klondike!"

Everyone around me was making plans, or wishing they could make plans, or angry because they could not make plans, to go to the Klondike. If a man was fancy-free enough, and had money enough to buy an outfit, he was the envy of his friends. If he could not go, if he had a wife, or God forfend children, or other responsibilities that prevented him from going, he swore and called himself a coward.

I saw more than one ragged man reduced to begging his fellows to grubstake him because he had not the pennies to rub together to buy an outfit. I saw children pleading with their parents to take them to the "K'ondyke." I saw women tearfully telling their husbands to go make their fortune and bring it back to them. It was all worse than a stage melodrama; worse because it was real.

I let the babbling crowd carry me back down the hill, but not to the Macombers' or to Miss Alice and my lowly position as a seamstress's assistant. No, I thought. This was my chance, and I was going to take it. I had been denied adventures since I was old enough to remember wanting them. But I made my plans in silence as I headed towards the streetcar to Seattle. I would not sound like a melodrama, even if there was anyone to listen to me. No one was.

* * *

My name is Karin Marie Myre. I was born in Norway in 1879, and when we immigrated to America we took as our surname the name of the town we had come from, as was the custom. I came here at the age of three with my two older brothers and my mother, who was pregnant with my sister Ronja.

I wish I could remember the crossing, even if my mother's tales of seasickness and cramped quarters and storms should have been enough to make me glad I do not. We arrived in New York City and boarded a train which I also do not remember except for my brothers' boastful recollections, for Washington territory. My father had gone there before us to find work in the timber.

My earliest memories are of the smell of sawdust and rain, of tree stumps large enough to build a house upon and logs bigger around than Father was tall being skidded down to the waterfront. By the time

I was ten there were six of us children in our small cabin. When I was fourteen, the year the world fell apart in what became known as the Panic of 1893, the mill closed and Father lost his job.

We left the woods and moved to the town of Ballard, north of Seattle, which to my eyes would have been an improvement had I not been put out to work as a seamstress's assistant before our few boxes were unpacked. I have always been good with a needle, and we needed the money. We always needed the money, since Father could not hold onto two bits to save his life, and now we were seven, with Mother showing no signs of slowing down. At least not so far as having babies was concerned.

It was not long after we moved to town that I received my first marriage proposal. Or, rather, that the man in question went to Father and asked *him* for me. Fortunately for me, Father turned him down. I do not think it was Mother's pleas that I was too young that stopped him. It was that he did not have enough money to suit my father. I was glad, because he was not exciting enough for me.

And so it went. My father could not find work. I have to admit it was not for lack of trying; because of the Panic thousands of men could not find work. But the reasons did not matter. If it had not been for the clams and mussels we children scavenged on the beach, we would have gone hungry more than once. Lars and John left home to go to sea, my younger brother and sisters were too young for anyone to want to pay them to do anything, and that left me.

Miss Alice took me with her when she went to pay calls on her customers, to fetch and carry and hold, and I saw the insides of big houses full of fine things and ladies whose servants received more pay than I did for less skill.

Oh, she was good to me, taught me how to make French tucks and gave me extra for the crocheted lace I made with the fine thread from the shop, but she was a working woman, too. All of the fine cloth and materials passing through our hands were for other people.

Miss Alice often talked about her Matthew who'd been a soldier, fighting the Indians before I was born. How he'd promised her all the fine cloth she wanted, and the house and whatnot, when he came home. Made him sound like a proper savior. And then he had died a hero, and left her with nothing.

It was, in its own way, as bad as my mother's own situation. If I was going to have any fine things, make anything at all of myself, it was going to have to be by the work of my own hands.

* * *

I was eighteen the day the *Portland* arrived. Eighteen and every penny I made went towards the care of siblings who kept arriving in spite of the fact that there was no money to pay for them. Eighteen, with four marriage proposals behind me, and thank goodness that was where they were.

I knew I was desirable. My face and figure are pleasing even if I am not overtall and not willowy enough for some. My eyesight is good, and I am more than capable of earning my own way. People will always need a seamstress, Panic or no Panic.

I do not know which of these characteristics men considered so well, or if it was my thick blonde hair and my blue eyes that made them want me, but I had no intention of sharing any of it. Fortunately, my father felt the same way, but I knew it was because he could not afford to let me go. But someday he would find a man who could meet his price, and unless I escaped before he could do so, I would never have a chance.

Right then, however, I was no better off than the ragged men pleading with their friends to lend them the money to buy a grubstake, whatever that was. I did not have the money to buy a steamer ticket, let alone whatever a grubstake or an outfit consisted of.

But I was not about to let that stop me. I took the two coins Mrs. Macomber had given me as a reward for some little extra thing I had done the previous day, money I did not have to account for to my father, and boarded the streetcar for Seattle.

* * *

I was disheveled, damp, and exhausted by the time I arrived at Seattle's waterfront. My hat was askew, my shoes were filthy, and I had absolutely no desire to know what the hem of my skirts looked like.

I envied the men milling about the streets in their mackinaws and woolen trousers, their sturdy boots and slouch hats. They moved so freely, while I struggled for good deep breaths even with my corset laced as loosely as would still fit under my dress.

I wondered if I told the merchants I was making the purchase for my husband or brother, if they would sell me clothing – but no. What would I purchase it with? A smile? I would need to earn my way north as it was. Surely some good captain would have need of a skilled seamstress.

Yes, I was naïve. Some of the offers I received from those "good captains" as I made my way from ship to ship down the docks opened my eyes wider than was quite necessary. Apparently, no lady going North who was not attached to a man was considered to be a lady, and the term adventuress had an entirely different meaning in this context than what I had aspired to.

Besides, I could not count the number of men who had perfectly good cash to pay for their tickets north. I could not help but wonder why, if they had ready access to the sums of money needed to buy passage, they felt they needed to go dig for gold in the first place.

Those sums seemed vast to me at the time. In some ways, they still do. But they could have been entirely reasonable and a ticket north still would have been beyond my reach. The sun fell behind the mountains across the Sound, changing the sky from bright blue to lit by more gaslights than in all of Ballard. Ships sailed on the outgoing tide, and I stood on the dock watching them, wanting to weep.

Instead I drew myself up and deliberately strolled away, as casual as you please. I knew I could earn my passage north if I had a chance. What I had to do was force that chance.

* * *

Her name (I am informed that referring to a ship of any kind as anything but she is a grave insult) was the *Tacoma Belle*. The name was slapped on her peeling, dirty, once-white prow in sloppy, mud-brown letters. She chugged in from the south and slid into a space along the dock still sloshing from the departure of the previous tenant. She was a steamship, with one smokestack and two wheels, one on either side. She looked no worse than most of the ships that came into Shilshole Bay to be loaded with lumber, and better than some, and those had seemed sturdy enough. Of course, the lumber ships were not overloaded when they arrived, nor even more overloaded when they left.

I am no more a judge of seaworthy vessels than I am of horses, and I know almost nothing of horses. I knew I would have to take my chance, and here it was. I slipped into the crowd on the dock. The gangplank went down, and people and goods started aboard. I found myself some large crates and tall men, and did my best to make myself inconspicuous.

It was far easier than I had thought it would be. People were cheek by jowl with animals, crates, boxes, bags, and every other sort of container or conveyance for goods imaginable. The smells were almost worse than the sights. And the noise! I thought the lumber mill where Father and the boys had worked was noisy, but my ears reverberated with the racket.

I was swept along with my company of crates, kept my eyes down, and ignored several plaintive shouts of "miss?" as I climbed down into the nether regions of the ship. It was both bigger and more jammed with goods and animals than I would have thought possible.

A voice behind me said, "Ma'am? Miss?" A hand came down on my shoulder. And I'd been so close.

I sighed, and turned to look at him. "Yes?"

"Where are you going?"

I thought quickly. What would a real passenger be doing? "To see that my goods are stowed properly." Naturally.

"Your menfolk should be doing that."

Of course. Drat him. I drew myself up. "I beg your pardon?"

"You shouldn't be down here."

I remembered Mrs. Macomber's sharp tones, so often aimed at me, and did my best at a fair imitation. "You, sir, are overstepping your bounds."

Well, that took him aback, but only for a second. "I will fetch the captain. Stay right there."

You do that, I thought. As soon as he was out of sight, a matter of a few seconds, I darted into one of the boarded divisions in the hold of the ship, and pulled the half-dozen planks nailed together serving as a door in behind me. A few seconds later, I heard a heavy slam as something thudded against it, but it did not open.

I sank down on a crate to catch my breath. To try, at any rate. Corsets, being made for women, do not allow for much physical activity without causing the wearer much shortness of breath. I have always hated mine. At that moment, had I been able, I would have torn it from my body and flung it out the window.

If there had been a window. I peered around the shadowy space. Light seeped in through cracks in the ceiling, which consisted of boards nailed hastily down to crosspieces in the same manner as the walls and doors dividing the hold. Sturdy enough, but slapdash. Booted feet thumped on them almost continuously, dislodging a drizzle of dust that made me want to sneeze.

The room itself was packed from floor to ceiling and side to side with crates of various sizes and shapes. The only reason I had space to stand and sit was due to the shape of the ship itself and the sheer necessity for the human packers to have at least some room to maneuver in.

Carefully I made my way to the outside wall, the only thing between me and the water slapping on the hull, leaned on it and listened. I could not hear much, certainly not enough to tell if we were on our way yet. Then a sudden vibration, almost a chugging, shook me off the wall as if it were a wild animal.

I sat down abruptly on the floor, and shook to my very bones, as if the vibration would jar them out of my body. The sloshing outside turned to churning, pounding against the hull as if it wanted in, a tenor counterpoint to the bass of the ship. The crates hummed and bounced in their constraints.

Over it all, completely out of place, a chorus of "baa"s pitched themselves to be heard by the deaf. They went on and on and on, rising and falling as I felt the ship move away from the dock. Both sound and motion were unmistakable. Those animals were not on the dock, they were here on the ship with me. It was God's own punishment.

I was stuck in the hold of a steamship with umpteen crates and a herd of – something. Sheep? Goats? I could not help myself. I was probably half-hysterical by that point, but, back against a crate, ears full of bleating animals, ship throbbing beneath me, I laughed till I cried.

I was on my way to the Klondike.

CHAPTER 2

After a bit I struggled to my feet, fighting to keep my balance. This was not easy, given the lumbering wallow of the hull beneath my feet. It made my stomach feel odd, not as if I was going to be sick, precisely, but as if my insides were bouncing in counterpoint to the rhythm of the ship.

I wondered if what I was feeling was worse or better than my mother's tales of the journey from Norway. It could not be much worse, I finally decided, or she would not have survived the trip.

Perhaps I would feel better up on deck, where the air was fresh and I could see my surroundings. The musty, ripe smell of dirt and animals was almost enough to overcome me. Surely now that we were underway it would be safe to show my face. I doubted seriously that I would be thrown overboard, at any rate. What would they do, turn around and take me back to Seattle? Not likely.

Simply getting back to the doorway took some time, as crates and boxes and huge canvas sacks, each heavier and most larger than I was, blocked my way at every step. I did manage it, climbing over or detouring around them. My person as well as my clothing suffered, but what else was to be done?

At last I stood before the door. I pushed. It did not move. I shoved harder, and it did move, but only a few inches. Not enough to slip out. At which point it lodged up against something, another crate, or a pile of them to judge by the resistance.

Well, I thought. I had not considerered that. I sank down onto the nearest container, which happened to be a canvas sack full of what felt like pots and pans, and considered the situation. Obviously, I could not stay down here for the entire voyage. I had no idea how long we would be under way. Equally obviously, I could not get out without help.

I swallowed a first small taste of panic. It would not do me the least bit of good. After all, it was not the first time something like this had happened to me.

I could not remember a time when Lars and John were not 'rescuing' – their word – me from some 'peril' – again, their word – I had been in. It was not my fault I was born a girl, and so not allowed to have adventures. It was not my fault I had been forced to find my own excitement against the wishes of everyone who knew me.

But this time I was forced to admit I had two strikes against me. First, my brothers were not here. Part of me rejoiced in that fact because if they had been I would never have made it this far. A niggardly part of me wished they were. That door would not have stood against *them*.

I dismissed that cowardly thought. I could take care of myself. The second strike was that no one knew I was down here in a cargo hold unlikely to be disturbed or visited until the ship made port in Alaska.

Well. And so. Just because I could not get myself out by main strength did not mean I hadn't any other options. I could hear booted feet tramping back and forth over my head. It was as if the entire population of the ship was so anxious to get where they were going they could not stay still. I knew how they felt.

I stood up again, one hand on a crate for balance, and looked around. Surely someone would have brought a shovel to dig gold with – there. And a nice long handle, too. I hefted it, handle end up, banged on the boards above my head, and shouted. I waited. The boots kept thumping, the ship's engines kept roaring. And nobody, it appeared, heard me. Certainly no one called down to answer my increasingly desperate shouts. No sounds of crates being shoved aside materialized at the door.

I took a deep breath, trying not to gag on the rancid air. I would survive the journey if it was the last thing I did. Surely someone would come down and take care of those animals eventually. Surely I would be able to make myself heard then. Until that time, however, there was nothing I could do. At least not to escape, although escape I would.

In the meantime I was utterly incapable of sitting there and feeling sorry for myself. Besides, I was curious. And hungry. What was in all those crates? And bags? And boxes? Some of them had rattled interestingly when I clambered over them, and at least one of them had sloshed. I started poking around.

The crates were all nailed shut, and I had nothing to use for a crowbar. The shovel was too long to maneuver in the space between them. I would come back to them only if I could find nothing of use elsewhere.

Some of the boxes were pasteboard, though, and while I did tear a fingernail prying one of them open, it proved to be full of packets labeled, "evaporated eggs." Ugh, I thought. I dug deeper. "Evaporated apples." Now those might be edible. I ignored the small voice in the back of my mind telling me that I was stealing, which was ridiculous. First, compared to stealing my passage this was small potatoes, and second, it was not as if I had a choice once I had been stuck down here.

I tore one of the packets open, tugged a slice out, and bit into it. Delicious, actually. Tart and chewy. Considering that I had not eaten since breakfast, I devoured the whole packet and went looking for more. Surely whoever's supplies these were had not been planning on surviving on dried apples and eggs alone?

I tried another box. And another. But I was not yet reduced to eating flour or oatmeal in their natural states. Nor had I found anything so far to open the cans filling several of them. I wished most sincerely for the latter, as the dried apples had made me thirsty.

I went back to the sack I'd sat on and opened it, but it was not full of cooking gear as I had thought it would be. Several large round tin plates, much too large for eating from. Another shovel, this one with a short handle. A pick. A saw. Several bags of nails. Nothing lent itself to the opening of cans.

I wondered briefly what the miners thought they would be using to get into them once they arrived, and almost sliced my hand on an axe.

I picked it up and hefted it. It was heavier than it looked, but I could handle it, barely. Perhaps one of the crates would have something I could open a can with, or maybe some bottles I could open without one.

I remembered how my father had used his to open the crates that held the gifts from family in Norway which made my mother cry when they stopped coming every Christmas. I slid the sharp edge of the axe carefully between the lid and side of one of the crates that had sloshed when I bumped it. Then what could I do? Father slid the crowbar in and leaned on it, but I could get no leverage. I was afraid to do too much because the bottles inside sounded like glass.

My mouth felt like someone had stuffed it full of paper.

"I don't care how many I break, so long as I get one," I said out loud, then wished I had not. I could barely hear myself over the ship's noise, even if the animals next door had finally quit bleating sometime during my reconnaissance.

I pulled the axe out of where I had wedged it in. I lifted it by the handle, staggering a bit as I regained my balance, and brought it down as hard as I could, sharp edge down, onto the crate. It stuck there, reverberating in a counterpoint to the throbbing of the ship. The crate itself was otherwise intact.

"Drat." I tugged at the axe. It would not give. "Double drat." Somehow the words I had been taught were more than enough for a lady did nothing to help. I took a deep breath. "Dammit!" Oddly, it did not sound in the least as effective in my voice as it did when Lars or John said it. Nor did it help, either, except to make me feel slightly better. "Dammit, dammit, dammit!" I tried out a forbidden Norwegian word. "*Farsken!*" It meant roughly the same thing, and still wasn't enough.

And with that I plunked myself down on the crate next to the embedded axe and leaned back. If I couldn't use it one way, I would another. But as I put more of my weight against it, I heard a distinct cracking noise, and the axe gave way so suddenly that I wound up on the floor, flat on my back and gasping.

"Ow! *Farsken! Farsken! Farsken!*"

But when I had picked myself up and looked myself over nothing appeared to be damaged any further except my dignity, with the possibility of another bruise or two to add to my collection.

But the axe was lying on the floor next to where I had been. And so was the side of the crate.

I leaned over and peered inside. Bottles! Just as I had thought. Big ones. Wrapped in some sort of padding that wasn't paper and wasn't cotton, that curled in little streamers when I pulled one out. It was heavy and full. The top had a cork in it, coated in wax, I supposed to keep it from popping out when the crate was roughly handled.

It was a simple matter to scrape the wax off, but the cork stymied me momentarily until I went back to the bag that had held my axe and pulled out the sack of nails. Using main strength and awkwardness, as Mama would say, I forced that nail into the cork until it broke through to the inside of the bottle, then pulled it out. A small gush of liquid followed it, wetting my hands. I licked them. The flavor made my tongue burn.

Oh, no, I almost wailed.

I knew what alcohol was. Anyone who grows up in a logging camp knows what demon whiskey, as my mother called it, is. I had only tasted it once, when I'd picked up Father's almost empty glass and managed to down the last slip before he could get it back from me. It had made me sick then. But I had only been five years old at the time.

It was liquid, though. And my mouth was so dry, and I was so tired of wrestling crates and boxes and bags and the heavy axe. I got a grip on the bottle and, putting the cork to my lips, drank. Or tried to. The liquor burned my lips and my tongue and clear down the back of my throat. It scalded away the dryness and what felt like most of the insides of my mouth along with it. One swallow was plenty. I dropped the bottle and it rolled into another crate, dispensing a small brown stream of liquid across the floor.

I stared at it. Oddly enough, the one thought that jumped to my mind was, "How on earth could Father enjoy that stuff?"

* * *

Nobody came down to my part of the hold, not even to tend the goats, so far as I could tell. If someone had, he kept utter silence and walked on cat feet. Or did it when I was asleep, for I did fall asleep eventually.

The ship churned on, mostly. The two times the engines did stop, it was not, apparently, at a port of any kind, because my sudden ability to hear the voices above me, if not their sense, sounded more consternated than anything else. I still could not make myself heard above them no matter how hard I tried. At any rate, both times the engine restarted after a bit and I could feel the motion of our passage again.

There was a small space between the curved hull of the ship and the first row of crates, and I used that as my necessary. There was not much else I could do, except wish I had a better way to hold my skirts out of the way when I used it. I ate apples and a lucky find of hard bread. I finally managed to figure out how to open cans with the nails and a hammer I found in the sack with them. This kept me from being forced to drink any more of that whiskey, which had added its stench to everything else.

I have no idea how long I was down there, days at least or so it seemed, when I finally heard booted thumps coming down the ladder, outside my door. I ran to it. Shouted. Banged on it with my battered hands.

"*Gode Gud*!" For a terrifying moment, I thought it was my father. It could have been, accent and all. "Is there a ghoul down here?"

"Give over, Hoel. You're hearing things." This one sounded solid American. And considerably younger.

He thought they were hearing things? I would give them something to hear. I threw back my head and screamed. It seared my throat and I stopped, almost choking.

Unintelligible noises ensued outside, and then a great deal of thumping and scraping. The door opened.

"Whew!" said the Norwegian man. He had my father's blond and fair coloring, but he was most definitely not my father. Or Lars. Or John. I swayed in relief. "This smells worse than the goats."

I stood gaping at my two rescuers as my surroundings began to spin. Hands grasped me. "Where did you come from?"

I looked up at the other man, the one who did not sound Norwegian, as he held me upright. He was tall and sturdy, and had thick hair the color of the mahogany furniture in Mrs. Macomber's parlor, not quite curling against the collar of his mackinaw coat. "Ballard," I told him. The world quit whirling around me and went black.

* * *

When I woke I was not in the hold of the ship, although I cannot say where I was lying was much of an improvement. I was flat on my back on some sort of hard bunk, covered with a stiff blanket, surrounded by a chorus of snoring bad smells. Not that I was smelling very sweet myself at that point. I opened my eyes and sat up.

A pair of hands propped me up against the wall. I looked up to find my brown-haired rescuer handing me a bottle. I stared dubiously at it.

"Don't worry. It's not liquor."

I sniffed at it. I was not sure exactly what it smelled like, but he was right, it was not alcoholic. I took a swallow, realized it was perfectly harmless if rather foul-tasting water, and drank until the bottle was dry.

"Thank you," I said, and handed it back. "I was so thirsty."

A wry chuckle. "I'm not surprised. How much of that whiskey did you drink, and how much did you spill?"

I stared up at him indignantly, but I could not deny I had at least tasted it. "Only a little."

He nodded. I was not sure he believed me, but it did not matter. I threw back the blanket and rose, or tried to. He put his hands on my shoulders and held me to the bunk, far too easily for my comfort. "How long were you down there?"

I started to answer, then realized I had no idea. "How long have we been under way?" Belatedly I added, "Where are we?"

"About a day out of Dyea, if the captain is to be believed, which I'm not sure I do. Are you trying to tell me you've been down there since we left Seattle?"

"Yes."

"Why didn't you yell before?" He was handsome, but apparently not very bright.

"I did. You were the first to hear me over the ship engines." I added, "Thank you."

He nodded understanding. "They are pretty loud." The door began to open, and we both turned to see who was coming in.

Whoever that was with my other rescuer, he looked important. And angry.

"– she is going to be all right. Wait." Hoel? my other rescuer, stopped in the doorway, but the third man strode forward, over and around bodies as if they weren't there.

I cringed back. Fear is what that sort wants, and I was hoping I could find a way to slip past him, out that door, and – who was I fooling? My legs were as jellied as lutefisk, and my stomach empty of everything but water, like the seas outside the cabin. I was lightheaded from lack of proper food. Maybe fear was not just what he wanted, but what he was going to receive.

My dark-haired rescuer took one look at me, then stood and planted his feet between the angry man and me. "She's with us, and I am damned glad that highway robbery of a fare we spent on her wasn't completely wasted." He turned back down to me. "You still haven't explained how you got stuck down there. We thought you'd been left standing on the wharf."

I stared at him. Behind him, I could see both Hoel and that man – the captain? – staring at him as well. Even some of the men were watching the whole play, although at least as many had thrown coats or hats over their heads to try to block the noise out so they could get back to sleep.

"I-I," I stammered, my mouth suddenly full of cotton again in spite of the water. Not that it mattered. I had not the first idea what he expected me to say after that speech.

My rescuer shook his head. "Come on. You can explain the whole mess later." He offered me his arm. After a moment I realized he wanted me to come with them. Hesitantly I stood and took that strong arm and, much as I did not want to, leaned upon it. His expression was as much of a glare as I've seen on any man, but as he turned back to the captain and Hoel he put a calloused hand on top of mine and tucked it in more firmly, and as he helped me over and around the men lying on the floor, I was almost positive he *winked* at me.

CHAPTER 3

We threaded our way down the hall, which looked as if the hold had been emptied into it. Boxes and crates and bags lined either side, the only empty spaces where doors opened into it.

All very interesting, but I was suddenly aware of certain personal issues I could not ignore. "I need —" I gestured, feeling myself turn bright pink.

"Oh." He headed to the end of the hall. "Come on, I'll show you."

My rescuer stopped at the last door and opened it for me. I went in and nearly choked at the stench. It was then I learned it is quite possible to deal with such things while holding one's breath, but I was close to fainting again by the time I opened the door.

He was still standing there. "Pretty bad, but better than the alternative."

I did not in the least want to know what he thought the alternative was. Nor did I have any idea whatsoever of the etiquette of the situation. "Thank you," I said in lieu of anything else.

"You're welcome." He smiled down at me. He really was rather tall. "Hungry?"

Do not misunderstand me. I was grateful for his rescue. But I did not wish to become beholden to him any more than I already was. Surely he did not want to keep up the pretense any further. "I do not wish to be any trouble."

The smile vanished. "You're now officially part of our party, at least until we reach Dyea. You need to act the part, unless you want us to leave you at the mercy of the captain." He firmly tucked my hand back onto his arm. "We've got plenty."

Oh, I thought. I had not thought of that alternative. For a moment I almost wished I was back in the hold. It would only have been one more day. It was too late now. "I will pay you back."

His eyes widened for a moment. Like his hair, they were a deep rich brown. "Sure you will. Come on."

He tugged me over to the ladder-like steps across from the necessary and nudged me up onto them, his hands entirely too familiar on my waist.

I tried to look down my nose at him. It was not easy. "May I ask your name, at least?"

"Oh." He chuckled, perhaps at the oversight. "McManis. William McManis. Most people call me Will." He cocked his head. "And you?"

You little ninny, I thought. Of course he's going to want your name in return. And probably plenty more. But was it safe to give my full name to him? Or to anyone?

His gaze went from friendly to cynical so quickly I missed the change. "Hiding's not going to work on a ship this small. You want to go back in your hole?"

No, I did not, even if it was safer. I did not even consider the propriety of giving him my first name. He had given me his, after all. "Karin," I blurted out. "My name is Karin."

"Nice to meet you, Miss Karen." He gave it the American pronunciation, and just like magic, his cynicism vanished. He smiled again, crookedly, as if he was enjoying our break with proper manners. He had a charming smile. Dazzling, I thought dizzily, trying to ignore it without much success.

"Let's go find Hoel, then, and get some grub." He nudged me on up the ladder.

I climbed. "It's a pleasure to meet you, too, Mr. McManis."

"Call me Will." He sounded amused.

Oh, no, you don't, I thought. Just because my brain had been too muddled to come up with a suitable pseudonym did not mean I was going to be overly familiar in return. I kept going.

* * *

I am forced to admit that without their help my situation would have been much worse than it had been when I was trapped in the hold. Food would have been the least of my troubles. If Mr. McManis and Mr. Hoel had not shared their rather dreadful provisions with me I would not have had a bite to eat but what I could steal, and the captain was suspicious enough of me as it was.

Even with their sponsorship of me, Mr. Trelane somehow found the time to stop frequently by the space my companions had carved out of the crowds on deck. He wanted to make sure I knew in no uncertain terms that he was watching me. He claimed, and with good reason, that he could not find a record of my fare.

"What does he expect me to do?" I almost wailed to Mr. Hoel after one of these visitations. He was bent over one of his cameras, paying very little attention to me. For that matter, he had not even paid much attention to Mr. Trelane except to tell the captain he would not trust the ship's records if his life depended on them.

Mr. Hoel was not, he had explained carefully to me, on his way to the Klondike to mine gold. He was a photographer, and expected to make his fortune selling his prints to both the miners and the press. He was quite convinced it would make him more money than mining, "and I will not have to dig for it," he'd added with a laugh aimed at Mr. McManis, who had merely shrugged and grinned.

"He expects you to give him payment for your passage, and he knows as well as you do that you do not have the money to give him, Miss Karin," Mr. Hoel said placidly. His way of saying my name made it sound as if he were treating it as a surname, not my Christian name. I did not know if that was because he thought it was, or because he did not approve of Mr. McManis's familiarity or my own lack of propriety. Not that it mattered. "He seems to think you should give it to him in trade, instead."

I swallowed. I knew what kind of trade. Contrary to my first impression, I was not the only woman on board this ship. Half a dozen adventuresses, in the local sense of the term, shared one cabin between them which they kept for themselves. It was a one-room red light district like the one in Ballard I was not supposed to know about, so far as I could tell. I had seen them inviting men down there, and the men going willingly, coming out with smiles on their faces.

But not, so far as I knew, either Mr. Hoel or Mr. McManis, for which I was grateful.

"I am not in that sort of trade," I told Mr. Hoel rather desperately. "And I am not here of my own accord." At least according to the story I had finally managed to conjure up when I was not within sight of Mr. McManis's smile.

I was rather proud of it, actually. I had been kidnapped, to be taken to the Klondike to earn money for my captors as a soiled dove, but had managed to escape and wound up shut in the hold of the ship. As for my kidnappers, I made a show, not entirely feigned, of keeping a wary eye out in the crowds of men on board. I also occasionally ducked away from men who, for all I knew, were perfectly innocent of the crimes I was impugning them with.

"No, you are not," he agreed.

"But the captain will not believe me. Or care even if he does."

"No." He reached over and patted my hand. "I could pay your fare. You could work it off by cooking and doing camp work for us. It will be some weeks before we will be ready to leave Dyea, and contrary to Will's opinion, his cooking is not what it should be."

"I cannot take such charity." Or become so much more beholden. "It would not compensate you nearly enough for what he would charge."

"It would be enough."

I shook my head. "I cannot." Besides, I meant to be on the trail as soon as I could possibly manage it, even if I could have taken any more advantage of his generosity.

He shrugged, but did not press the matter, much to my relief. "You stay with us until we reach shore, then. We will protect you."

I nodded. What else could I do? This was not working out as I had planned when I so casually strolled on board in Seattle. I was forced to admit I had not thought that far ahead. Or, I thought ruefully, ahead at all.

The last thing I wanted was protectors, whether I needed them or not. Even if I knew these men well, which I did not, I would not want to trust them.

They had no reason to want to help me. I still did not understand why they had. And even if they had a reason I did not want to know it.

I had not been able to trust my own father and brothers as protectors. But they wanted to pass you on to another man, to get you off their hands, I thought. These men do not have that control over you.

It was not my choice to make until we arrived in Dyea, at any rate, even if I chafed at it. I must wait until then to get free of this new debt. Most of my fellow passengers, male and female alike, thought I 'belonged' to Mr. Hoel and Mr. McManis, in a sense that outraged me when I dared think about it. It was only the captain who had decided not to 'respect' that relationship. Much as I detested the situation, I needed them. At least until I was off this horrible ship.

I would learn how to defend myself, or I would never be able to stand on my own two feet. I might as well have stayed in Ballard and married whoever Father chose for me. At least then I would have kept my respectability.

But I would not have kept my self-respect. If I had to battle for it every day of my life, I would. But I would have to win every day, too.

* * *

It was already damp and dreary outdoors when I escaped my prison. But the farther north we traveled, the colder and rainier and windier it became. A thick overcast draped itself over the gray and white mountaintops as if hiding something to be ashamed of.

A gleaming black and white whale leaped out of the water not fifty feet from the ship, and Mr. Hoel moaned that he did not have one of his cameras in his hands. A bear standing on shore was more fortunate, immortalized a bit blurrily on a glass plate.

Indians came out of their villages and stood on the rocky beaches watching idly as we floated by. One or two even rowed to the ship in dugout canoes, but the captain would not stop long enough for anyone to see what they wanted.

We did stop at the village of Wrangell, where a few men unloaded their grubstakes and waved jauntily as they strode down the gangplank.

"Where are they going?" I asked Mr. McManis curiously.

"Up the Stikine River to Telegraph Creek."

It was the first I had heard of either place. "Is there gold there as well?"

"No, just another trail to the Klondike." He sounded dismissive.

"Why aren't you taking that one?"

He glanced down at me. "Is that the one you wanted to take?"

I shook my head. "I am not —"

"Right." He scowled at me. For some reason known only to him, any mention of my kidnapping story made him angry, although since it did not prevent him from helping me I paid no attention, even if I wished I knew why it did. "We're not going that way because the guidebook says it's not the best way to go. Besides, our passage is paid to Dyea."

I gazed out at the town, which seemed to be built half over the water, and more noisy and raucous than shipboard. Suddenly, Mr. McManis was right behind me, his hands one on either side of me on the railing.

"Just like yours," he said loudly.

I started to look up, but he nudged my face forward again with his shoulder. "Is he —?"

He interrupted me with a whispered, "Yes."

I laughed, trying to make it sound carefree. "Just like mine," I said, then I did smile up at him. His eyes widened, and he took a breath. From behind us someone shoved into Mr. McManis's back, and the careful space he had kept between us vanished.

I could feel my own eyes going wide. "Mr. McManis!" He didn't move. "Mr. McManis, I must ask you —"

His breath brushed my ear. "Shh."

"I will not —"

"For pete's sake, will you hush, woman?" He twisted his head around and glared at something. Or someone. I stared out across the water, trying to ignore the feeling of being surrounded by someone who could, I thought, toss me overboard without even breathing hard.

But then I forgot about trying to escape. The carving appeared as we rounded a narrow bluff, which stuck out like a finger into the water not twenty yards from the ship. The carving was tall, so tall I had to crane my neck to see the top of it, roughly the size and shape of a telegraph pole. But it was far more elegant than any telegraph pole I had ever seen, elaborately sculpted from ground to tip.

At first all I could see was the eyes, picked out in black and white, which seemed to be staring directly into mine, watching me with disinterest and disapproval. Then I saw that the column of eyes belonged to a series of, were those animals? A bear, perhaps, and an eagle, and was that a beaver? A wolf and at the very top a solid black bird with white eyes and spread wings.

As I watched a live raven flew in and took a seat on its image, and emitted a cry that sounded to me as if it were berating us for disturbing its peace.

I let out my breath. The unending roar of the ship and its passengers flooded back into my ears. Mr. McManis had backed off a few inches again, and I could no longer feel the heat of his body behind mine. I shivered.

"What is that?"

"I don't know." He sounded indifferent. I could not see how anyone could be indifferent to such a thing.

"It's beautiful."

"Somebody put a lot of work into it." He shrugged. "He's gone now."

"Thank you," I said, but he had already disappeared into the crowd. I held onto the railing and watched the carving disappear as the ship moved on.

"It's a totem pole," said another voice behind me, an unfamiliar one. "Indians carve 'em. To tell stories, or use 'em like gravestones."

"Oh."

"You'll see 'em all over up here."

I turned to look at my informant. He was old, older than he ought to be if he was headed north to dig gold. His beard was dirty and his clothes looked like the photographs of the men who'd dragged bags of gold off of the *Portland*. "Do the Indians have that many stories to tell?"

"More'n we do, I expect." He held out a hand. "Name's Tripp. I'm headed back to my claim."

I didn't take his hand. I don't know what he saw in my face, but his expression was wry. "Thank you, sir."

"Better go catch up with your men." His face had gone from wry to cynical in a split second, then he let out a laugh. "If that's who they are."

I nodded and hurried off through the crowd, wishing Mr. McManis had not left me behind, and that I was not in the position of having to think that way.

* * *

We arrived in Dyea the next morning, in a heavy fog. I was not sure there was even anything out there when the lighters came out of nowhere to convey the passengers and their grubstakes, as I am informed the enormous piles of supplies are called, to the shore. All I could see was gray water as still as the pearly clouds floating motionless above the surface. Only the seabirds skimming between them made the scene appear to be anything more than two-dimensional.

The sounds of the crowd onboard rose to a fever pitch when the first boat appeared out of the mist.

"About time," Mr. McManis muttered as he stood next to me.

I glanced up at him. He was positively vibrating. "Why were you so worried about having to build a boat? These will be adequate to the purpose."

"Not where we're going, they won't." He turned from the railing. "Come on. The gear won't get into one of those all by itself."

I followed him. I owed them that much. We climbed the ladder down to the hold. It was the first time I had been back down there since I had escaped, but now it was an entirely different place. Pushing and jostling and shoving, animals as well as men, horses being led up via a ramp created from the planks that had been my prison. Voices, human and otherwise, echoed off the metal hull, and every booted footstep rang like a gong.

We found Mr. Hoel trying to gather the goats and rope them all together so he could lead them up the ramp and out. Mr. McManis took one look at the problem, plucked the billy up, threw the protesting animal over his shoulder and began barging his way through the crowd. Mr. Hoel, using Norwegian vocabulary I had not heard since the last time I had been near my brothers, picked up one of the nannies and followed him. I sighed, looked over the remainder of the little herd, and went for the smallest of the lot.

She did not cooperate. That is the most succinct description of the next fifteen minutes I can come up with. I wrestled with her, my hair falling in my face, my corsets digging into my ribs, my skirts attempting to trip me with every grab I made.

The laughter behind me made me whirl, and the little nanny got away again. "And what do you think is so funny?" I put my hands, bleeding in more than one spot from the nanny's sharp teeth, on my sore hips and glared at him. It was Mr. McManis, of course. "I do not owe you being laughed at."

"If you could just see yourself —"

"Carry them up yourself!" I headed towards the ramp.

"I'd intended to."

"Then I will get out of your way."

"Thank you."

Halfway up, I stopped to stare back at him. "For what?"

"For trying."

"Humph." I strode back to the nanny and glared at her. She glared back at me. "Hold still," I told her, ignoring his smothered laughter and her attempts to butt me in the knees. This time I managed to wrap my arms around the nanny's ribs. Before she could escape again I hoisted her, legs forward, and headed towards the ramp. Trying was not doing. I would do.

Mr. McManis's evil laughter followed me all the way to the deck.

* * *

Mr. Hoel had managed to secure one of the boats in spite of the great clamor for them. He had also managed to talk the owner of the boat, a short stout dirty little man I realized must be an Indian, into allowing him to place the billy goat and the first of the nannies into it. The moment he caught sight of me was quite obvious. His expression would have been comical if I had not had to apply all of my effort to keeping the goat from butting me in the chin with the back of its head.

"Miss Karin! I will have words with McManis. He should never have allowed you to do this!" He strode forward and snatched the goat from me, then carried it to the boat as if it weighed less than my little finger. He dropped it in, where its fellows greeted it with annoyed-sounding bleats.

I ignored his actions and his commentary, and headed below again. Halfway down, I crossed paths with Mr. McManis, his arms full of goat. "Did it get away from you?"

I drew myself up. I might have owed both of them for saving me from the captain's wrath or anything else he might have wished to visit upon me, but my debt did not include putting up with insults. "The creature is in the boat along with its companions. They appear to be complaining bitterly about their lot in life. I for one do not blame them."

Mr. McManis snorted, then gave me a closer look. "I didn't realize I was challenging you. You've proved yourself, at any rate. Go on and get in the boat. Hoel and I will fetch the rest of them."

I kept going. "I might as well take another while I am here."

I think he would have thrown up his hands had they not been full. "God save me from a stubborn woman. Go ahead. Just don't blame me if you get knocked on your –" I ignored the last of what he said since I was already in the hold by then, but as it sounded rather vulgar, it was probably just as well.

I sneaked up on another goat, grabbed it, and headed for the deck. I had nearly succeeded in elbowing my way to the railing when a large hand clapped onto my shoulder.

I dropped the goat.

CHAPTER 4

I tried to duck out from under the hand and catch the goat again at the same time. The hand was joined by a second one on my other shoulder, both squeezing tightly enough that my skin and muscles felt ground against my bones. "Ow! Let me go, you great lummox!"

"Not till you pay your fare." I jerked my head around to stare up into the furious face of the captain, then glanced frantically about. The goat had long since skittered off. Neither Mr. Hoel nor Mr. McManis were anywhere to be seen in the crowd.

"Let go of me!"

He squeezed even tighter. "You're not going anywhere until I get paid."

"But I was kidnapped –"

"Well, isn't that just too bad – umph!" And just like that, his hands flew up and away. I heard a jarring thud as I was swept up into another pair of arms, and the next thing I knew I was plummeting over the side of the ship.

Fortunately, the waterline, and the hired boat, were only a few feet below. I landed with a thump hard enough to jar my teeth, but was otherwise unharmed. I jumped up just in time to keep a pair of goats from landing on top of me.

"Go!" I heard Mr. McManis shout. "Get on shore and send him back."

I stared at the Indian. He stared back at me. "You heard him."

I don't know if he understood me or not, but he shrugged and picked up the oars.

* * *

The small boat wallowed in water nearly up to its gunwales with two people, four goats, and as many canvas bags, boxes, and crates as could be crammed in. I must admit the Indian handled the crude craft skillfully, much to my surprise. I was even more astonished when, having grounded the boat in shallow water still yards from shore, he gestured to me to get out. He grabbed one of the goats and dumped it overboard to demonstrate.

There was no hope for it. As the Indian kept throwing goats overboard I stood up on a crate, and jumped.

The icy water shocked me clear to the roots of my hair. Oh, it was cold. Painfully, rawly cold, and even if it only came up to my knees I was wearing enough clothing to serve as a boat anchor, most of it wet from the splash.

The Indian was already tossing bags and boxes and crates overboard, too. I tried to corral them and push them towards shore, but it was not easy. The same scene was replaying up and down the beach, thousands of pounds of supplies bobbing everywhere I looked.

I was lugging boxes onto the muddy beach by the time the Indian arrived back again, this time with Mr. McManis on board. I was wringing wet and panting, my hair straggling every which way. I had never been so exhausted in my life.

Mr. McManis, curse his black heart, took one look at me and broke out laughing. It was a big, rolling laugh I could have enjoyed had it not been aimed at me. As it was, I had no time for the likes of him. I had headed back for the last two crates when I heard his curse and a large splash.

Serves him right, I thought, and kept on going. This time, when I made it to the cobbled beach, I did not go back for more.

The shore was a strange combination of desolation and cacophany, with dozens of boats plying their way back and forth to several ships, horses and dogs swimming white-eyed towards the beach, the wide expanse of mud disappearing under piles of soggy goods, and the crowds of men everywhere.

Above it all, the gray sky hung low enough to touch, almost the same somber gunmetal shade as the water. Tall, dark evergreen trees surrounded the shingle like prison walls, and the low mountainsides behind them shone white as the mist lifted momentarily. White? But it was still September, and these mountains were not the high peaks of Washington. Surely it was the natural color of the rocks and not snow. But it looked like snow –

Never mind, I thought. I caught a glimpse of one of the goats, heading off into the woods. A quick glance back at the sea told me Mr. McManis was still splashing about in the water.

I owed them. This was why I did not want anyone doing me any favors, but I owed them. I went after the goat.

It was the billy, of course. If it had been any of the females, he would have corralled her himself, but since he was the adventurer, no one was going to tell *him* where to go. Including me, apparently, or so he thought. And what he wanted was a bid for freedom, at least until his beady yellow eyes spotted a clump of grass and his tiny brain could no longer compete with his stomach.

I caught up with him and grabbed at his collar. He ducked. I tried again, and this time I was successful.

The goat stretched and twisted his neck, trying to reach me with his wicked yellow teeth, almost as dark as his eyes. "You would not dare," I told him, and stared into those eyes.

"You tell him so," said Mr. Hoel, so close behind me that I sat down suddenly. I did not let go of the collar, however.

"He is not listening," I replied as Mr. Hoel came around in front of me and slung the goat over his shoulder. The goat bleated in protest but did not even try to escape his master.

"Samson is not a gentleman." He reached out his free hand to help me to my feet. "But I am. Thank you."

The goat was watching me with malevolent eyes. He certainly did not smell like a gentleman, either. The stench emanating from him was a vile combination of seawater, slime, and ammonia. "It was the least I could do."

"Is there anything further we could help you with?"

I shook my head. "You have more than enough to do for yourselves."

"You caught him, I see," said another voice. I turned to look at Mr. McManis, whose expression, I was surprised to see, was faintly disappointed.

"Miss Karin captured him for us."

Mr. McManis gave me a wry look. "Thanks, I think. Those goats are more trouble than they're worth."

"They are not," Mr. Hoel said firmly. "I will show you." He headed back toward the beach with his now-squirming armload. Mr. McManis and I followed.

"What on earth does he plan to do with them?" I asked.

"Everything you can think of, from using them as carthorses to selling their milk in Dawson City." He reached out a hand to help me over a fallen log. I avoided both him and the log and went around. I narrowly missed acquiring yet another tear in my skirt from a plant with leaves larger than my head and thorns up and down its gangly stem, which looked like an invention of the devil himself.

I looked longingly at Mr. McManis's trousers. He caught my glance and smirked, obviously assuming the worst. Why did men do that? "I wish you luck with the beasts, then."

"Thanks. I think we're going to need it."

We came out from under the trees. "I suppose I should be on my way."

His smirk went to a scowl. "You'd better settle up with Hoel first."

My heart sank. "Settle up?"

"He paid your fare," Mr. McManis said flatly.

I stopped dead, staring at him. "W-why would he do such a thing?"

He stopped, too, waiting in some sort of exaggerated politeness. Or perhaps because he was not about to let me flee without paying up? As if my wobbly knees would have carried me. "Because the captain wouldn't let us take the rest of our outfit off the ship until he did."

My stomach suddenly went hollow. "You are joking."

"I wish I was." His scowl deepened. "I'd never have tossed you into the boat if I'd known he was going to pull a trick like that."

"You would have left her to his mercies?" Mr. Hoel sounded angrier than Mr. McManis as he strode up to us. But, I realized with some wonderment as I watched him, not at me.

"You won't get your money back from her," Mr. McManis stated flatly.

I drew myself up. There was absolutely no help for it. I could no more leave this debt unpaid than I could give him the cash to pay for it. "What may I do to repay you?" I asked stiffly.

Mr. McManis snorted. Mr. Hoel shot him a sharp glance, then looked me up and down. I bore it, though I squirmed inside. "Can you cook?"

What did he think I was, an imbecile? Of course I could cook, and better than either of them if what I had eaten on shipboard was any indication. "Yes, I said impatiently.

"Can you tend camp?"

How hard could it be? "Yes."

"Can you tend the goats?"

There I faltered, but only for a moment. My family had always kept a cow and chickens, and I had done my fair share tending them, but I quailed at the thought of dealing with Samson, herding him and the nannies to the Klondike – to the Klondike? Was Mr. Hoel offering a way for me to pay my passage to the gold fields?

"Don't bait her, Hoel. She's scared to death of him."

I rounded on Mr. McManis. "I am not. Was it not I who just brought him back for you?"

"Right." But his sarcasm rolled right over me.

"I can tend the goats. I can tend camp. I can cook." I eyed Mr. McManis. "Better than you, I'd wager." His grimace made me want to crow, but I had higher goals in mind. "And I can sew, which means I can earn more than my keep. If you will let me travel with you, I will more than repay you the price of my passage –"

But Mr. Hoel raised a hand. "We will make our way over the pass and build our boat in a few weeks, but I wish to ply my trade here for a while first. If you will be so kind as to fulfill those duties I have mentioned while we are here, we will discuss our arrangements again when we are ready to leave."

So he wanted me to earn my place in their party. I could do that. I ignored Mr. McManis's muttered, "She'll have stowed away on another ship south by then.

I told Mr. Hoel, "I would be happy to accept your offer. Thank you."

* * *

It took the rest of the day for the men to finish gathering all of their goods into one place above the high tide mark. In the meantime I set up a makeshift camp at the edge of the trees, not that I had much to work with that was not soaked or packed away or otherwise unusable. Starting a fire was impossible.

Mr. McManis went by, almost bent double by a waterstained crate, and set it down next to our makeshift goat corral. He came over and stood looking down at me as I struggled with the damp wood, which was all I had been able to find. "That's never going to catch."

I bit my tongue. Constant arguing, no matter how much the man provoked me, was not going to earn me a place when they left for the gold fields. "It was all I could find."

"Come on." He grasped my hand and pulled me to my feet. "I'll show you where to get some dry."

I followed him. If he was able to conjure dry wood in this place, which was wetter than Ballard in November, I needed to learn the trick of it.

He headed for a cluster of trees. When we were standing under them, he peered up at nothing I could see. "There." He pointed, an expression of satisfaction on his face. "See those dead branches?"

Now I did. I also saw they were out of his reach, let alone mine.

"They're dry as a bone."

"But how do we get to them?"

"We bring them down to us." He glanced around at the ground, evidently spotting something useful to his eye, although I did not see what.

He picked up a stick. It was longer than it had looked on the ground, and it had a spread end where it had broken off of the tree. Hefting it, he jabbed that end at one of the dry branches.

It was more than long enough to reach the pieces he was aiming for, but surely simply poking at it would not be enough to dislodge –

"Watch out. There's a reason they're called widowmakers." He stabbed at one of the dry, needleless branches several times, and lo and behold, with a cracking noise it came loose and fell, right in front of me.

I leaped back. He grinned, and handed me the stick. "You try it."

I did. As it turned out, there was a trick to telling what sort of branch was truly dead and ready to fall and what sort of branch would simply shed debris all over me when I poked at it, but I was soon able to tell the difference. Mr. McManis picked up another long stick and it was not long before we had an armload of dry wood apiece.

As we walked back to our makeshift campsite, I knew I must say something, even at the risk of inflating his head even further. "Thank you. It would never have occurred to me to try to find dry wood in that way."

His expression was smug, but I could not begrudge him. "I know."

"How did you know how to do that?"

"My dad taught me. He used to be an Army scout."

My father had not even taught such tricks to my brothers, let alone to me. Perhaps he had not known himself, in spite of working in a logging camp. "Your father was in the Army?"

"Sort of." But we had arrived back in camp, and he dumped his armload next to the firepit. He began clearing my wet wood out of it, setting it along the edges. "Your wood'll be fine once it dries."

I set my own armload down next to his, and began arranging branches in the emptied firepit.

"Here." He broke several into smaller pieces, not that they were all that big to begin with. "Use this to get it started."

I glanced up at him. He was watching me with an expression I did not wish to see on his face. It was rather like the expressions I had seen on the faces of the men who had asked my father for my hand. I must be mistaken, I thought, but there was no point in taking chances, even as my bargain with Mr. Hoel brought us into closer proximity than I would have liked.

"I believe I can manage on my own now, Mr. McManis. Thank you."

"What? Oh, sure." The expression vanished from his face, leaving only the frustrating man I recognized. He stood up, dusting his hands off. "How long till supper?" He grinned at my indignation. "I'm starving."

* * *

The next few days saw us settled, after a fashion, in the town of Dyea. I use the term town in its loosest sense. It was a gathering of tents and mud and noise, with more ships full of gold-seekers arriving every day. Mr. Hoel and Mr. McManis commandeered a patch of ground along the river of mud ambitiously called Broadway. They set up two tents, one facing the street to which Mr. Hoel promptly attached a sign reading "E.A. Hoel, Photographer," and the other behind it where we slept.

Yes, all three of us. With all of Mr. McManis's goods and those belonging to Mr. Hoel which were not part of his photographic materials stacked between us, I might as well have been in a convent with regard to my virtue. Still, I felt a good deal safer knowing they were a few feet away.

It was all highly improper, but I had to admit I had forfeited all hope of keeping up the appearance of propriety the moment I set foot on that ship. My rescuers had not planned for a third, distaff, member of their party and I had not planned anything at all. It was a situation I was attempting to rectify as quickly as humanly possible, but in the meantime it was either share their tent or sleep outside with the goats. This certainly would have been a much more dangerous proposition no matter how one looked at it.

I, too, with Mr. Hoel's help, put up a sign on the street-facing tent, within a few days of our arrival. It stated simply, "Mending," and before the next day was out I had more than enough torn mackinaws, ripped shirts, and holey trousers to fill the hours not taken up with camp tending, cooking, and goats.

I was forced to assume another loan, this one considerably smaller, from Mr. Hoel for thread and a few other materials, the prices of which apparently doubled with every hundred miles they traveled north from Seattle. It was, however, the only way I knew of to earn the extra money I would need to both pay him back for my passage and to purchase an outfit to continue my journey.

I could not go back now.

CHAPTER 5

I learned several things over the next six weeks as the days became shorter, the weather worsened, and the crowds of argonauts came and went.

I had thought it rained far too much in Washington, that the wind which was sometimes strong enough in the winter to knock down trees could be frightening, but I was wrong. The wind in Dyea was constant, making the trees creak and groan, and it brought deluges of stinging, icy rain with it.

The clothing I took in was, as often as not, soaking wet when it arrived in the arms of its equally dripping owners. My own clothing was entirely inadequate to the purpose, but until I earned enough money to purchase more there was little I could do about it. I borrowed a coat from Mr. Hoel when I absolutely had to go out of the tent. It hung to my knees and the sleeves ended at my fingertips, but it was better than the alternative.

Dry wood became impossible to obtain after the widowmakers had all been picked clean. It would have made cooking even more a trial if I had not used Mr. McManis's trick about lining the firepit with damp wood. And if he had not strung another canvas over it all.

Mr. Hoel could not complain about the muck my customers brought in, although I think he would have liked to. But he tracked in as much mud and dripped as much water as any of them. He came back in the evenings with his cameras and plates carefully draped in rubberized canvas and retreated to his darkroom tent within a tent to develop his plates.

Mr. McManis, too, went afield every day and came back to our camp exhausted of an evening, but his activities were not as obvious to me.

"Where do you go to wear yourself out so?" I asked one evening almost two months into our sojourn in Dyea.

The men had just inhaled the supper I had prepared, and were relaxing by the fire, or at least no longer singlemindedly filling their stomachs. I had quickly learned to double the quantities I had originally thought adequate. Both of them ate more food, proportionately, than Samson, and he was the most gluttonous animal of my acquaintance.

"Working," Mr. McManis said shortly.

I looked at him quizzically, but Mr. Hoel smiled. "He packs goods on the trail for other men while he waits for me."

I stared at Mr. McManis, who leaned back and ignored me.

"He earns good money," Mr. Hoel added.

"It's better than sitting on my thumbs," Mr. McManis said, and shot Mr. Hoel a resentful glance. Was he getting impatient with Mr. Hoel's continued delay? I was torn myself, but then I needed to earn my place in both senses of the term. As anxious as I was to be on my way, I had to appreciate being given this time to prepare.

But my curiosity was still getting the better of me. "How far have you been?"

He grinned, and pulled out his book. I shook my head. He had brought the flimsy papercovered penny dreadful from Seattle, hot off the press, he said. It was supposed to have been written by someone who had interviewed the passengers of the *Portland* and gleaned all of their knowledge.

I did not see, then or now, how the reporter had possibly had time to do so, or how anyone from the *Portland*, which had, by the accounts I had heard, floated down the Yukon River almost to Russia and then steamed across the Pacific to reach Seattle, could know anything about the Chilkoot Pass.

But *The Seattle Post-Intelligencer Guide for Gold Seekers, being a compendium of all information for argonauts*, as the book was grandiosely titled, was the Bible so far as Mr. McManis was concerned. He referred to it whenever the opportunity arose, and many times when it did not.

Apparently seeing my expression, he said, "I was going to show you, but if you don't want to know –" He made to put the book back.

"Show me?"

"The maps in here aren't half bad. They got a few things wrong so far that I can tell, but not many." He gave me an I-told-you-so look. I frowned back at him. "Want to see?"

Curiosity probably did kill the cat. I had to see. "Yes."

He opened it and carefully unfolded a page from the back. It was much bigger than the book itself, and was, indeed, a poorly-drawn map with far too many blank spaces on it.

He pointed. "We're here." The small dot near the bottom of the page was labeled Dyea, and the channel of water stretching south from it had Lynn Canal written along it. A small line wavered its way north, zigzagging and twisting, until it reached another, cross-hatched line.

He put his finger on where they crossed. "That's the Chilkoot Pass." He traced the solid line further, down to a chain of oddly-shaped ovals and blobs labeled Crater Lake, Lake Bennett, and Lake Lindeman. Beyond that, the line became thicker with hash marks across it at intervals. "Those are rapids," he told me and Mr. Hoel, who was also peering over his shoulder in interest. Another blob, this one labeled Lake Laberge. More rapids.

The line grew wider and split into two parallel lines, I supposed because the river was growing bigger from the other lines feeding into it at intervals from either side. It was cryptically labeled Thirty-Mile at that point. Another set of hash marks. Past that the line was labeled again: Yukon River.

At last, his finger came down on a small dot named Dawson. Above it the words "KLONDIKE GOLD FIELDS" were written in an arc covering what must have been several hundred square miles, in fancy type rendering the letters practically illegible. "That's where we're going," he said triumphantly.

"You haven't been that far already, have you?" I demanded in disbelief.

He burst out laughing. If he had not been so fond of aiming that laughter at me, I would have liked the sound, but as it was – "Dawson's over six hundred miles away. Even I'm not capable of traveling that far and back in a day."

I knew my eyes were wide. "Six hundred miles?" Even to my own ears my voice sounded faint.

"It's a long way. More than you can handle," he told me.

I gulped, but no. I had come farther than that already, and gone to a great deal of trouble to get this far. I would not stop now. "I see it is a long journey, and will take much hard work. And you will not want to work hard all day and then tend your own camp and cook your own food at the end of it."

Mr. McManis rolled his eyes and folded his map back up. "I have been as far as the base of the Golden Staircase once or twice. Anyone who goes over the Chilkoot has to climb it. Right, Hoel?"

Mr. Hoel nodded. "It is difficult." He got up and left the tent. I looked after him, wondering where he was going, but he was back in a few minutes, shaking the rain from his clothing. In his hands he held one of his glass plates. He unwrapped it and handed it to me.

It was the first time he had allowed me to handle one of his photographic negatives, but I had watched how he did it often enough. I took it carefully by the edges and held it so the firelight shone through it.

It was difficult to make much sense out of it. All I could see at first was an expanse of black, which would be white in the print, and a white line streaking diagonally across it.

I brought the plate closer to my eyes, and the ragged trail resolved itself into dozens of small figures one after the other, hunched over by heavy boxes and packs on their backs. Almost at the very top I could see piles of pale lumps and squares, and above that a lighter gray patch that appeared to be a familiarly gloomy sky in reverse.

"That is the Golden Staircase," Mr. Hoel said. "Over a thousand steps to climb in deep snow. At the top is Chilkoot Pass, where the men leave their goods while they go back and get more, again and again. The only way to deliver an outfit to the top is to carry it. Or to pay someone to carry it for you."

"Is that what you have been doing?" I demanded of Mr. McManis.

But he shook his head. "No. The Indian packers have a monopoly on the Staircase, and won't let anyone else compete. I've been packing as far as Sheep Camp, though." At my questioning glance, he added, "That's within view of the base of the climb, and far enough for me for now.

"But you see," and his gaze was oddly pleading, "why you can't go any further. You'd never make it to the top."

"Other women have," I said stubbornly. "Mrs. Berry and her sister Miss Bush, and Miss Mulroney. My customers have told me. And I have seen other women pass by our shop on their way to the gold fields." Not many, to be sure. Dyea's male population appeared to outnumber their women by a considerable margin.

Mr. McManis looked helplessly, I thought with triumph, at Mr. Hoel. Mr. Hoel shrugged, as if to ask what did you expect, then said, "I will be ready for us to leave next week. Do you have funds enough now to buy your own supplies?"

I faltered. I did, but not if I paid him the money I still owed him.

"You may wait to pay me what remains, if anything, of your debt at the end of your journey," he told me. "If you accept those terms, do you have enough money to buy an outfit?"

I let out a grateful sigh. "Yes, I do. Thank you, Mr. Hoel."

He nodded. "You will go with us to the base of the Chilkoot Pass, then," he said, ignoring Mr. McManis's sputtering. "If you still wish to travel with us after that, we will discuss it again."

I nodded. "Thank you. I accept."

* * *

Our last few days in Dyea passed by in a blur of work. I took down my sign and stopped accepting any new mending, but it took me two days to finish up what I had already taken on. I would have returned it undone but I needed the money, and so I sewed by firelight deep into the night until my eyes ached from the strain.

I was extremely glad when my last customer walked away with his garments. If I never saw another piece of 'Klondike' clothing it would be too soon.

Honestly, never in all my years, and I first held a needle in my hand at the tender age of four, have I seen such shoddy workmanship as I did in any article of clothing labeled 'Klondike.' Seams that split, fabric that tore at the slightest tension, and fastenings that fell apart if a person even looked at them sternly. Poor design and poor construction. Even here in Dyea, where the worst the garments were forced to endure so far was a dunking in the sea, 'Klondike' clothing had been more than enough to keep me busy.

I gazed around the tent with satisfaction. The tools of my trade were packed away, and my purse was full. It was time to make some purchases.

But when I stepped out of the tent, I was startled to find Mr. McManis standing there, as if he was waiting for me. I had thought that today, like every other day, he would be on the trail earning his own way. I looked up at him in inquiry.

"You thought I was going to let you go off and spend your money by yourself?" he demanded.

I considered him. He stood there in his muddy but sturdy boots, flannel shirt, and wool coat. Only his lap-seamed blue denim jeans differed from the canvas trousers most of the men wore. I had never mended his clothing, except to replace a loose button or two. It had never needed it. Nor had I ever heard him refer to anything he owned as a 'Klondike' item.

I nodded in approval. I could rely upon his judgment, in this area at least. "You could be useful." Before he could smirk, I added, "You have had plenty of practice as a pack mule."

He grimaced. "If that's what it takes." He helped me into Eric's oversized coat, and we set out for the shore.

If that seems like an odd destination for the purpose, it was not. Many would-be argonauts, as Will's book called them, had taken one look at the barren shoreline and ragged town of Dyea, and decided they had seen the elephant. This meant they needed to sell all the goods they had brought with them to acquire the funds for a steamship ticket back to Seattle or Victoria or wherever it was they had come from.

We strolled from amateur merchant to amateur merchant, where the going rate for most of the goods was as much as ninety percent less than what their owners had paid for them.

I was tempted to ask what they had expected to see when they arrived here, if mere cold and wet and wind had frightened them so. But some, I knew, had been lucky to arrive here with their goods and not just the clothes on their backs, given the condition of the ships they had traveled in.

I did not even glance at the outfits covered in coal dust mixed with seawater into a concrete-like coating as we walked past. Nor did

I peruse the goods that had obviously been immersed for a long time rather than simply dunked in transit.

At last I found what I was looking for.

The man standing behind the neat piles of his outfit was only a little taller than my own height, a small, wiry fellow with a long black mustache almost as big as he was. He was neatly turned out in spite of the conditions, another point in his favor, and his piles of goods were actually sorted into clothing, food, and other categories. I stopped in front of his clothing.

Mr. McManis walked on a few steps, only then seeming to realize I was no longer with him. I paid him no attention when he came back and looked at what I was inspecting.

He snickered. "Just your size, Goldilocks?"

I glanced up at him before going back to my inspection. "I would prefer to wear clothing that fits me, yes." They were well-made, too, unlike most of what I had seen, and reasonably clean and unworn except for what must have been a relatively brief soaking.

Even his boots, when I sat down on a sack and tried them on, fit me better than I had expected, although I would still need extra socks to keep them from rubbing my feet raw.

The little man watched me with an anxious expression. I held up a pair of trousers. Mr. McManis commented dryly, "You know, even my aunt Anna quit running around in Uncle Martin's cast-offs by the time she was your age."

"You do not expect me to climb the Golden Staircase in my trailing skirts, do you?" I turned to the amateur merchant. "How much for the lot?"

I did not buy most of the rest of the man's goods, just his clothing and some blankets. His foodstuffs revealed a finicky, impractical taste which was not to mine at all. But some of his tools were of use to me, being of a size I could handle, and I purchased them as well.

Mr. McManis watched, and even nodded as if he approved occasionally, although he balked when I added two of those large plates used to sift the gold from the dirt of the stream beds.

"What are you going to do, eat from 'em?"

I ignored him.

He removed them from my pile. "Don't waste your money."

I put them back. "It is my money to waste." I added several other mining tools to the pile, and when he made to grab them I put my hand on his arm. "It is my money to waste," I repeated.

"You're not going any farther than Sheep Camp."

I smiled. "Perhaps not. If I do end up back here, I am quite sure I would be able to sell them to someone else." But I would not end up back here. This morning's work had made it ever more clear to me that I would not become one of the cowards on the beach running home with his tail between his legs.

In the end, I picked and chose my new outfit from half a dozen different men, and we made a number of trips back and forth to the tents, our arms full of goods. Not just clothing, but more blankets, a few more cooking utensils and other domestic necessities. I also bought as much food as I could afford, given the men's appetites and the fact that I had been eating their supplies for some time now.

Mr. McManis also purchased more foodstuffs with his own money, which I was glad to see. He also insisted I make a few other purchases I would not have thought of, which upon further consideration did make sense, so I made them. The variety of goods available on that rocky beach was quite amazing. It was more than equal to the stock of the largest store back home in Ballard.

Mr. McManis laughed hard and long when he saw me eyeing the sewing machine, however. Somehow its owner had prevented it from acquiring a saltwater soaking, and it was in remarkably good condition, its mechanism well-oiled and the treadle gliding smoothly. Its stand was of an ingenious make that folded the whole works up into a large rectangular box, about eighteen by fifteen inches by two feet. I thought of all the sewing I had done laboriously by hand in the last two months, and how much faster I could have worked and how much more money I could have earned had I owned this machine. I almost wanted to cry.

I had to have it.

Its owner was more than happy to part with it, and his efforts at bargaining were almost perfunctory. In a shorter time and for far less money than I would have thought possible, I was its proud possessor. I also purchased part of his stock of fabric, thread, needles, and other supplies. With them I could broaden my services and earn more along the way. Miss Alice would have been envious.

"Well, that's the final proof you're not going with us," Mr. McManis commented as he hefted the machine to his shoulder and we started back to our tents with the last of my outfit. "I'm sure as shootin' not hauling this thing over the Chilkoot for you."

I glanced up at him over my own load. "No one is asking you to."

He took one look at me and burst out laughing again. "I won't be there to catch you when you fall over backwards down the mountain trying to lug it up there yourself, either."

I did not favor him with a reply, but trudged back to our tent in silence.

* * *

It took several days to dismantle our camp and prepare for our departure, which consisted mostly of packing our outfits into loads that could be carried upon a man's back. We stacked as many of the bundles as would fit onto the cart. Mr. Hoel had obtained it from somewhere and he proposed to hitch the goats to it. I had my doubts as to the practicality of this. Since Mr. Hoel's photographic supplies alone took up an appalling amount of our cargo space, however, I rather looked forward to watching him try.

I do not think Mr. McManis was expecting me to have any say in how things were arranged, but I was to be their cook. The foodstuffs and cooking utensils for the journey itself would need to be readily accessible, even more so than Mr. Hoel's precious cameras, which would not feed us directly. After some grumbling, both men agreed and I was able to arrange at least that part of the packing to my satisfaction

We woke to the first sea level snow of the season the day we left Dyea. It was the first day of November, 1897.

CHAPTER 6

We set out before light, which that far north at that time of year was not as early as it sounds. Mr. Hoel hitched his goats to the cart and he led them, or rather pulled them, with Mr. McManis pushing from behind.

I carried a pack of my own with the bare minimum of what I would need to carry out my cooking and camp tending duties, over Mr. Hoel's protests. Mr. McManis had apparently decided to save his breath and confine his commentary to sardonic glances in my direction when he thought I was not looking.

The trail was wide and flat, and well-trodden to the point where I would have called the first few miles of it a road, even if it was ankle-deep in snow-covered mud. I had walked much worse in the logging camp as a child, and Seattle's city hills were much steeper than this. The road ran along the Dyea River, which was a tidy little stream chuckling over rocks and through more of that thorned plant I had learned was called devil's club, appropriately enough. Dark evergreen trees hid the sides of the canyon as it narrowed until there was barely room enough for both trail and river as they wove over and under each other several times.

There were, of course, no such things as proper bridges, so we were all forced to pick our way across the river when the trail ended on one side and began again on the other. I was glad for my new trousers, which dispensed with my corset. I packed it along, of course, and I had plans to make a new dress out of some of the material I had bought. I wanted to look a decent woman when I arrived in the Klondike, and the dress I had been wearing for the past few weeks was fairly beyond repair.

But I already suspected it would be difficult to give up my new clothing. The freedom of movement those trousers gave me was downright indecent. If it had not been for the coat covering me to the knees the view from behind me would have been indecent as well. But I found I did not care. I might even set a new style once I arrived back Outside, as the argonauts said. I could not help smiling at the thought, even as I stepped gingerly from stone to stone in my new boots.

"What's so funny?" Mr. McManis demanded. He did not look at all pleased, as he and Mr. Hoel fought with the cart.

"I am not amused, Mr. McManis. I am happy. I am traveling again. Every step now I am coming closer to the gold fields. And the trail is not nearly so terrible as I thought it would be."

He snorted. "You do realize this is just the beginning."

I wanted to stick my tongue out at him, then thought why not, did it, and grinned at his stunned expression. Oh, yes, this freedom was wonderful.

I started up the river bank, planting my staff with each step. "I know. We have six hundred miles still ahead of us. You want me to turn around because you think I will become a burden to you. I will not."

He gathered himself back more quickly than I would have liked. "What? Turn around? You will be a burden if you don't."

"No, I won't." Having achieved the top of the bank, I leaned down to grab the harness alongside Mr. Hoel, dodging Samson's teeth. The least I could do was to help the men get the cart up the – "Oh!"

It happened faster than I can describe it. My pack overbalanced me, and I landed face first on Samson's back. He bucked me off, I slid down the muddy bank, and sat down straight in the river.

Oh, it was cold! Colder than any ice I had ever touched, and my trousers and coat acted like wicks. By the time I scrambled to my feet, I was soaked to my waist and beyond.

Mr. McManis was doubled over in laughter. I glared at him.

But even Mr. Hoel's eyes were dancing as he fought a smile. "Are you all right, Miss Karin?"

I let out a breath. "It's only water. I am sure I will get wetter than this by the time we reach the Klondike." I scrambled up the bank for a second time and watched cart, goats, and men as they achieved the bank themselves while I wrung out the skirts of my coat. The rest would have to dry as I walked.

I headed up the trail without another word, my boots squelching with every step I took.

* * *

My trousers were still damp, no, wet, by the time we reached a haphazard collection of tents called Finnegan's Point, five miles upriver from Dyea. The men unpacked the cart and went back for another load, as it could only hold part of the almost 3000 pounds of goods we must take to satisfy the Northwest Mounted Police. The Mounties, as everyone called them, insisted that each person carry enough to make him self-sufficient for at least a year. Otherwise we would not have been allowed to cross into Canada, according to Mr. McManis's book. I would not have believed it, except that every customer I mended for back in Dyea had complained about the requirement. It seemed ridiculous to me. Were there not shops in Dawson?

This meant that the men would have to cover the same ground several times each day, but it could not be helped. The cart and goats did not seem so nonsensical now. Because of them we were much better off than the men who had to carry everything they were taking upon their backs, and cover the same ground twenty times or more before they could move further up the trail. I watched the empty cart rattle back down the trail and set to work.

This is the only place I will ever admit it took me the better part of two hours to set up our tent that first day. And I am still of the firm belief Mr. McManis hid one of the poles, or at least did not put it in the first load with the rest of them. It was just as well my staff was of a correct length since he probably would still be reminding me of my status as a cheechako, or newcomer to this country, to this day. As if he were any more a sourdough than I was back then.

My pack was also missing the one pot I needed, as well as one of the long forks. I had been exceedingly careful to make sure the canvas bag carrying the rest of the cooking was on top of the cartload where it would be accessible when we stopped for meals. Not that we had.

We had not eaten much of anything besides bread and dried beef for luncheon, and that as we continued up the trail.

What I had not counted on was that what was last added to the load would be first off, and what was first on, as last off, would be piled atop what was first off, and, oh, I refuse to explain it further. It took me almost as long to set ourselves up for the evening, find wood dry enough to feed a fire, and start some semblance of supper as it took the men to make the second round trip, and instead of praising me for having a hot meal ready for them, Mr. McManis had the temerity to complain I had "messed up" his organization of the first pile of goods!

"If you had not," I told him stiffly, cutting his tirade off in midbellow, "buried what I needed to perform my duties underneath your careful organization, I would not have had to 'mess' it up in order to cook you a decent meal."

Mr. McManis stomped off. Mr. Hoel burst out laughing. I turned on him, but he waved his hands at me. "Your decent meal deserves our attention," he said, but he said it in a way that made me understand he was not laughing at me. Or at least I was not the only one he was laughing at. He meant no harm. I was not sure Mr. McManis realized it, though.

"Next time get what you need out of the way before it gets buried," was all he said when we sat down. But he ate as if it were his last meal, scraped his bowl even after seconds, and seemed in a better humor after his share of the dutch oven cobbler I made with a can of cherries.

"Living high on the hog, aren't we?" he asked, although it didn't sound like a complaint.

It was my turn to be startled. Even in the worst times, my mother had always made making do taste good. "Was I not to use the provisions we bought?"

"Sure, sure." He added, "You're almost as good a cook as my mother."

That was probably a high compliment in his book. "I can do better with a proper stove."

He smirked, but not meanly. "I'm sure you can. So can she."

Did the poor woman not even have a stove? Was that why Mr. McManis was out here, to dig enough gold to buy his mother a proper house? I could remember a time when all we'd had was a rough cabin at the logging camp, but still my father had found the money for a stove, even when we had very little to cook upon it.

"Are you that poor, Mr. McManis?"

He gave me an odd look. "No poorer than you."

Which was not saying very much. But where, then, had he got the money to come north? He had paid for his steamer passage, unlike me, and he'd possessed goods when we arrived. I decided I was better off not knowing.

Mr. Hoel stood and stretched. "I will check on the goats." Since our supper had been accompanied by the racket of their chomping as they demolished any and all greenery inside their makeshift crate corral, I could not see what needed checking on, but I did not say anything. Neither did Mr. McManis, who shifted several times as if he were uncomfortable, then stood as well.

"I'll help you clean up," he said abruptly, and reached out a hand to pull me to my feet.

"Thank you." I had put a pot of river water to heat on the fire before we ate, and the warmth felt good on my hands as I scrubbed and rinsed, and Mr. McManis dried and put everything away in its sack. When we were done, I went to arrange it to my liking, and found, to my astonishment, that everything was just the way it should have been.

I glanced over at Mr. McManis. He shrugged. "My mother has a place for everything and everything in its place. It makes sense to me."

Then he spoiled it by adding, "So don't mess up my packing arrangements tomorrow."

I sighed and ignored him. After a moment he left the circle of firelight. I wished I could hope the devil's club or some equally nasty thing would attack him, but he was a necessary evil. In a few weeks we would be in the Klondike, and I would not need him any longer. I wiped my hands as dry as I could on my still-damp trousers and headed into the tent.

* * *

It was long past dark, which was coming earlier and earlier these days, when the men came back from wherever they had gone. I had changed into a dry outfit of clothing, my trousers and coat draped over a rope tied to the poles propping up the tent. The fire outside

59

had died down to coals, not even casting shadows as Mr. McManis ducked into the tent – and straight into a faceful of wet coat.

"What the hell–" He backed up, missing the opening and hitting the canvas wall. The whole tent wobbled. Almost in slow motion, I could see it fall, the posts giving way, and then the heavy damp canvas crashed down on top of me before I could move.

Mr. McManis was flailing about, I was trying to get the cloth off my face so I could breathe, let alone get out from under it, and over the rest of the racket I could hear Mr. Hoel laughing again.

"Damn, Hoel, get me out of here!" At least Mr. McManis had gotten his breath back. Even if he did not seem to care he was cursing in front of me.

I scraped the canvas off of my face. "*Hælvetes teltskit!*" I cursed the tent in Norwegian, not having any English words strong enough for the purpose. I scrambled to my feet and out of the mess that had been my neatly-pitched tent.

Mr. Hoel was staring at me as if I had grown a second head. "*Gode Gud.* You should not know such words."

I did not look at him, but grabbed a corner of the canvas. "Come on."

Mr. McManis fought his way free and got to his feet. Even in the faint moonlight through the clouds, I could see his face had darkened to a dusky hue. He took a deep breath. "What were you trying to do, boobytrap it?"

"I was trying," I said with as much dignity as I could muster, "to give my clothing a chance to dry."

"You might warn a fellow before you start setting up clotheslines right in the middle of his path."

"You might watch where you're going."

"It's dark in there, in case you haven't noticed."

"All the more reason not to go barging about as if you had all the space in the world."

"All the more reason not to hang your unmentionables where nobody can see 'em."

"My unmentionables! That was my *coat* you plowed into, in case *you* hadn't noticed." We were standing toe to toe by now, and I had no doubt all of Finnegan's Point could hear us, not that I cared in the least. "*Fórr nån toskhau!*"

"*What?*"

A throat cleared behind me. "I believe she just called you a cod-head."

Mr. McManis's eyes went wide, the whites gleaming in the dark.

Mr. Hoel added, "I do not think I wish to know how you learned such curses, Miss Karin."

"I lived in a logging camp until I was ten," I said, still glaring at Mr. McManis. "My father was a foreman there. And I have two older brothers."

"Ah." He sounded as if he were choking.

"So you see. I am not a delicate flower."

Mr. McManis found his voice. "A *cod* head?"

"McManis," Mr. Hoel reproved him.

Mr. McManis shrugged. "I've been called worse." He glanced down at me. "Never, I admit, by a," he coughed, "delicate flower."

I scowled at him. "Are you going to stand here all night or put the tent back up?"

Mr. McManis said nothing more, but set to work. He did not need to. His expression said it all.

* * *

The next day was almost a repeat of the first. The men left before light to go fetch the last load while I fixed a meal for them and broke camp. We then wound our way further upriver, through a canyon so steep and narrow that no daylight at all reached us at its bottom.

We passed another tent settlement in the gloom, but Mr. McManis, Mr. Hoel, and I were of the same opinion as to its suitability as a camping ground, so we went on. We eventually came out of the canyon into a patch of woods bright with golden leaves quivering with each passing breeze. The men unloaded the cart and headed back down the canyon. I unloaded my pack of cooking gear and began my work.

"Hello, ma'am. "

The strange voice made me jump. I ignored it, as I had no spare time to be sociable.

"Ma'am? Are you the lady who does mending?"

That made me pay attention. I turned.

The stranger was tall and broad, much more so than either Mr. Hoel or Mr. McManis. He loomed out of the trees like a stray bear in his gold-seeker's uniform of dirty mackinaw and canvas trousers, boots and slouch hat. His face was half-hidden with what I would have called a luxuriant beard if it, too, hadn't been filthy, as well as tangled and full of twigs.

"They told me you were here."

I asked cautiously, "Who did?"

"Fellers on the trail."

I thought he was referring to my companions, but his thumb jerked up the trail, not back towards Dyea.

"What do you want?"

"Ain't it plain?"

He turned around. I blinked, suddenly feeling less threatened. "That must have taken some doing."

"What'll you charge to fix 'em?"

"Remove them and let me take a look."

His face went red. "Ma'am, I couldn't do that."

Decidedly less threatened. "I cannot mend them in their present location. Mending is what you wanted, is it not?"

"I was hopin'."

"Then remove them. I will not watch you." I turned around. A few moments later a pair of canvas trousers, which did not smell as bad as I had feared, landed on my shoulder. They were not, thank goodness, of the 'Klondike' variety, so it had taken a good bit of effort to cause the rip from waistband to knee in the back.

I fetched needle and thread, and sewed them up to the sound of heavy breathing behind me. I did not turn around. When I was finished, I put them back on my shoulder. They disappeared.

In a few moments, a tiny stone landed in my lap. I picked it up. It was about the size of my smallest fingernail, heavier than it looked, oddly shaped but smooth, as if it had been polished. It shone with a luster I had never seen before but recognized immediately. It was gold.

My breath caught. "Thank you."

"Thank you, ma'am." I heard his footsteps retreating behind me down the trail, but I only had eyes for the nugget in my hand. So this was what gold looked like in its native state. And this was what I, and all those I saw on the trail, were pursuing.

Until that moment my vision of what gold would be like had been abstract. This was the first time I had seen a nugget, held a nugget, in my hand. Was this what Will insisted the streams of the Klondike were paved with? If so, now I understood. Now it was no longer a vision. I wanted more nuggets like this. I wanted them more badly than I had wanted anything in my life.

I sat there with that little nugget in the palm of my hand until the sun came over the cliffs, and I realized with a start that the men would be back soon. I had not even started a fire yet. I tucked the little golden stone carefully into the pocket of my flannel shirt. It felt like a talisman there, and I vowed I would not spend it, even if I was dying. Then I got back to my tasks. After all, it was only my first nugget. I would possess many, many more before my work was done.

CHAPTER 7

The trail became progressively steeper and more narrow as we progressed, and the snow deeper where it was not trampled down to the ground. We abandoned the cart when the trail steepened too much for it at Sheep Camp, where I saw no sheep whatsoever, just more tents, mud, and men.

From that point on I assumed the disagreeable chore of herding the goats up the trail while Mr. Hoel and Mr. McManis ferried our goods crate by 100 pound bag. Our progress dropped from five or six miles a day to one or two, as the men had to make what seemed like dozens of trips over the same piece of ground to bring everything along.

I saw Indians on the trail, packing for other men, but when I suggested this to Mr. McManis, he caustically asked me how I planned to pay for it. When I offered to help with the carrying, he looked me up and down and walked away without a word.

Fine. If he did not want my help, he would not receive it. Mr. Hoel graciously received my offer to help with the goats, and I divided the cooking gear into smaller bags on their backs and herded them onward, feeling rather like the goose girl in the fairy tale.

We reached a place called the Scales at the foot of the Golden Staircase in four more days time, and it was then I realized why Mr. McManis had given in on my accompanying them even after Mr. Hoel showed me his photograph.

Mr. Hoel had told me the photograph did not do the place justice, and he was right. Mr. McManis obviously expected me to take one look at the men threading their way up the snowy slope like black cording along a blank white expanse of cloth and run back for Dyea leaving everything behind, but he was wrong.

I will admit, here if nowhere else, the place did give me pause. The Scales, so called because this was where the Indians took off their packs to be reweighed and where their poundage rates for packing goods doubled, was littered with abandoned goods of all types. If a person had the wherewithal to cart it all back down to Dyea and put it on a ship, that person could have made a tidy sum selling everything back in Seattle. Here it was utterly worthless, the castoffs of yet more foolish men who did not realize what would be expected of them when they had started out so blithely weeks ago.

It all seemed so wasteful. I poked through the detritus while I ostensibly guarded our own growing pile of goods and kept an eye on the goats who were searching in vain for anything edible, the whole place being nothing but a wasteland of rocks covered in drifts of dirty snow.

The ideas some people had as to what constituted bare necessity utterly amazed me. I saw enough pots and pans to fit out a hotel kitchen, and a complete set of beautiful rosebud china, at least eight place settings, scattered from their crate as if flung in anger. I saw a crate of cans labeled 'Finest Caviar' and dozens of bags of flour moldering in the snow. I saw a Victrola, the wax cylinders cracking in the cold. There was enough furniture to furnish a good-sized house, and enough trunks to fit out several steamships.

One could have set up housekeeping right there and then, if the location was not so forbidding. And if there had been a stick of firewood within miles.

I did rescue a few yards of lovely wool suiting fabric from a trunk that had kept it dry, and a pretty piece of blue calico, but reluctantly left the rest behind.

A crate taller than I was drew my attention, and I went over to inspect it. A piano. Someone had decided the Klondike needed a piano, but not badly enough to haul it up and over the pass. I wondered what would happen to it, if anyone would rescue it and carry it in one direction or the other, either back to civilization or on to the goldfields.

When I went back to camp, the men had just arrived, with the last of the goods according to Mr. Hoel. Mr. McManis was sorting through them. I suddenly noticed most of my outfit was in a separate pile.

"What are you doing?" I asked.

He did not deign to look at me. "Sorting out what's going and what's staying."

"You could have done that in Dyea and saved yourself a great deal of trouble."

"Staying with you," he added.

I let out my breath. "Oh, for once and all, I am not staying."

He shrugged, and pulled out my sack of fabric. I took it from him. "This is my livelihood," I told him.

"Which is why you need it."

"Yes, you *hæstkuk*."

"If you're going to call me names, have the decency to call me something I can understand."

"I was not calling you names. If you do not wish to be called a horse's cock, then you should not act like one."

"Ha, ha." He sounded tired. Which I supposed I understood, but at the moment I was angry enough I did not care. I opened my mouth to tell him so, when he plunked my sewing machine atop the pile.

"Be careful." I grabbed for it before it could slide down into the snow, which would ruin it. "If I told you you would be free of me if only that machine went over the pass, would you think it worth the trouble?"

He actually looked tempted, but shook his head. "You're never going to make it over, even without that thing weighing you down. Haven't you had enough by now?"

"You owe me a trip to the Klondike."

"We owe you to take you as far as you can go. This is as far as you can go."

"No one said you were to determine how far I will go. I have determined that I shall go all the way to the Klondike, and you have no right to stop me."

"She is right," said Mr. Hoel. He, as usual, sounded quite amused. "I wish to go back down and take some more photographs. I will be back tonight. You will have solved the problem by then."

He lifted one of his cameras, which did not weigh much less than my sewing machine, to his shoulder. The pole attachment stuck out in front of him like some odd counterweight. He tossed back over his shoulder, "You might think, Will, about tools of the trade. Is her machine any different from my cameras? Or your shovel and pick?"

"Revolutionary," Mr. McManis muttered. But he did not mutter it very loudly.

I held my peace.

"You two are going to be the death of me," he said, not much more loudly.

"Oddly enough, I feel the same way about you," I told him.

"I'll bet you do." He eyed me in that unnerving way of his. "Why?"

That surprised me. "I do not understand your question."

He waved an arm, ostensibly at the men still climbing in the fading light, apparently at the whole adventure. "Why are you doing this?"

I blinked. "Why not?"

He frowned.

"Why are you here?" I asked.

"I'm here to make my fortune." He turned away.

"As am I."

"But you're a woman."

What did that have to do with it? "May a woman not have the same goals as a man?"

"Not the women I know."

"Who are these weak-spined women? And are you not ashamed of them?"

He looked taken aback. "Why would I be ashamed of them?"

I turned away. "You and Mr. Hoel will want my women's work done by the time he returns. So I'd better get started."

The silence ran on for a bit, then he stalked off. Sounds of canvas being shaken out and put over tent poles came to my ears. I did not go to help him. He would not have welcomed my help in any case. Well, and I had told them I would no longer need them once I made it over the pass. It was time I proved it. This night would be my last beholden to Messrs. Hoel and McManis.

* * *

Mr. Hoel had not returned by suppertime. Mr. McManis and I ate in silence, then I set aside Mr. Hoel's share to keep warm by the fire. A fire, I had to admit, we would not have had without Mr. McManis's foresight in adding to one of his loads that day with a bundle of wood. Because, he said, brandishing his precious guidebook, there would be no wood available at the Scales.

I suppose we could have found something wooden to burn amongst all the discards surrounding us. Somehow, though, in spite of the hundreds of men – and a few women – camping in the snow, no one touched the furniture, or the crates, or anything else that would burn. No one took anything. I wondered at that.

Mr. Hoel had not returned by the time the fire burned down to coals, either. The piles of his photographic equipment reassured me that he had not abandoned us. I left Mr. McManis to watch for him and took to my bedroll, setting my sewing machine carefully beside it on a piece of rubberized canvas.

I reached into my shirt pocket and pulled out my little nugget, rolling it between my thumb and forefinger. My other hand reached out to run along the edge of the sewing machine crate. The one was a pathway to the other. Carefully I replaced the nugget in my pocket, and, my other hand still resting on the machine, I went to sleep.

* * *

I woke in the middle of the night with ice-cold fingers. I could hear the sounds of Mr. McManis's deep breathing on the other side of the tent. I pulled my hand under the blankets and listened, but, no, I did not hear Mr. Hoel, whose slight snore I had become accustomed to in the last weeks. So he was still not back. I rolled over and went back to sleep, cradling my hand next to my breast to warm it.

* * *

He was still not back next morning. When Mr. McManis woke up sufficiently to realize it, he let a stream of invective out under his breath. He did not look at me, nor I at him.

"Look, will you stick around here and keep an eye on those stupid goats until I can go find Hoel and figure out what the hell he thinks he's doing?"

"I need to finish packing my things," I said neutrally. "That should take me most of the morning."

"Good. So you've decided to see reason."

I saw no point in arguing with him any further. He would do what he thought he had to do, and I would do what I needed to do. With any luck, I would have packed my first load to the top by the time he got back. And I knew exactly what my first load would be.

It did take me most of the morning to prepare for the next stage of my journey. I took my share of the food, and of the cooking gear, and picked from the tools I both knew how to use and thought I might need. Surely I could purchase what else I needed along the way.

I had no tent of my own, thanks to Mr. McManis, but I took a piece of the rubberized canvas, and I scavenged several makeshift tent poles from the abandoned piles so as to have something to prop it up with. I would manage. I began packing and experimenting to see how much I could carry, and how best to manage it so I could put my goods at the top of the pass in the shortest amount of time.

I would show him. By the time Mr. McManis reached the Klondike, I would already have enough gold to fill a sack I could barely lift. No, *two* sacks. And he would stare at me in astonishment, and he would never again tell me that a woman could not have the same dreams as a man.

It was dark by the time I had everything in readiness. Too late to start up the trail today.

I was still alone. I built myself a fire with the last of Mr. McManis's wood, and cooked myself a meal. I was just washing the pot and plate I had used, ready to pack them into one of my canvas bags, when I heard two voices that had already become familiar, over the cacophony of several hundred people setting up camp in the middle of nowhere.

"I am not taking her along," Mr. McManis said. Shouted, actually, since his voice was loud and clear above the racket.

"You gave your word that you would."

"Because I thought seeing what she'd gotten herself into would make her realize she was in over her head, dammit."

"She does not appear to be in that state, my friend."

"Well, she ought to be."

"But I am not," I said as they appeared in the firelight. Mr. Hoel lifted his camera from over his shoulder and set it down with a sigh. Mr. McManis dropped another load of firewood on the ground, picked a piece up, and flung it into the fire. It landed heavily, scattering both sparks and ashes. I brushed both off of my clothing and glared at him. "I will be carrying my goods over the pass tomorrow, and you cannot stop me."

"Go ahead. I won't need to." He sat down and added more sticks to the fire, but at least he did it gently. "I've done my best to keep you safe. If you're that determined to kill yourself, it'll be on your head." He stopped, and his face, in the firelight, went from resigned – resigned? I wondered, baffled – to angry all over again. "Don't tell me you spent the whole day messing up my organization."

I lifted my chin. "I have every right to pack up my own goods."

"Oh, hell." Hoel glared at him, and he added, "Look, Hoel, if she's the cause of the cusswords she can damned well listen to them. And you're not exactly at the top of my list at the moment, either, wasting two days taking photographs of mudslides. But I'm too tired to do anything about it now. We'll re-sort the mess in the morning.

"And you," he shook his head at me, "can wait until I arrange packers to get you back down to Dyea. With the sewing machine if you won't leave without it."

I would be at the top of the Golden Staircase for the second time by the time those two crawled out of their bedrolls. I did not dignify his statement with an answer. Instead I went to my bedroll, not to sleep, but to wait for dawn.

* * *

I was up well before the gray sky began to lighten. The snore chorus muffled as I dropped the tent flap behind me and headed for the clump of rocks affording me as much privacy as I was going to find in this place.

They were beginning to stir by the time I got back. No time to stop and think. I slipped back into the tent and squatted with my back to the sewing machine, my staff in my hand. I had fixed straps around it to secure it to my back, and I fastened them as tightly as I could around my bulky clothing, over my shoulders and around my waist like the straps Mr. McManis used.

Then I pushed up with my staff. Nothing happened, except that I almost fell over backwards. I grunted, and tried again. I made it halfway this time, and hung onto my staff with everything I had. It would be easier once I was walking, I told myself. The rhythm would carry me, and it would be easier to keep moving than to stop.

Stifling a groan, I pushed until I was upright, or as near to upright as I was going to get, and took my first step. Then my second. Then I was at the tent flap, and I reached to push it out of my way and almost knocked myself over.

Regaining my equilibrium with some effort, I stepped outside and looked up. The staircase was already crowded with men. Slowly, carefully, working at my balance every step of the way, I made my way over and fell in line.

CHAPTER 8

I will never forget that climb. I do not know how much that
sewing machine weighed, but I do know it gained a pound with every
step I took. It rubbed against my shoulder blades until I was sure it
was drawing blood even through my heavy coat and flannel shirt, and
it bounced against me lower down until I knew I would be black and
blue.

The steps hewn in the ice were steep and uneven and slippery, and
there was nothing beyond a ragged rope rigged to poles driven in the
snow to hold on to. I did not dare trust my doubled weight with it, nor
did I dare look down as the milling crowd at the Scales grew smaller
and smaller below me. Instead I dug my boots and my staff into the
snow, watching only the feet of the man before me.

Before I was a quarter of the way up I was gasping and sweat was
trickling down my neck. I did not dare try to stop for fear those behind
me would simply push me down and walk over me, or, worse, simply
shove me out of their way over the cliff to my death. I did not dare do
anything but keep going. Whether I could or not, it was too late now to
turn back.

The rhythm took me over, straining my legs as I lifted each one to
its limit on the steep climb, pushing me blindly up the mountain. The
wind-whipped snow slashed at the bits of my face that were the only
part of my body exposed to it. I climbed over ice formed from snow
crushed under thousands of bootsteps, up another step, and another,
until at last there were no more.

I had made it. I had made it to the top, to the windiest, coldest, most desolate place I had ever been. The gale almost knocked me off my feet and back down to the bottom. If it were not for the man behind me, who pushed me forward and said, "Out of the way, bub," I would have gone over backwards completely.

Instead, I staggered out of the way over to a spot between the white mounds that were the piles of someone's grubstake. I sat down on what turned out to be a rock under its white disguise, and, after several tries, managed to unhook the straps from my person. I felt as if I were lighter than air, as if I would float up into the clouds and see the entire world, from Seattle to the Klondike.

Instead I sat and tried to catch my breath, rub my shoulders, and gather up the courage to head back down for my next load.

"I'll say one thing for you," said a familiar, detestable voice, as two canvas sacks thumped down beside me. "You're the most determined woman I've ever met."

"I, " I gasped, "told you I was going to the Klondike."

"Yeah, you did." He rubbed his own shoulders.

I glared up at him. "We had a bargain, and you were prepared to break it, simply because of your antiquated ideas of what a woman cannot do."

He sat down heavily on the rock next to me. "I know what a woman can do. My mother –" He broke off, and his expression changed. I had not seen that look in his eyes before. He looked – he couldn't be *proud* of me, could he? It was gone as soon as it came.

"Look. You're up here. You've proved yourself. You may look like a good wind would blow you over, but that's obviously not the case."

I could have sworn I heard my back creak as I straightened. "It is not. Especially carrying that much weight."

He snorted. "Oh, so that's the trick, is it?" He pushed himself to his feet again and gazed down at me, his very stance resigned. "Look, you stay out of the wind as much as you can, keep an eye on everything we bring up, and I won't fight you again. There's no turning back after this."

I eyed him. "You won't make me abandon my machine?"

"After that stunt? Hauling it all the way up here? No." He gave me an assessing look. "I ought to put you back to work, but you're more use right where you are." He glanced up and waved a mittened hand. "Hoel! Over here!"

I did not need to ask how he knew the man in question was Mr. Hoel. In addition to the load on his back, his arms were full of goat.

* * *

I had thought the camp at the Scales was crowded, but as the day wore on, pile after pile of goods jammed the small level area surrounding the little customs shack adorned with the British flag. Around it men ebbed and flowed like the wind's constant buffeting.

By the time the men were finished for the day, having brought up five loads each, I had recovered after a fashion and gone about my usual duties as best I could. There was no wood up here, nor any shelter to speak of, so a fire was out of the question.

All eight goats arrived throughout the day, dumped by one or the other of the men into yet another makeshift crate corral. I had nothing to feed them, but they huddled together into a mound at one side and ignored me. I returned the favor. Surely we would be down into more reasonable country soon.

"And I thought winter camping with my dad in Yellowstone was bad," Mr. McManis commented as he dumped his last load of the day on the pile. "At least there the wind wasn't trying to blow me to kingdom come." He bent over to re-anchor one corner of the tent into the snow before it came loose altogether and started flapping again, then settled down. I handed him a plate of dried beef and apples, that having been the best I could manage to fix.

"How long before we can move on?" I asked.

"Until we get everything up here. At least three more days, at a guess."

Mr. Hoel nodded. "I cannot entrust my glass plates to packers. I would be fortunate if half of them arrived unbroken."

Mr. McManis sighed. "Which leaves me with the rest of it, if we're not going to be stuck here till spring."

"I can help," I heard myself say and immediately wished I hadn't.

"You've done enough," Mr. McManis said flatly. "I can manage."

I bristled, though part of me wondered at my sanity in volunteering to make that climb again. I ignored it. It was the principle of the matter. "I will not be a, what did you call it? A deadweight."

"That was your choice."

"No, it was—"

Hoel interrupted. "If you two do not mind, I would like to get some sleep before tomorrow's work."

I swallowed my last bite of dried beef. It stuck in my throat, as did what I was about to say. I swallowed again. "Just one more question, Mr. Hoel. Mr. McManis, exactly what are you going to do to stop me?"

Mr. McManis shook his head. "You want to kill yourself over this, you go right ahead." He chomped down on his own food as if it would bite back.

Principles could be very foolish things. "I do."

"Fine."

* * *

The next morning, with the sun barely up, not that we could see it in this weather, I followed the two men to the edge of the drop off. Mr. Hoel laid a small piece of canvas on the snow, at the edge of a U-shaped trough disappearing down the hill, and sat down on it. He pushed off with his foot, and suddenly he was gone. Mr. McManis set down another piece of canvas in the same place and gestured at me.

"You're next."

"But I—"

His eyes took on a wicked gleam. "Haven't you ever been on a sled before?"

I stared at the canvas. "That is not a sled."

"It's the same principle."

I was beginning to hate that word. Suddenly that drop off looked as if it would take me all the way to Dyea and beyond. "How do I make it stop?"

"Dig in your heels. But not too hard or too sudden, or you'll end up on your head." He took me by the arm. It felt like a challenge. "Nobody's saying you have to do this."

"But if I do, it will be one less load for you and Mr. Hoel."

He gave me an odd look, and pushed me down onto the canvas. I landed with a thump. My feet went out from under me, and suddenly it was as if I was flying through fog so dense and white I could not tell where I was headed or how fast.

My head was dizzy. My stomach knew I was falling, and tried to save itself by leaping out through my mouth. I hung onto the canvas with both hands and tried to put my feet out to slow down, but all that did was spray more snow into my face, as if I hadn't been half-blinded already. I jerked them back against my body, and hung onto the canvas as it slid faster and faster and finally dumped me against a rock, slightly larger and less half-buried than the rest. I rolled several times before I could stop altogether.

A large, gloved hand took me under the arm and raised me to my feet. I blinked snowflakes off of my eyelashes and looked up to see Mr. McManis, who had pulled his scarf off and shaken the ice from his breathing out of it, grinning down at me.

I could not help myself. "Can we do that again?"

The grin broadened into a laugh as he wrapped the scarf back around his face. "I'm beginning to think Aunt Anna was right." He took my arm again and led the way to what remained of our outfits.

"What was she right about?"

"Never mind. Come on and I'll get you loaded up."

I made two more trips up the Golden Staircase, one that day and one the next. I will admit it here and nowhere else, but I might well have given up if I had been forced to go it alone. And it became ever more obvious that I was doing more good by staying above to mind the goats and watch over our possessions than I was carrying them up that mountainside. But I proved I could do it, and that was what mattered.

I achieved Mr. McManis's grudging respect, even if he would not admit it yet. Just because he was expert in all things outdoors did not mean I could not do as well, given time and learning. But after my third climb, I went back to making sure they had food when they needed it, and a place to sleep when they staggered in from the last climb of the day. There is a difference between proving something to oneself or someone else, and being ridiculous. I had accomplished the one and did not need to do the other.

* * *

"Duty?" I asked blankly.

Mr. Hoel sighed. "Yes. Fifteen per cent of everything, and some items more than that."

"The Klondike is in British North America, not the United States," added Mr. McManis. "The book says so." He waved it at me.

We were in our tent, during what we all hoped would be our last night on the summit. Every single ounce of our three thousand pounds of grubstake was stacked around us like a barricade, all eight goats had piled themselves together in one corner to stay warm, and the three of us were sitting around the spirit lamp, our only source of heat in this benighted place.

No, not benighted, even as the daylight wound down to just a few hours before night swept in again. This cold was damp, blowing in off of the ocean below, pushing the laden clouds up and up, until they slammed against the cliffs and dumped their almost constant burden of heavy, wet snow. But snow meant we were closer to our destination, even if the rumors coming down from the north were that the river was already freezing over. We would get through somehow.

But fifteen per cent? And more on some things? "I haven't that much left in currency." I could not set up shop here and make more, either. Even if it was not obvious my companions were more than eager to be on their way, this was not a community the way Finnegan's Point and the Scales had been, let alone Dyea. What would I do, sit under my canvas shelter sewing until my fingers froze?

"You can pay us back," Mr. McManis said, with an expression I had seen before, the one that said he knew I would rather chew firewood than be beholden. The scoundrel was reveling in my situation again. Back on his superior footing that said he was in charge.

I bit my tongue. I am surprised I did not make it bleed, but perhaps it was frozen. The rest of me certainly felt that way. "I will pay you back," I said.

"I know, I know, from your first sack of gold." He waved a mittened hand, it being far too cold in the tent to undress even to that extent. We were all still wearing the same stiff clothing we had first arrived here in, and, I thought with some disgust, with no chance to do anything about it in the forseeable future.

"Before then, if I can manage it."

Mr. Hoel put in, "I will pay the Mounties. You two will do as I tell you to."

"What?" said Mr. McManis, as I said, "How?"

"You are not the only one with a skill to sell, Miss Karin. I spoke to one of the young men yesterday. He is quite lonely for his home, a place called Kitchener, Ontario, I believe. He wishes to send a picture to his sweetheart there."

"And how can you develop a glass plate?" demanded Mr. McManis, waving his arm to encompass our miserable situation. "Here?"

Mr. Hoel just shook his head and laughed. "You will let me talk with him first. And with his superior. Others have bartered for what they owe here. I see no reason why we cannot as well."

In the end, however, it was my skills as well as those of Mr. Hoel that paid our way over the border into Canada after all. And some of Mr. McManis's dwindling supply of cash. "At the rate I'm going, I'd better strike it rich the minute we arrive in Dawson City," he said ruefully.

He was loading the sled he had built from pieces of wood he had painstakingly hauled up the Golden Staircase, as I sat putting a last few stitches into yet another pair of ripped trousers on the customs station's "front porch," a mere few boards laid down under the shelter of the shack's overhanging eave.

The goats were tied together and waiting, looking as eager as we were to get away from this place. The only food they had to eat was the evergreen boughs and brambles we had been able to gather and carry with us for them along the trail before we reached the point where nothing, not even the odd scraggly bush, grew.

It was the one advantage, as Mr. Hoel kept pointing out, of goats as opposed to the dogs, of every size and breed, most completely out of place as sled dogs, that men hauled or dragged or pushed or carried up and over the summit. Mr. Hoel, who had taken the time while still in Dyea to scout and photograph the White Pass route, had told us of the fate of the horses on that trail as well.

"They call it the Dead Horse Pass," he had said, and showed us some of the plates he had taken. I could not look after the first few, and I dreamed, no, had nightmares about them for several nights after. I was extremely glad I had chosen the Chilkoot instead, stairs or no stairs. At least the dogs were not being used until they dropped dead, and then trampled into oblivion.

The ride, so to speak, down the north slope of the Chilkoot Summit, was a shorter, less steep version of what we had done while fetching our outfits up the Golden Staircase. I sat my piece of canvas like an old hand, and sailed down the slope out of the constant gale and wind-driven blizzard into another world.

The heavy gray clouds stopped just past the summit almost as if there was a barrier holding them back, and I slid out from under them, blinking in the bright sunshine. The sky was a kind of blue I had never seen before, so deep and pure it was like looking up from the bottom of a lake.

I only had a few seconds to enjoy it, though, as I slid past Mr. McManis and out onto a real lake, admittedly one that appeared to be frozen solid at the moment. He drew up beside me and helped me to my feet, and we watched Mr. Hoel guiding the sled down the hill at a more decorous pace, several of the goats perched behind him on the first pile of our goods. We tromped back to shore, unloaded our packs and the sled, and all three of us headed back up the hill.

By the time we had most of our goods ferried down to Crater Lake, as the tarn was called according to Mr. McManis's guidebook, even though it did not look like a crater at all, the exhilaration of the ride had worn itself out. Mr. Hoel and Mr. McManis climbed back up to the pass for the last load, and I set about what had become my normal routine.

After I set up the tent, I found some scrubby looking bushes growing up through the snow. As I pulled them out, it being easier to bring the food to the goats than to round them up later, I heard a very odd snorting sound. Thinking nothing of it, I turned to head back to our camp. A shadow crossed the snow ahead of me. An enormous shadow.

I did not wait to find out what it was, but ran back as best I could in my heavy boots to warn the men, who would not listen.

"It wasn't a bear," Mr. McManis said, sounding exasperated. "Bears hibernate this time of year."

"Then what was it?" I demanded.

"Probably a shadow from the trees."

"Oh, yes, trees," I said. "This is such a forest, I must have been mistaken. *Farsken. Farsken, farsken, farsken.*" The Norwegian was much more satisfying than a mere English 'hell.'

Mr. Mc Manis burst out laughing. "You're in America now, Miss Karin."

"Miss Karin," Mr. Hoel said to me in a shocked tone, pointedly ignoring Mr. McManis, "that is not a word for a lady."

I knew that. I also knew the term lady felt like a straitjacket, at least as much as it did at home. I might not be an adventuress in the usual use of the term, but I was having an adventure, and, besides, I had not used half the vocabulary I was capable of. I turned, looked Mr. McManis straight in the eye, and said, "Goddamn son of a bitch."

Mr. McManis blanched.

"Is that phrase American enough for you? You seem to be very fond of it." Especially when he thought I had not been listening. He sputtered. It was quite amusing to watch. "You look as if you expect God to strike you down on the spot."

He actually swallowed. "Either Him or my mother."

"Neither of whom knows your exact whereabouts at the moment."

"Miss Karin," Mr. Hoel said slowly.

"Yes?"

"Your pronunciation of my language is very good."

I nodded. "Thank you."

"Far too good for a mere imitation. You sounded just like my mother would have, if she ever used such words."

Was that praise, or censure? "I listen well."

"I am quite sure you do, but," he paused and reached under his cap to scratch his head. "What is your surname?"

I did not answer.

He watched me for a moment, and added, "Where did you say you were from?"

I was more than aware of Mr. McManis's sudden attention, too. "Washington."

The silence stretched after that. I did not rush to fill it, although I wanted to. Who I was and where I was from was none of their business.

At last, Mr. Hoel spoke. "Ah, yes. Many Scandinavians have settled in Washington. I arrived there myself at the age of seventeen. How old were you when you came to the United States?"

I let my breath out. I supposed it would not hurt to answer that. "Three."

"What town in Norway does your family originally come from?"

Now that *was* none of his business. I folded my arms in front of me.

But he was persistent. "Was it your mother's people then?"

"Does it matter?"

Instead of answering me, he said, "*Du e trygg her med oss.*"

"Safe with you? *Safe* with you!" I stood, nearly knocking the tent over. "I am safe because I make sure I am safe." I pushed open the flap, brushing away the snow that fell in, and stepped back out into the cold dark world.

Not quite dark, actually. Filmy curtains of green and blue swayed across the night sky, half-obliterating the stars. It was not the first time I'd seen the northern lights on this journey, and I stared up at them, lost in my own thoughts.

I could not stay out here forever. I knew that. I could not strike out on my own, not here. I would have to go back in and face them sooner or later, even if I could not think of anything I wished to do less than go back in that tent to face their questions. Questions I did not want to answer.

For a few moments, I heard voices, muffled into unintelligibility by the canvas. Then the tent flap opened, and Mr. McManis came out, a gun I had not known he possessed in his hands. He glanced up. "Pretty." Then his gaze landed back down on me. "You'll freeze to death out here."

And why did he care? He had not wanted me here in the first place. "Perhaps my imaginary bear will come eat me."

But apparently he was not to be sidetracked. "Is that what you want? To die? After what you've done to get this far?"

"Better to die than go back."

"You think we'll send you back now?" He came up behind me, blocking the wind. It was still cold, but it was different, somehow. He was not touching me, not anywhere, but he was protecting me, as if it was his right to do so. It was not.

"You do not want me here. You said so. Many times."

He let out a disgusted snort. "Oh, for crying out loud."

Incredulously I stared at him. "You tried to prevent me from crossing the pass."

To my surprise he wouldn't meet my eyes. He positively shuffled his feet. "That was before I – never mind. You've earned your right. "Go on back in. I'll get Hoel to shut up if you don't want to talk, but I think he liked the sound of home. It's all this snow, I guess, but he's homesick. Or at least that's what it looks like to me."

"Oh." So it was not about me at all. He's given in, I almost chortled, weight lifting off as if I'd been carrying my sewing machine again. He's given *in*. "Are you homesick, too?"

"It's too cold to stand out here talking. Go on back inside. I'll go take a look around and make sure there isn't a bear." He shuffled the rifle to one hand, then he did touch me, but only to grasp my mittened hand with his. I could have slipped out of my mitten and gotten away, but what would I have then? A cold hand and the wind blowing down my back again. After a moment he let go.

I went back into the tent.

Hoel looked up from the camera in his lap and smiled at me. "I am sorry if I upset you, Miss Karin. I did not mean to."

"So Mr. McManis told me."

"You do sound very like my mother when you speak Norwegian," he added, his eyes twinkling.

"Å veit mor di kor du e hænne nu?"

"No, my mother does not know where I am at this moment. But I am too old to be holding apron strings."

Given that he had to be almost as old as Mr. McManis and I were put together, I had to agree.

"Myre," I told him. This little bit would not hurt, I thought. No one could trace me from here to Ballard now. "My grandparents were fishermen from Myre." I was about to say more, when the sound of a rifle shot brought both of us to our feet.

CHAPTER 9

His face brightened. "Now I understand why you sound like my mother. She was from the north."

I scowled at him, but he was not paying attention.

"I grew up in Telemark, not far from Oslo."

That certainly explained things to me. No point in frowning at the likes of him. "A soft Southerner, are you?"

"I suppose you would think so." His brow furrowed again. "Do you use Myre as your surname, then, or did your family keep their traditional name?"

I shrugged. Mr. McManis, who had been listening as if curious while he turned the skewered meat, asked, "Traditional name?"

Mr. Hoel turned to him. "In Norway, one takes one's father's Christian name as one's surname. Anderssen, or Svensdottir, for example."

"Oh." Mr. McManis appeared to think this one over. "Like McManis. Mc means 'son of.' Although the Scots don't differentiate between sons and daughters. My family's been over here long enough that I have no idea who the original Manis was to begin with." He winked at me, and I smiled at him gratefully for deflecting Mr. Hoel's question. "Not that it matters. I prefer Will to Mister in the first place. Mr. McManis is my father."

But Mr. Hoel was not to be distracted. He looked expectantly back at me.

I sighed. "My family took Myre as a surname when we arrived in the United States. But like," I hesitated, but only slightly, "Will, I would rather you called me Karin."

Now Mr. Hoel looked scandalized, but only briefly. He glanced around the tent, barely big enough to hold the three of us, bundled to our eyes as we were, to the inward bulge in the canvas caused by the pile of goats trying to stay warm in their makeshift corral, to the shadows dancing about from the spirit lamp, and chuckled.

Mr. McManis –Will – looked up from his guidebook, which he'd been idly thumbing through as was his habit. "What's so funny?"

"It does seem a bit odd to cling so to formality in our current situation," Mr. Hoel admitted. "I must claim a preference for Eric myself."

I asked, I admit simply to be polite, "How long have you been in the United States, Eric?"

That was all it took to set him off, which was a great relief to me. He had arrived here not long before my family had, traveling alone across the sea and the country when he was a year younger than I was now, unhappy with the narrow choices facing him in Norway, learning photography and turning it into his life's work. He was a brave man, and I congratulated myself on attaching myself to the group he led.

I don't know what Will thought about it because he said very little himself, whether he was bored or cared because Eric was his friend or had his own reasons for not saying much. I willl say that by the time sleep finally overcame all three of us and we put out the spirit lamp for the night, I irrationally felt far more comfortable in my situation.

I think, even if he had been lying, and it was perfectly obvious he was not, his stories being far too artless and ingenuous, it would have been a relief to me simply to have a story, any story about at least one of my companions. And, much as I would have liked to hear Mr. McManis's – Will's – story, too, his reticence made my own seem less obvious. I did not know whether to be grateful or curious.

* * *

We all slept too late the next morning in our warm blanket rolls. If it had not been for the goats nudging us awake I am not sure we would have resumed our travels before midday. But goats have an innate sense of time better than that of most humans and are extremely difficult to ignore. The men left the breaking of camp to me and Will began to pack the sled. Mr. Hoel – Eric – took a piece of the canvas from the tent and two of the poles and, to my astonishment, began constructing a sort of sail.

Will watched him for a moment, then shook his head and went back to loading the sled. But when Eric propped the makeshift sail in the middle of the sled and started piling canvas sacks around it to hold it up, Will began to object. Then Eric climbed aboard, the canvas caught the everpresent wind, and as I watched the sled began to move. Faster and faster it spun down the frozen lake, becoming smaller and smaller in the distance.

Other men nearby watched this performance, and I noted with some amusement, went looking for canvas and poles of their own. Sooner rather than later a small flotilla of sleds skimmed one by one down the lake, some more successfully than others.

Camp was thoroughly broken and packed up when the sled I recognized, the one with "E.A. Hoel, Photographic Views" written on the side in black paint Eric had conjured up from somewhere, came zigzagging back up the ice.

"You're going to like this better than you did sliding down the hill," Eric told me, his face chapped red with wind. "But wrap yourself up well first. You do not know the meaning of cold until you have been out on that lake."

I removed my mittens and pulled my woolen muffler up from where it had been tucked around my neck. I wrapped it snugly around my head so only my eyes showed, then pulled my collar up around it so it stood straight up, almost to my ears. I pulled my cap down and tugged my mittens back over my quickly cooling hands. "Will that suffice?"

"I beg your pardon?" Eric said.

I reached to pull the muffler down so I could speak more clearly, but he put out a hand and stopped me. "Don't spoil your handiwork."

"If you're finished fussing over her, I need your help," Will said. And then he came over and inspected me head to foot and back again with an attitude I recognized from my older brothers. It annoyed me even more coming from him. I did not want to examine why.

"She'll do, Hoel." He smirked. I scowled at him, although I am quite sure he could not see it.

"Yes, yes," Eric said. "We do not want to lose any part of our excellent cook and seamstress to frostbite."

I took the seat Eric indicated, on the surprisingly soft canvas bag I realized must be the one containing our bedrolls, tucked all loose ends of my clothing into place, and found a strong mittenhold on one side of the sled.

Then Eric raised the sail again and we were off. The wind whipped the scream out of my lungs and the tears out of my eyes. Was the entire journey to the Klondike to be one unending thrill? It seemed so at the moment, as the shores of the lake passed by in a blur.

After a few moments I realized another sled was sailing next to ours, and that its captain was shouting across at us. Eric shouted back, and suddenly we were traveling even faster. It took me a moment to realize the two sleds were racing.

I did not know if wagers had been taken in those unintelligible shouts over the ice. Perhaps it was simply for the glory, but what I could see of Eric's crouched form as he maneuvered both sled and sail made me realize that no matter what the reason, he was not going to allow the other man to reach the far shore before him.

As we teetered first on one runner and then the other, I only hoped he would not dump the entire sled in the process.

We never did learn who would have won. The other sled went over with a crash that made the ice moan and vibrate, and Eric dropped our sail. As we coasted to a stop mere yards from shore, we both turned to look back. I blinked wind tears out of my eyes. As we watched, the man climbed from the wreckage of what had once been his sled. Eric made to turn our sled around, but the man waved us on.

I pulled my scarf down to uncover my mouth. "That could have been us, you know."

Eric looked surprised. And offended. "It could not. I have been ice sailing since I was a boy back in Norway. Do you think I would have risked your life as he risked his? Or my plates?"

"Oh." I considered this. "I suppose you think I should apologize."

He simply waited.

After a moment, I said, "I am sorry."

He snorted. But then he slid the sled neatly to shore, and we both had it unloaded in short order.

I did not ride back with him, preferring not to take the chance he would decide to challenge any other sail-sled captains along the way.

The first of the goats came on the next trip, the wind carrying their panicked bleating well ahead of them.

I noticed Eric was not racing anyone this trip. As a matter of fact, as I watched, he swung the sled around to stop it while still some distance from shore, and jerked one of them by its hind legs – Samson, perhaps? – back into the sled from where it had been about to leap to its freedom.

It was only a matter of seconds, and he was on his way towards me again. He was still cursing in Norwegian as the sled came to a halt, but stopped as he saw me waiting for him.

"Now are you wishing you did not bring them?" I asked.

"No. You will see." His eyes, which were about all I could see of his face, were sheepish. "I was wishing you did not understand Norwegian quite so well as you do."

The goats were well on their way to scrambling up the bank. I corralled Samson and led him by the collar to the usual makeshift crate and bag corral I had built on the frozen shore. His ladies, of course, followed him docilely. I shook my head, watching as all of them headed for the pile of twigs, branches, and moss I had managed to collect.

"Why do you disapprove?" asked Eric.

I turned, startled. "Of what? Oh." I shrugged. I knew what he was talking about, but it was not something I wished to discuss. "They are so singleminded."

He looked disappointed for a moment, then began unloading the sled. "You would be hungry, too, in this cold with nothing but your own skin between you and the wind."

"I would be frozen solid," I corrected him, and went to help him.

It took three more trips to bring everything across the lake. Will came on the last trip. He and Eric raced another of the flotilla, flying so fast across the ice I feared they would not be able to halt before crashing into the shore. I did not mention this fear to Eric when the sled came to a skidding stop so suddenly the runners threw up crystals of ice onto the rocks at the edge of the lake. I did not want to have to apologize again.

The last load was the smallest, and the men did not bother to unload it, but instead lifted the sled bodily up over the rocks and began adding to its load in preparation for portaging down to the next lake.

According to Will's guidebook, and, more reliably in my opinion, what Eric had learned in his photographic jaunts, we had two more lakes to traverse before we reached the Yukon River proper.

We quickly ate the food I had prepared. The men hitched the goats, who having finished their own meal were more inclined to bed down for the afternoon than haul the sled. Especially over three miles of non-existent portage trail, so far as I could see.

I remained behind after they pushed away, but I was not alone by any stretch of the imagination. All around me other groups of argonauts were busy wrangling their own outfits on shore and preparing them for the overland trip to the next water crossing.

Most of them did not have animals, and dragged their sleds themselves. Because of this they could not carry as much weight each trip, and I began to see Eric's point. Not that I would ever say such a thing to him. He thought enough of himself as it was.

The travelers came and went in waves, sliding up on shore and heading down the trail, leaving the now-familiar piles of goods in caches wherever they could. In between, it was quiet, protected from the wind by the first trees, small and scrubby though they were, that I had seen in days. Peaceful, as the snow scrunched beneath my boots. Almost beautiful in its own austere way, all shaded in gray like one of Eric's photographs, black lace against the trampled snow. And over all, the only note of true color, the deep blue sky.

I could even hear birds, invisible back in the trees, until another wave of gold seekers arrived on shore and drowned their slight music with shouts and the squeaks and groans of their sleds and cargoes.

Will arrived back sooner than I expected, his hand on the harness of a recalcitrant Samson and his ladies, the empty sled bouncing behind them. He was alone this time. "Damn goats," he commented. "And Hoel."

"Where is he?" I asked, although I was quite certain I knew the answer.

Will shrugged. "One guess. When I asked him if we were going to leave you here tonight, he told me that was my job, and went off without a backward look.

"Which," he added with a grimace and a hand to his back, "is more than I could say for Samson. It was bad enough pulling them along, but getting them to keep moving when I'm not up there dragging them's going to be a trick."

This was not what I had envisioned, but I heard myself saying, "I will help."

He gave me an incredulous look. "You think you could get them to do any better?"

"I think two people could, no matter who they were." No one had ever said I did not believe in cooperation, as long as it was only temporary. Look where I was now. Besides, I did not relish waiting in the dark cold alone for them to come back for me. It was already well past noon, and the tent had gone in the first load.

"All right," he said at last.

"Eric can come back with you next time," I added.

"If he's there when we get there."

He had a point.

"Or he can handle the varmints himself," Will muttered.

I could not help smiling, but he was concentrating on the last few sacks and did not see me.

We had been loading the sled as we spoke, while the goats fidgeted in their traces. Will had possessed enough sense to tie them to a tree while we did so. It was a good thing, because as soon as he untied them, Samson tried to take off and nearly choked himself when neither his ladies nor the sled went with him. I stepped up, took the harness, and waited for Will to go round to the back of the sled. "Ready?" he called out.

In answer, I began pulling on Samson's harness. Will pushed on the back of the sled, the goats started moving whether they liked it or not, and we were on our way.

It was a long, long three miles, when I had to walk it bent over to hold on to the harness every step of the way. Samson never did come to the understanding that he had no choice but to haul the sled, and he kept trying to butt me. His horns were like skewers, and it was not easy to both stay out of his way and keep pulling him along. But I managed, and comforted myself with the fact that Will's back was probably aching at least as much as mine was as he leaned over the sled and pushed. And he was the one who was having to tramp through what the goats occasionally left behind.

The trail was not difficult to follow, as well trampled as it was. It was not quite as crowded as the Golden Staircase had been, but we still wound up jockeying for position with other travelers, and even passing more than a few of them, since we had animal power and most of them did not. They did not show much imagination in their curses, especially once they figured out I was female. They were much more interesting before they came to that realization.

We finally arrived at the shore of another lake, this one long enough that I could not see the farther shore. Much to my surprise and that of Will, Eric was waiting for us. The men unloaded the sled. I watered the goats and myself from the snow Eric had melted on the fire crackling in a bare spot of ground under a tree. Will came over and drank from the tin mug I handed him.

"I will have coffee waiting for you next time," I told him. "And a hot meal."

"All the more reason to get going again." He smiled down at me. He really was a tall, well-built man. Not that I had any intention of telling him I admired his looks. "Thanks for the help with Samson. I'm pretty sure I'd still be fighting with him halfway back to Crater Lake if you hadn't volunteered."

"All the more reason for me to have done so," I said lightly. "Go on."

"Yes, ma'am." He nodded decisively, and they headed back down the trail. I set about my usual chores, but his smile danced in front of my eyes until I purposely chased it away.

This lake, as he told us that night with his precious guidebook in one hand and his fork in the other, was called Lake Lindemann, and it was more than twice as long as Crater Lake, with one more portage at the other end.

"There's a river between Lake Lindemann and Lake Bennett," he said, "but the guidebooks say the rapids aren't passable."

He put another bite into his mouth, glanced up at Eric, and swallowed it. "Want to prove 'em wrong? We could save a day if we don't portage around. We're going to be lucky if the river isn't frozen by the time we get there, anyway."

I wondered how many broken sleds we would see at those rapids, the route attempted by others as sure as our partner was. I think Eric felt the same way, because he only remarked, "perhaps," and went back to his meal.

"If the lakes are frozen, won't the river be frozen by now as well?" I asked.

"The book says," Will began, but for once Eric interrupted him. "Moving water does not freeze so quickly as still water does. But it is November, and the ice is thicker here than I expected."

"The book says," Will began again, but I interrupted him this time.

"I have noticed this on rivers and ponds I have seen near the logging camps in the mountains. But we are much farther north than they are, and I have never seen ice so thick so early in the season as here."

"The book says," Will said loudly, "the Yukon does not freeze completely until mid-November."

Eric and I both glared at him. Eric asked, "Who wrote your book, Will, and is he here now?"

"It's supposed to be compiled from the reports of experienced men," Will said defensively.

"Am I not experienced?" Eric asked mildly. "For that matter, you grew up in a cold climate. Does this not look like an early winter to you?"

Will hunched a shoulder. "There's not much in the way of big rivers in Montana, or at least not in the part of Montana I'm from."

I put in, "I have never seen lakes frozen this solid."

Now Will glared at me. "Do you want to beat everyone else to the Klondike or not?"

I started stacking our empty tin plates. As was his custom, Will went to lift the large pot of wash water out of the fire for me.

Eric, whose usual evening chore was to bed down the goats, left the circle of firelight without a word. His very back was eloquent, however.

"If we don't make it down the river before freeze-up, we'll be stuck at Lake Bennett all winter. The book says —"

"The book says, the book says. Do you know how much I wish to use your precious book as kindling?" I demanded, plopping the wiped plates into the wash pot firmly enough to have him jerking the volume out of reach of the splash.

I did not look up at him as I reached in after the first one and began scrubbing it as if I wished to rub a hole through the tin.

"Call me when you need me," he said, and went into the tent. A few moments later the light from the spirit lamp lit the canvas.

I finished the dishes and sat by the dying fire, wondering how anyone could put printed words before what was plainly in front of his eyes. And what we were going to do for an entire winter as we waited out the ice.

CHAPTER 10

I will not describe the next day's ice-sailing, if only because it was so much like the first. It took longer because of the distance. We did not travel any further once we had ferried all of our goods to the other end of the lake, partly because it was too late to make much progress, and partly because Will insisted on scouting the river at the lake's outlet.

He did not arrive back until well after dark, with a sober look on his face, the first I'd seen on it without a hint of sarcasm or irony. "Looks like we just missed our chance to run the rapids. The ice is jumbled around like boulders. We'll have to portage around them tomorrow." He went to fetch the tent from the sled without another word.

I followed him. "How do you know we just missed it?"

He stuck out a mittened hand. I handed him one of the tent poles, and he put it in place and reached for the next one. "Will?"

"I just know, okay?"

It was not 'okay,' but, try as I might, I could not get an answer out of him. I supposed tomorrow was soon enough to find out.

For the first time since we had begun traveling together, our camp was a sober, quiet place that night. Will's mood seemed to have struck us all, even Eric, who tended to laugh his way through almost everything and took nothing too seriously.

After supper, Eric volunteered to help with the clean-up instead of fussing endlessly with his cameras, which was not at all usual. I welcomed the help, however, as Will had gone to a corner of the tent with the spirit lamp and did not look up, even with our splashing about.

He did lift his gaze from his book when we came in after bedding the goats down for the night. I sat down on my bedroll and watched him right back, but still he did not say anything. I am still not sure if he did give a tiny shake of his head at me, or if it was a trick of the light, but after a few moments he blew the lamp out.

He did not respond when Eric and I said our goodnights, either.

* * *

Will seemed a bit more like his normal self in the morning, as we packed up and made ready to portage our outfits once more. At least he was talking again. I could hear him arguing with Eric over something as they loaded the sled. My ears pricked up as I heard my name, and I left the tent to see what was going on.

"– nobody listened to me, no sir."

"What's done is done, young man. You cannot prevent her –"

"Cannot prevent me from what?" They both jerked straight up as I spoke. "If you wished to discuss me out of my hearing, you might have waited until you were on the trail. What have I done now?"

Will scowled. "You're here."

That was obvious. "Yes, I am."

"I wish you weren't."

Was it to be that argument again? What set him off this time? "So you have told me on numerous occasions."

If anything his scowl deepened. "You won't listen."

That stung. "Only when you do not make any sense. I know something is bothering you, but it is not my fault you will not tell me."

It appeared that he was not about to tell me now, either, as he let out a gusty sigh and leaned over to pick up another crate. "Did anybody ever tell you you talk like somebody's maiden aunt?"

I could hear Eric's laughter as he headed back to the tent. "I do not, you *hæstkuk!*"

"That's right, you only swear in Norwegian." He smirked at me.

"Oh!" I tromped back to the tent, wishing for something more solid than snow to stamp my booted feet on.

It was not until the men had left with the first load that I realized he had distracted me. But I still did not know what it was he was distracting me from.

* * *

This portage was longer than the last, judging from the amount of time it took the men to come back for the second load. I remained behind until the last load, and it was near dusk before I followed the sled into the mouth of the canyon. There was barely enough room between the tall cliffs on either side for the ice-covered river, leaving no room at all for a real trail.

I followed the men as they maneuvered the sled around boulders both rock and ice and over the rough surface of the frozen rapids. After we had gone what felt like miles into the murky dimness, I heard Will's rather breathless voice.

"Wait a minute, Hoel. Come on up here and help push, will you, Karin?"

They had come to a stop. I supposed a runner had gotten stuck, but when Will made room for me beside him at the back of the sled and we pushed, it moved forward without undue difficulty. I glanced at him curiously, but I could not see his face as he pushed, head down, so I did the same.

"Thanks," he said, his voice husky. "It's been a long day."

I supposed that explained his need of my help. Fair enough. "That it has."

"I sure hope the river to Dawson is still passable."

There was not much to say to this. I suspected it would not be, and I also suspected that pushing a sled down six hundred miles of frozen river by hand, multiple times, was not a practical way to reach the gold fields.

"You're a brave woman," Will said completely out of the blue, so far as I could tell.

"What?" I almost squeaked the word, and in my astonishment I forgot to watch my footing and nearly went down on my face.

Will grabbed my arm and steadied me. I could not feel the warmth of his hand through his mitten and my clothing, but, oddly, it seemed as if I did. "Thank you."

Eric's voice floated back. "Why have you stopped?"

Will dropped my arm as if he thought I would slap him for the familiarity. I would not have done so. I knew he was only trying to help, and it was certainly not the first time he'd done me a similar turn.

"Coming!" I called back. We all resumed our measured pace forward, but as we did so I glanced around. My eyes had long since become accustomed to the lack of light, and it was then that I saw them. A pair of legs, too still, sticking out from behind the far side of a boulder. I pointed. "Will –"

"Don't look," he said, and kept pushing.

"But –"

"Don't look."

"But he might be –"

"He's not." Will gave a mighty shove, earning him a shout from Eric for apparently running the sled up against the goats. "Come on. We're almost there."

"Will, is he –"

"Yes." The word was chopped off, final.

I could not help it. I glanced back. I could see better from this angle, the snow in front of what remained of his head was rusty brown, and – I could not help it. I swallowed hard, but it did no good. I turned my head and leaned my shoulder against the back of the sled as my last meal splashed over the snow.

Will called up to Eric and the sled stopped. I felt myself being lifted and set upon one of the crates atop it. I leaned forward, resting my elbows upon my knees and my face in my hands. Will called out again, and put a hand on my knee, steadying me as he pushed and the sled began to move forward once more.

I could not say anything. At last I lifted my head and looked into his face, which was just below mine and close enough I could see the worry line between his thick eyebrows.

"I told you not to look." His voice was gruff.

"You did." And he had been right to tell me so.

We moved on in silence for a bit. After a few moments, he added, "You shouldn't have seen that."

I could not disagree with him, but – "You tried to keep me from doing so." He peered up into my face, as if trying to figure out if I was angry or not. "That was honorable of you." I could see the relief in his countenance. I shook my head. "That was honorable of you, but you cannot keep protecting me here."

"I can damn well try." His voice was gruff.

"You can break your heart trying," I told him, then wished I could take the words back.

His gaze became piercing then, for a second. It was as if he could stare straight through me and see everything I did not wish him to see. "If I do," he said, and lowered his head again to push, "it won't be my fault."

I was still trying to figure out how to answer him when the canyon opened up and Lake Bennett spread out before us.

* * *

It was full dark by the time we found a bare spot of ground to pitch our tent. I knew we were only three of thousands of argonauts headed north to seek our fortunes, and I thought I had seen crowds at Dyea and climbing the Golden Staircase, but once over the pass the companies had spread out and it had been almost possible to forget we were part of a migration Eric persisted in calling one of the greatest in human history.

I was too tired to care, and my stomach was still unsettled enough that I dreaded cooking our evening meal, let alone eating it. When I finally fell into my blankets that night, however, I found I could not close my eyes for seeing that poor man, face gone, lying in the snow, wondering if he would lie there forever or if someone would take pity on him and bury him. But how? The ground was frozen, where it was not solid rock –

I do not know what time I finally lost the battle, but I must have been too exhausted to dream, because when I woke I was ravenous and I wasted no time in cooking flapjacks and bacon over our little fire. Will watched me pour yet another pancake from the bowl of batter. "Feeling better, are you? Can I have another, or are you planning on eating them all?"

I had been planning on eating that one, but it was my fourth, and when it was flipped and finished, I slid it onto his plate and poured myself another.

Eric was already in the tent sorting out his cameras. Will took his last bite of pancake and joined Eric into the tent. I could hear them talking again, even over the racket that surrounded us. I stood, too, and took stock of my new surroundings for the first time.

The place was a city of tents. Large tents, small tents, new tents, old tents, billowing sheets of white canvas laced between half a dozen trees and tightly-strung lean-tos so small a single man would barely fit beneath one. Smoke from hundreds of tiny fires spindled up into the bright blue sky, the scent smothered by the odor of freshly cut lumber. The sound of saws tore through hundreds, no, thousands of voices, shouting, calling, laughing, and cursing.

The greatest migration in history, indeed. Eric burst out of the tent with a camera over his shoulder and a grin on his face as he saw me staring about, and aimed his steps down to the crowded lakeshore. I decided my camp work could wait a few minutes more, and followed him.

"This lake must be deeper than the others," he told me, watching as a foolish young man stepped out onto it and then very quickly stepped back as a starburst of cracks developed beneath his feet. "The ice is not thick enough to sail on here, even near the edge."

"Not thin enough to sail through, either," Will said from behind his other shoulder. "We'll have to go round."

"Even if we had a boat," Eric agreed. "You understand," he went on, his sharp gaze belying the mildness in his voice, "that if your book is correct," and it had been, at least in the distances we had covered so far as we could tell, "by the time we rest the goats and make our way to the other end of this lake, the river will be frozen over. They are not in condition for yet another portage. They need a few days before they will be able to pull the sled again."

Surely Will would not argue with that last point. It had been all we could do to push the goats through that last trip the previous evening, and I was fairly sure the men had actually done more of the work than the animals had.

Will looked mutinous. "Conveniently for you and your damn photographs."

"You knew my plans before we left Seattle."

"You didn't tell me you meant to hare off after every step we took."

"This is how I earn my living," Eric stated flatly.

Will stepped forward. "I can't start earning mine until we get to the Klondike."

"We cannot leave here until the river breaks up."

"We need to leave before it freezes up."

"It is already frozen."

"You don't know that."

They were standing toe to toe now, their voices having risen with each sentence. I stared from one to the other of them in some dismay as I began to wonder if Will would leave us rather than put up with any further delay. "We can't leave," I said, quickly. "Until we can make plans for moving on."

Both of them turned to stare at me as if they had forgotten my existence.

Will's breath huffed out in a wordless "Hmph."

"Yes." Eric's voice lightened. Or did it simply seem that it did because that was how I felt? "And when I get back, I will purchase a boat, and if the river is still open, we will be on our way."

"Buy a boat? From who?" Will demanded.

Eric shrugged. "There is a sawmill at the end of the trail from Skaguay. At the very least we can buy lumber there." He turned away.

"Go on," Will said, disgust clear in his voice. "But I am not staying any longer than I absolutely have to."

Eric shrugged again and, apparently deciding he had forgotten something, went back to the tent. When he did not come back out right away, I started towards the tent myself.

Will put a hand on my shoulder. Then he glared down at me. "You don't think we should keep going either, do you?"

I shrugged, wishing he'd let go. "I don't know enough to make the decision, but I see no sense in trying to make one until we have enough information to do so. And," I added as he let go of me to unlace his pack, "I don't trust your book any more than I do the rumors I hear, so do not wave that penny dreadful at me as if it were Holy Writ."

"Fine." He gave me a look of utter disdain and gestured further down the shore towards what I recognized from my experience with the other tent cities along our route as the business district of the place. "I'm going to see what I can find out about the trail north. Want to come along?"

I looked around at our camp. I thought about what needed to be done if we were to spend the winter here. I wanted to wring both men's necks for leaving all the work of it to me. I scowled up at him.

He shrugged. "Suit yourself." And off went my other traveling companion, to return only heaven knew when.

CHAPTER 11

I watched Will's retreating back, then sighed and took stock of my surroundings. They could have been worse. Eric had chosen reasonably well, given the options to hand. The tent was on a relatively flat space a few feet back from an indentation in the lakeshore, with the hillside and a jutting boulder behind it. The fire ring he had built from water-smoothed rocks was not directly in front of it. This gave me room to set up my work, so I could share the heat and light from the fire.

With the days growing shorter and shorter, I would need candles and more oil to stretch the time I could work beyond a few hours daily. I wondered if I would be able to find them for sale here, let alone purchase them. Well, and I could do many things by firelight alone. But not sewing.

As I set up my canvas shelter, Eric came out of the tent, camera over one shoulder and haversack over the other. He watched me for a moment. "Do you need any help?"

It was obvious he wanted to be gone, so I waved him off. He shrugged and strode off down the shore. I did not waste time watching him leave. When he wanted a hot meal he would come back.

A few hours later I had things arranged to my satisfaction, my bedroll on the end of the space in the main tent nearest my makeshift shop, the bulk of our goods between me and the men's bedrolls on the other side. I put the goat corral on the other side of the canvas beyond that. Let them deal with Samson butting them for his food every morning.

I had just set my sewing machine up on a plank filched from the sled and was draping my sign over my shelter, when a pair of hands took it from me. I glanced up.

"Here. I can reach higher than you." And Will fastened my sign to the very top of the tent, where it was visible up and down the shore.

"Thank you."

"Looks like you've got things in good order. What else can I do?"

I stared at him. This was not the man who had left camp this morning determined to head downriver as soon as humanly possible. "Don't you have your own work?"

He did not answer me, but said, "The lake's frozen more solid than it looks. The ice is thin enough to crack near shore only because the lake itself is so shallow there."

"So we are too late to go on?" I knew it was a miracle we had come as far as we had by now.

His face bore an expression I had not seen in him so far. I had seen him in a myriad of moods, angry, pleased, unhappy, frustrated, even exuberant. But I had not seen this sort of resignation in him before.

"Not till the ice breaks up. God knows when that will be."

I wasn't happy about it, either, but some things are intractable. "It is already November. Spring is not too far away."

"That might be true in Seattle, but not here." He actually sighed.

Privately I agreed with him. "At any rate, Eric has gone off again, and we can't leave without him."

Now he did frown, and I recognized the frustration fueling his attitude. "Damn Hoel, anyway. If I'd known what he was going to be like, I'd never have thrown in with him." He looked around our camp. "At least you pull your weight. And then some." He shook his head. "I never expected it of you."

Well, I thought. And he'd surprised us both. "Would your aunt Anna approve of me?"

He snorted. "Aunt Anna would say you waste too much time doing chores. My mother, on the other hand..." He gave me an approving look, then changed the subject so abruptly I blinked. "There's a fellow carrying mail back and forth to Skaguay once a week for ten cents a letter. They say if someone will mail a letter to Skaguay marked for

Lake Bennett, he'll pick it up and bring it here. And he'll take any mail from here to the Skaguay post office."

And was that not a waste of time? "I'm sure there are many who appreciate it."

"You could write your family. Let them know you're all right. I'll get stamps and make sure he takes it when he takes mine."

I had no intention of doing so. It had only been since we'd crossed the pass that I finally stopped looking over my shoulder as if I expected to be dragged back to Ballard at any moment. But – "Yours?"

"I promised to write my folks when I could." But then his idle tone sharpened. "I never did believe you were kidnapped, you know. You want this too badly."

What was the harm in admitting it now? "No, I wasn't. I simply walked on board and down into the hold. The next thing I knew, someone shoved several heavy crates in front of the opening, and the ship was underway."

He laughed. "Just like that?"

I smiled, remembering. My predicament then seemed so mild compared to everything I had been through since. "Yes."

"That took gumption." He paused. "Were you running away or to?"

"What do you mean?"

"I know you've got gold fever now, and no mistake. I've seen you playing with that little nugget too many times. Where did you get it?" He held up a hand. "Never mind. Somebody paid you with it, I'm sure."

I nodded. I had not realized I'd been so obvious about it.

"Can I see it?"

I supposed there could be no harm. I fished in my pocket and pulled it out. It was a tiny thing, but it was mine. He plucked it out of my palm and examined it. "Huh. It is real."

"Of course it is real!" I snatched it back.

"All right, all right." He watched me tuck it carefully away back in my pocket. "What I meant was, did you have gold fever when you left Seattle, or were you running away from something?"

I bit my lip. But before I could figure out how to answer that question, my first customer at Lake Bennett, a tall, burly man with a bright blond beard, strode up and wanted to know if I was the sewing lady, and though thankfully Will stayed within sight as I spoke with him about his the badly torn mackinaw coat, Will was gone, with the goats and sled, by the time I went to work on it.

* * *

Will came and went twice that day. He stopped once to eat then left again right away and I saw nothing of him again until evening. Since the entire community of Lake Bennett had apparently been hoarding their damaged clothing since they'd left Skaguay and Dyea, I did not have time to be curious about what he was doing. I recognized at least some of the men as customers from my former location, which should have surprised them less than it did.

When I tied the tent flap shut for the day, I had a nice stack of work awaiting me. If this kept on, paying for my share of the boat in the spring would not be a hardship. And, I thought triumphantly, I would not be doing all my sewing by hand this time.

It was full dark when I stepped outside, and had been for some time. The stars were a carpet of light across a pitch-black sky, and the northern lights played off and on as if someone repeatedly lit and snuffed a lamp. What must have been thousands of campfires along the lakeshore looked as if some of those stars had fallen to the ground, and many of the tents were illumined by candles or lamps as well.

I raised the spirit lamp to light my steps as I walked around the tent to check on the goats, and almost ran headlong into an enormous stack of, branches, I supposed, although they were large for it. Too large to feed the goats or to use as firewood unless they were chopped down to size. Twisted and knotty, they would not be much use otherwise.

"Watch out."

"Is this what you have been doing all day?"

"Yes," Will replied. "A few more days and I'll have enough to start on our boat."

I let out my breath. It hung in a frosty cloud before me for a moment before dissipating in the cold, cold air. "Eric said he would buy one when he got back."

He snorted. "You want to know something, Karin? I wouldn't trust Eric so far as I can throw him. If you want to be sitting here next summer waiting for him to show up and buy you a boat, you go right ahead. Me, I'm going to build us one. And if you want to ride to the Klondike in it with me, I'll be glad to have you."

It was the first time he had called me Karin, without the Miss in front of it. I don't know if he meant anything by it, or if he had simply decided to finally take me up on my offer of informality.

But did he really believe he could build a boat from that tangle of twisted, bent, undersized logs? I opened my mouth, but it was obvious he could see what I was thinking, even by lamplight, and beat me to it. "Fine. If I have to prove to you I *can* build a boat you'll feel safe in, I will. If it's the last thing I do. I don't want to drown, either."

He stalked off towards the tent, leaving me standing there staring in consternation at the raw materials for our next means of transportation, piled in a haphazard heap. I wished I knew how to swim.

* * *

It seemed very odd next morning not to be in an enormous hurry to break camp, harness the goats, load the sled, and see how many miles we could put in that day. As I settled down at my sewing machine I could feel curious eyes watching me as men came and went up and down the shore.

While I plied my treadle, frequently warming my cold hands over the fire I had started for the purpose, I listened to Eric, who had arrived back at the tent last night just in time for his hot meal, arguing with Will about boat construction.

Inevitably, Will had dragged his book into the discussion, and was waving it about like the Bible of a preacher at a revival. Honestly, I wished Eric would find a way to throw the book into the fire. I was afraid I was going to have to do the job myself to preserve their partnership.

"I," said Eric at last in a tone I had not heard from him before, "am going to work. I will return when I return. And when I get back, I will see what you have accomplished in the way of plans, and I will make the corrections needed to –"

"You won't need to make any damned corrections," Will all but snarled.

Eric did not answer.

"Besides, it's going to take two to saw the damned boards before we can even get started. How do you expect me to do that by myself?"

"I told you I will buy a boat when I get back." Eric went to the back of the tent and came out with one of his cameras. He sat down by the fire to prepare it for his day's work.

"No, you won't. Those are perfectly good logs, and if you don't want to do your share of the work, then maybe I need to find new partners. Fellows who don't think something's stupid just because it comes from a book."

He stomped off. I stopped sewing. "Please don't chase him away. We need him."

Eric looked up from his camera. "Would you rather drown with him next spring or arrive safely in Dawson without him?" He went back to fiddling with the insides of the camera. "Because if he will not see reason about the boat, those will be our choices."

I turned back to my own machine. I did not want to look at him any more than he wanted to look at me. "I do not want any of us to drown." I rose to my feet, the trousers I had been working on gone from my attention. "Not you, not me, and," I added, "not Will."

I ignored his snort as I, too, left our camp.

* * *

Will hadn't gone far, only down to the shore, where he stood staring out across the ice. I stopped next to him and followed his gaze. All around us the sound of sawing and shouting, of booted feet tramping and canvas snapping in the wind, drowned out the creaking of the ice and the sighing of the wind in the trees. This could have been a beautiful place. It probably had been before this winter, and perhaps it would be beautiful again one day. But now it looked as if its new residents were determined to tear it to shreds down to the very bedrock, no matter what got in their way.

Wasn't all of this journey like that, though? We were all headed for riches, no matter what got in our way.

"He doesn't mean it, you know."

Will did not reply at first, not even acknowledging my presence. Just as I was about to try again, he said angrily, "Oh, he did. And does. And has every right to."

That was not what I had expected. Before I could think of anything to say to that, he went on. "This wasn't what I expected. None of it."

He rounded on me. Before I knew it, he had grabbed both of my hands and squeezed them hard enough to make me squeak. He dropped them as if he'd broken them. "Sorry. But you – both of you, you and Eric – You cook and keep camp and on top of everything else you plunk yourself down wherever we are and you start earning cash with a sewing machine you carried over that pass by yourself.

"Eric has those damned goats, which I thought were the most stupid thing in the world to try to bring on this trail, but if it weren't for them God knows where we'd be but not this far, and he can plunk himself down wherever we are and start earning cash with those cameras of his.

"Then on top of everything else he has the gall to try to tell me what to do, when I've been living in the wilderness for most of my life."

I swallowed. His eyes were hot, his shoulders stiff, and his back as straight as a tent pole. Straighter, since ours had not had an easy time of it in the last months. "Most of your life?"

He laughed. It was one of the most unhumorous sounds I'd ever heard. "My dad singlehandedly rescued my mother and her kid sister from being kidnapped by Indians back before I was born. Oh, he doesn't talk about it much, but Aunt Anna told me what really happened. We lived in Yellowstone National Park most of the time I was growing up, because he worked for the army helping keep the park safe. You know about Yellowstone?"

I shook my head.

"Most beautiful place in the world. I'd like to take you there someday –" He shook his own head at me. Heaven knew what he saw in my face, but I certainly never thought he would want to take me anywhere. "Most of it's wilderness, geysers and hot springs and wild animals and thousands of square miles emptier than here. We used to camp out there. Explore. I've seen things you wouldn't believe."

I let my eyes roam, taking in our surroundings.

He watched me and laughed again, the sound softer than before. "Well, maybe you would." He took my hand again, and I could feel the warmth through both our mittens. "You remind me of Aunt Anna. She does what she wants and damn what anyone else thinks, too."

No matter what it took. I wondered if his aunt would have stowed away as I had.

Will was still talking. "Well, so am I. I can build a perfectly good boat, but I can't do it by myself. So now here I am stuck for the winter with a partner who doesn't give a damn when or if we ever get to Dawson and no way to keep going. How the hell am I going to get there in time to stake a claim before they're all gone?" He stopped, apparently out of breath since he'd practically been shouting. More than the familiarity of my name had changed in his language as well. I do not know why I found that reassuring.

"Am I not your partner, too?"

He eyed me up and down. I knew what he was going to say before he even opened his mouth. "Look, Karin, I appreciate the thought, but you couldn't lift that saw if your life depended on it."

Since I had no interest in wasting my time with the saw, I let that one pass. "So you will give up? Because things did not work out as you wanted them to?"

He stared down at me. "Hell, no."

"Then what are you doing?"

He let out his breath in a steamy cloud. It hung there for a moment, then dissipated. "Got me."

"Then do you blame me for wishing you would hush up and get back to work?" I asked him tartly. "There is a great deal to do before we will be ready to float down the Yukon River next spring, and a great deal to do to survive until then.

"And you, because Eric has proved over and over again that he cares more about his photograph business than he does anything else, are the only man I have to rely on to get the work done. If you are going to abandon me I wish you would do it and get it over with, but if you are not, then I wish you would spend your time and talents making sure we get to the Klondike safely, and not waste your time whining at me."

His eyes were wide now. They really were a beautiful shade of brown, like the dark amber beads I had seen one of Miss Alice's customers wear once.

"You didn't hear anything I said, did you?"

"I heard you feeling sorry for yourself, if that is what you mean," I retorted.

Will opened his mouth and closed it again. "I don't know how to build a boat," he confessed at last, "and I think Eric's right about the instructions in the book."

Hallelujah, I thought. Perhaps that book of his might become kindling after all. I hesitated, then told myself it could not do any harm to ask. "Do you have any objection to learning from something other than a book?"

"You mean eat crow?"

I looked up at the ubiquitous large black birds that flocked around every place humans camped in this country. Will always insisted they were ravens and not crows, but I was past quibbling. "Better than having them eat you."

His laugh, this time, was genuine. It made me want to smile. But there was work to be done.

"Come on," I said. "We don't have time to waste."

Chapter 12

Eric was gone when we got back, as were his bedroll and more of his things than I had supposed he could carry. Will stared at their side of the tent for a moment, then shrugged and went to harness the goats. I supposed he considered himself lucky Eric hadn't decided to take the sled, too.

He hauled logs all day, down from who knew where – trees were already getting scarce around the lake and in the surrounding hills – to the growing pile next to our tent. I consoled myself watching his 'progress' thinking perhaps he could pay for his share of the boat by selling it all as firewood. And I wished he would take his gun with him and bring us some more fresh meat, but he simply shook his head when I mentioned it and took his axe instead.

It was a hard way to earn his portion, however. He started work by moonlight, and ended it in starlight. He ate ravenously when he stopped long enough to do so, and fell into his bedroll every night with a crash like a falling tree.

I too was working hard, but there was only so much daylight to sew by, and lamplight was a poor substitute. I tried to make up for this by utilizing every bit of the daylight time I could, but even then I found myself with hours of dark on my hands.

The lack of daylight did not hinder my growing desire to take a look around the haphazard community of Lake Bennett, however, and one moonlit afternoon I blew out the lamp and went to explore.

If it seems odd that I felt comfortable leaving all of our worldly goods unprotected in camp, I will only say that we and everyone else had been doing so for varying lengths of time since we left Dyea. People here were much more likely to abandon goods they had deemed necessary before they had realized what they were up against than they were to try to acquire more along the way in any manner. Every man and woman here had, thanks to the Northwest Mounted Police and their ironclad rule about entering British North America with a year's worth of food and supplies, more to eat than they knew what to do with. We might be marooned here for the winter against our will, but no one would starve.

* * *

The panorama unfolded before me as I strolled along, the human cacophany on the shore a sharp contrast to the empty, completely unpopulated stretch of the frozen lake. No one seemed to be at all willing to risk stepping out there. I did see one group of men shoving an empty sled out as far as they could reach, laughing and yanking it back to dry land even though it had showed no signs of cracking the ice.

One of the more curious things I saw, repeated over and over again on the more level ground farther back from the lake, were strange scaffolds constructed of scrawny logs like those Will had been hauling, upon which another log was laid as if waiting for a flood of Biblical proportions to rise to it. One man stood balanced atop this odd contraption and another below, with a familiar, long, two-handled saw like the one in Will's baggage between them.

The saw bit through the log on its way down, then was pulled back up for another pass, propelled mostly, so far as I could tell, by the cursewords accompanying the work. The man below was covered with sawdust, and the man above was perched precariously enough it was a wonder he did not fall off at any moment.

Indeed, as I strolled by one did, and landed flat on his back in a cloud of sawdust. He did not appear to be seriously injured, judging from the language issuing from his mouth as soon as he got his breath back.

The men in the lumber camps where I had grown up used these kinds of saws to topple the enormous trees that had brought them there, but here no tree was worthy of the name, let alone big enough to require such a tool. I had begun to wonder how Will had thought to use the one in his luggage, or, rather, how foolish he was to bring such a thing along. Now I wondered who he would get to wield the other end since it was clear it would not be me. For which I was grateful.

The whole venture seemed even more ridiculous when I reached the sawmill at the head of the lake. It was not a large enterprise, but the pile of planks it was producing looked good enough to my eye. They certainly seemed to suit the team of men slapping them together into what looked to me like oversized crates with one end slanted up into what I assumed was supposed to be a prow. Ungainly and awkward, they did not look particularly riverworthy. If this was what Eric intended to purchase for us... My confidence in his plan slipped a bit.

It slipped even more when I spotted the price list scribbled in grease pencil on the side of the mill. I blanched at the numbers, and that was just for the planks. It wasn't that I did not understand the laws of supply and demand. I had raised my own rates by fifty per cent over what I had been charging at Dyea and thought myself brave, but the fact that none of my customers so far had batted so much as an eyelash at them made me think I should have raised them more.

Now I knew I must, or I would never have enough money to pay for my share of the boat. I wondered if I could hold that enormous pile of garments I had already taken in to ransom for higher rates. I supposed it would do no harm to try.

I had seen enough, and more than enough. I turned to make my way back up the shore to our tent. As I walked along, picking my way among the cobbles, an odor, sweet and light, penetrated both my dismayed calculations and the normal stench of too many people living too close together without adequate cleanliness. For a moment I was back in Ballard, in my mother's kitchen, the smell of frying lefse so strong for a moment I thought it was real. Then the wind shifted and the stench came back.

I shook my head and went on, paying far less attention to my surroundings than I should have been, I suppose. I was not homesick. I had nothing to be homesick for. But why I should be smelling lefse now, and out here, made no sense.

Except for that tent back away from the shore. It was somewhat larger, and certainly in better repair than most of the others scattered randomly up and down the beach, with a stovepipe sticking out of one end and a line of men trailing out of the other. And the sign, as simple as my own "Mending" at the ridgepole of our tent. "Baked Goods" it said.

How I had missed it on my way down here I could not fathom.

The odor drew me closer, and while I had no conscious intention of standing out here in the cold and the dark waiting for something I was probably imagining anyway, I fell into line behind the last man. I tapped him on the shoulder. "What are you waiting for?"

He jolted slightly, as if out of a reverie. "Potato doughnuts." He sounded positively worshipful. "Real yeast potato doughnuts. Best things I've had to eat since I left home."

"Worth standing in line for?"

The man in front of him chimed in. "Worth waiting hours for."

Surely they hadn't been out here for hours. But just then the tent flap opened, and the first man ducked inside. The rest of the line moved forward, and the man in front of me sighed. "Won't be long now."

The line did move quickly, and I stayed in it. My curiosity would not allow me to leave even though I knew it was high time I returned to my work. In a few moments I was at the entrance to the tent, and another moment after that I was inside.

The scent now was strong, exactly like my mother's kitchen on baking day. I was drawn without conscious intent close to the makeshift table. The planks resting on two crates held tin trays with actual tea cloths draped over them, and on top of those pristine white tea cloths rested small stacks of lefse.

Doughnuts, indeed. Those were not doughnuts. Those were circles of perfectly golden brown fried dough spread with what to my amazed eyes looked like blackberry jam and rolled into cylinders of buttery goodness.

At home, as my mother said, in the old country, lefse jam was lingonberry, and lingonberry only. But in our new country, lingonberries were unknown, and blackberries were everywhere. So we adapted, as my mother said, always with her wistful in-the-old-country expression. As a child of our new home I had never had what was to me the mythical lingonberry, but lefse with blackberry jam was the treat of my childhood. My mouth watered even though I was perfectly well, if rather monotonously, fed, and not hungry at all.

"How much?" I heard myself ask.

The woman who was simultaneously ladling more dough into the pan, smoothing it out to cook evenly, and spreading an already cooked lefse with jam out of a mason jar said, "two bits," then stared up at me.

"Do you not know how to make these yourself, young woman?"

The voice was home, too. Not quite my mother's northern Norwegian accent, but enough like it that I had to swallow. I pulled several coins out of my trouser pocket and handed them to her. "Two, please."

She humphed at me, but took my money and gave me my lefse, still warm, wrapped in a piece of newspaper. I think she would have said more, but the next man in line pushed up and asked for half a dozen. I ducked out of the makeshift bakery with my prize, and wandered back to our tent in the starlight, eating ambrosia and, manners be damned, licking my fingers before I put my mittens back on.

* * *

"You must come with me tomorrow," I told Will that evening after our supper, now flavorless to me. "You would not believe how delicious they are."

"Can't you bring some back for me?"

"No, you must eat them warm. Fresh from the pan. You have never had anything half so good."

He laughed. "And here I thought your cooking wasn't bad, given the circumstances. Not my mother's, mind you, but decent."

"They're almost as good as my mother's —" I began, then stopped.

His eyebrows rose. "Oh?"

. And what could be the harm in talking about my mother's cooking? "My mother makes the best lefse in Ballard," I told him. "And I'm told, although I find the stuff vile, the best lutefisk."

"I've heard of lutefisk. Some joker tried to sell me some in Seattle. Told me it would keep forever. It surely smelled bad enough to, if only because no one would ever eat it."

I grimaced. "Mother says in Norway it was only eaten at the end of winter when all the other supplies ran out, but my father likes it, so she makes it for him.

"But lefse really are delicious. If you will not come with me, I will bring some back to you, and try to keep them warm, but if I eat your share because I cannot bear to watch them get cold, it will be your fault."

* * *

I went back at the end of the next day, and the next, and the next. I could not help myself. Each lefse cost me the equivalent of one repair. I raised my rates until one repair would pay for two lefse, then for three, and kept going back. My customers began to grumble at my new prices, but paid them. I did not care. I needed the money to pay for my share of the boat, and I was not going to forgo my daily treat for it. I had something to look forward to at the end of the day, and if it seems a silly thing, well, I'd had very few silly things to look forward to in a very long time.

I suppose it was the third or fourth time I took the walk down the shore that the baker, a plump woman, said more than "How many today?" to me. She wore her light brown hair in a knot at the nape of her neck, wisps escaping to cling to her warm, pink face, and the white apron over her dress was far cleaner-looking than it should have been under the circumstances

"You're worse than the rest of them," she commented as I traded my coins for my treat. "For them, they are simply something sweet. For you –" she turned the statement into a question.

"My mother made lefse," I confessed.

She nodded, and gestured me around to her side of the plank table. Surprised, I went before I thought about it.

"You look Scandinavian, but your accent has worn thin," she commented as she handed me the jam jar and spoon.

"We came over from Norway when I was small," I answered, and bemusedly began to spread blackberries and syrup onto one of the steaming circles.

"Here, not so much." She stopped to tend to another customer and another, as I tried to spread the lumpy jam thinner. She took another look. "That is better. My name is Mrs. Thielsen. I come from Christiania."

I supposed I could get away with giving her my first name. She was half a generation older than I was, if I could guess, and would not expect to use Miss. "My name is Karin. My family is from Vesterålen."

But she only said, "Vesterålen. That is far north indeed. The snow and the dark must seem slight indeed to you."

I supposed she would not know Ballard. It surprised me she spoke English as well as she did. "I myself am from Seattle. It seems very cold and dark to me here, and sometimes I wonder if spring will ever come."

She laughed. "There must be seasons here, as there are anywhere else." Then, to a customer who was about to leave without paying, "Here, hold up."

The man dropped his coins into the half-full bowl. "Thought you weren't payin' attention."

"I always pay attention. And you are no longer welcome here."

The man scowled, but he left.

I stared at her. "But he paid."

"He would not have, had I not been watching."

I shrugged agreement. "It is not as if you haven't enough customers."

She laughed, and spread more batter in the pan. "We women, and we Norwegians, must cling together in this place."

I had no idea how long I had been standing there, spreading jam and chatting, but I suspected it was longer than it should have been. "I need to get back now. I have work of my own to do."

"Come again, Karin. And when you do, do not stand in the line, but come to the back." She gestured at the flap behind her. I nodded thanks, and ducked through it.

* * *

I should not have kept going back, but I did. The lefse were delicious, but the real reason was the motherly baker. I had not realized how much I missed the company of another woman. Every afternoon I ducked through the back entrance of the bakery tent, spread jam on warm potato pancakes, and chatted.

Mrs. Thielsen, I think, was as glad for the company as I. We talked about Norway, or rather she did and I listened to her stories, which reminded me so much of my mother's wistful tales of the old country.

She told me about her arrival in Minnesota, and of the stump-cleared farm her husband had dug out of the north woods. I did not ask what had happened to her husband. He was patently not here with her.

She did not ask uncomfortable questions of me, either. I told her about my own small business, and she said she had guessed it already – "You always have loose threads about your clothing" – and gave me a few pieces she said she did not have the time to mend herself. I took them, and took far more time over the slight damage than I did over anything else I worked on that winter.

She never said anthing else to me about my attire. I had expected her to condemn it. Certainly many of the men I did business with looked askance at my trousers and shirts, but I did not care what they thought. I did care about what Mrs. Thielsen thought. More than I should have.

Because the day she finally met Will, I found I did care. Very much indeed.

Chapter 13

It was not to happen the next day, however, or the next, or the next. Will came back to the tent that evening with an expression on his face bordering smug, and, grabbing my hand, dragged me to my feet away from my cookpot and out of the tent.

"Wait! What-"

"Look at that," he crowed, leading me around to his pile of sticks and branches, which was now higher than the tent. "If that's not enough to build us a boat, I will eat my hat."

Since the hat in question was very dirty and worn, I said, "I would not eat it; it will make you ill."

"Very funny." He gestured. "What do you think?"

I did not deem it a good idea to be honest with him. "It is a very large pile." No one could dispute that. "What will you do next?"

"Start sawing planks, of course."

Eric had not yet returned. I was beginning to doubt if he ever would. "How do you propose to go about it?"

He grinned, then followed me when I headed back inside the tent. "Met a fellow up on the hill. He's traveling by himself. The deal is, he helps me saw my planks, and I help him saw his."

"Are we about to acquire another partner?" I inquired dishing up stew, more than a bit concerned. Another partner would add to my workload, and complicate our situation, especially if- when Eric came back.

"Nah. The only reason he's willing to work with me is because he can't figure out any other way to do it." He scowled and took the bowl I handed him. "Which is about where I am, too."

I nodded and began to eat. I knew what he meant. We had not seen Eric in weeks. We hadn't spoken of him much. What point was there? He would come back before the ice broke up and we left. Or he would not. He had left a good many of his possessions with us, not to mention the goats. I could not imagine him abandoning them all.

Then again, I had not imagined him taking such advantage of Will and me, either. I still owed him for my passage. But Will – Well. I owed him, too. More than I owed Eric by this point. "Is there anything I can do?"

He looked me up and down, then shook his head. "Not answering that one. You've already done way more than I thought you could."

I could not help smiling. "That is not what I meant."

"I know." He had already finished inhaling his meal, and he rose to lift the water pot off the fire. "You need anything else?"

I could tell he wanted to get back to work. "Go on."

Bemused, I watched him as he left, his steps almost bouncing. In some ways, he seemed so much younger than I was, so eager and full of energy. I was fairly sure we were the same age, give or take a few months, but I felt much older. To him this was all a game. To me it was an all-or-nothing proposition. I wondered what he would do if he did not strike it rich. I did not want to think about what I would do if I didn't.

* * *

A strange man was standing near the goat pen when I went out to care for them after breakfast the next morning. He was built on the proportions of a barrel, not much taller than me, with a broad torso and limbs short out of proportion. I had to admit he looked sturdy, however, and his hand, as he pulled one battered mitten off to stroke one of the goats in a surprisingly gentle manner, looked as if it had seen hard work.

He glanced up at me as I picked up the armload of twigs and moss and other gleanings from Will's logging efforts. "So you are the goatherd." His voice was more cultured than I expected it to be, given his looks and the circumstances, but I did not like the tone of it. For one thing, he had obviously meant goatherd as a derogatory term, and for another, I did not like the way he looked me up and down when he said it.

I was about to reply and put him in his place when Will came around the corner. I dumped the goats' meal in their enclosure and headed back to the tent.

Will put out a hand. "Wait a minute."

"I need to get to my work."

"Well, hang on a second. This is Matt Lawson," Will said, gesturing at the man. "He's going to be sawing planks with me. Matt, this is my partner, Miss Myre."

"Miss Myre," Mr. Lawson said. My name sounded no different in his mouth than did the word goatherd.

"Mr. Lawson." I nodded.

As I headed back to my worktent, I heard him say, "Now I see why you were looking for real help."

Will laughed. I could not hear his answer. I did not want to.

* * *

I supposed it did not matter who cut the wood for our boat as long as the resulting planks measured up to the need, but I did not like Mr. Lawson, and I told Will so that evening.

"I'm lucky I found him," was all Will had to say as he plunked himself down and took the bowl and spoon I handed him. "I asked him if he wanted to eat with us, but he said no, he'd rather go back to his own camp."

I glared at him. "You might have asked me first."

He glanced up from his bowl. "Asked you? This food's as much mine as it is yours."

"You do not prepare it. Would you have had him eat my share, or yours?"

I could see the understanding suffuse his expression. "Oh. I hadn't thought of that."

It was not all I wanted, but it was something. I nodded.

"Okay." He shoveled in a mouthful, chewed and swallowed. "I'm going to ask him again tomorrow. It's only neighborly. He's been traveling alone, all the way from some little town back East. He's got to be lonesome for company by now. And someone else's cooking."

I held the sigh in. "Please let me know if he accepts before you both show up at the end of the day."

"Yes, ma'am." He said it in a playful way, but I was in no mood for it.

"And tell him he is not to loiter around here when he is not working."

That sobered him up. "Why not?"

I thought about it for a moment, then decided the truth was probably all that would do. "He makes me uncomfortable."

Will hooted. "You? Miss Damn-the-torpedoes?"

"I beg your pardon?"

He waved the odd phrase away. What on earth was a torpedo? "You haven't been fazed by anything since we left Dyea." He scooped the last spoonful of stew out of his bowl and swallowed it. "As a matter of fact, you haven't been bothered by anything since Captain what's-his-name tried to take your fare out in trade."

He stopped. Stared at me. Shook his head. "No. You've got to be joking. Lawson? The fellow looks like a tree stump."

I shrugged helplessly and took another bite of my own cooling food to cover my embarrassment.

"You're *not* joking. What did he say to you?"

"Never mind. It was nothing." At his dubious glance, I added, feeling foolish, "It wasn't anything he said." I didn't add that it was how he said it. "I suppose I am being oversensitive."

"If it'll make you feel any better, I won't ask him to eat with us." He shook his head, then waited as if he expected me to take back what I'd said. When I didn't, he added, "I think you're making a fuss over nothing, though."

"I probably am." But I did not think I was. I had dealt with a great many different men in the last few months, on my own, as a businesswoman. I had dealt with men who looked askance at my attire, at my circumstances, and at my independence. I was who I was, and even now I am still proud of it.

But Will was right. I had dealt with them without batting an eyelash. I had not been uncomfortable around any of them and none of their opinions of me had made me feel small. Except for Captain Trelane. And now Mr. Lawson.

* * *

Mr. Lawson did not eat supper with us the following evening. The only time I saw him that day was when I went out to care for the goats while he and Will were working at the sawpit. Even at that distance, I could see his gaze fastened upon me, and I hastened through the routine of feeding and watering them, using the mining shovel I had purchased in Dyea to scoop their frozen manure onto the heap beginning to rival Will's logpile.

Will saw him watching me, too, or perhaps noticed me watching them, and frowned as he pulled the saw down through the log perched on the scaffold. Or I suppose he could have been scowling at the sawdust landing on his head. He had ended up on the bottom somehow, although I knew if he truly minded he would be on top. Neither position seemed to be desirable, but after the first two or three planks they both seemed to have gotten the hang of it.

I supposed if I stayed out of the way, nothing untoward would happen. Mr. Lawson had no excuse to search me out.

* * *

What with one thing and another, it had been a while since I had gone to visit Mrs. Thielsen. Including yet another escape attempt by Samson which took me the better part of a day to resolve, and then only when he was dragged back to me by an irate man who claimed the beast had tried to eat his boots. One evening in February, when the days were finally beginning to lengthen noticeably, I made my way back over to the bakery tent.

"And here I thought you had forgotten me," said Mrs. Thielsen as I ducked in through the back of the tent. "Watch yourself," she added, as I miscalculated the space and bumped into the plank table.

I grasped the table to steady it and me. "I had not forgotten you. My own business has kept me too busy for anything but work."

"This is good?" She glanced up at me, poured a lefse, took coin, and gestured me to the jam jar, all without missing a beat.

I smiled. "Yes, although had I realized I would be earning my living doing exactly what I did at home, I would have had second thoughts about bothering to make the trip."

She almost bobbled the batter bowl. "Do you think your menfolk would have given you a choice?"

Now it was my turn to be startled. I dropped the spoon. Fortunately, it landed bowl down onto the lefse I was rolling. "Menfolk?"

"You are not here alone." It was not a question.

"You are." At least I had not seen a Mr. Thielsen. Unless he was as irresponsible as Eric...

"I am. But I had no other choice." She smiled at the curiosity I did not voice. "My husband was unable to make the journey. His health would not allow it. But we needed – well. So I came. But I am not going any further. Six bits." This to the first miner in about a dozen customers who did not seem to know how much the lefse cost. She went on. "I did not realize I could make my fortune right here." She spread more batter, I spread more jam. "Here, you eat that one."

"Thank you." I picked it up and took a bite. How had I stayed away?

"Are you not making enough money you need go no farther?"

I licked my fingers. "I do not intend to mend other people's clothing for the rest of my life."

"Why not? It is an honorable calling."

"For some, perhaps."

"You are good at it." She all but laughed at me. "You thought I did not inspect the work I gave you? You should be making elegant dresses and suits, not mending holes in canvas trousers."

"I would rather go to the Klondike and find enough gold to pay someone else to make those elegant dresses for me."

She did not say anything. She did not need to.

"When Will and I get there –"

She gave me a sharp glance. "Who is this Will?"

I faltered.

"Your brother, perhaps?"

"No." Will was anything but my brother, even if he did treat me in a brotherly fashion on occasion.

"You are not married."

"No."

I risked a glance over at her. She looked positively thunderous. "Your – protector?" The tone with which she imbued that word, and, yes, I knew what she meant, put my back up straight as a ramrod.

"No!"

"What other choice is there?" she asked, her tone calm but icy.

"We are traveling together. I keep camp and do my work, he builds our boat."

"You are traveling with him, unchaperoned?"

I thought about Mr. Lawson, and, for the first time, wished I was not on my own. Perhaps another woman would have kept him from thinking – what he was obviously thinking.

"Yes. But in the most proper manner possible," I added hastily.

"How can such a thing be proper?"

"You are here alone."

"But I am a married woman." She said it with great conviction. Almost as if she were trying to convince herself, I realized suddenly. As if 'Mrs.' allowed her to do things, be places she did not feel she could do or be without it.

"And I am not an adventuress," I replied firmly. "I can take care of myself." As if it had just occurred to me, which I supposed it had, I said, "Would you like to come to supper? We would be happy to have you." And I could show her that my circumstances were as proper as it was possible to make them.

She looked taken aback. "I do not close shop until late."

"Will does not usually finish work until he can no longer see what he is doing, and we do not normally eat until he is finished."

She nodded decisively. "Someone should watch out for you, young woman. Yes, I will come."

"And you will see I am watching out for myself quite well." After all, I thought, I am inviting you. Surely that will set the odious Mr. Lawson straight about who, and what, I am.

"Would tomorrow night suit?" I asked.

"Tomorrow night would be lovely."

"Then I suppose I should get back to our – my camp, and prepare."

"Two bits." She looked almost apologetic. But she was earning her living, too.

"Oh. I am sorry." I dropped the coins in her jar.

Suddenly she laughed. "A dinner party. Here, of all places. I will look forward to it."

All my anxieties aside, so would I.

CHAPTER 14

I was on my way back to our camp when I began to wonder how Will would react to my invitation to Mrs. Thielsen, so soon after I had objected to his invitation to Mr. Lawson. But he was not the one doing the cooking, I told myself. And if he objected in his turn, I supposed I could put up with Mr. Lawson for one evening.

It would be worth it.

Part of me resented having to care what others thought of me. I didn't want to care. Not about what Mrs. Thielsen thought. Certainly not about what Mr. Lawson thought. Except that inexplicably I did care about her opinions, and it was a matter of my safety that he realize I was not an adventuress.

I tossed him out of my mind. He would think what he would think. As long as he stayed away from me, it did not matter. I had a dinner party to plan.

I had never invited a guest to supper before. But it wasn't as if I had a dining hall, or even a proper table, out here at this godforsaken way station en route to the Klondike. Part of me wished I did. Part of me was glad I did not. At least if everything was not exactly as it should be, it would most likely be the fault of my surroundings, not anything I could have done differently.

I walked back to our camp absorbed in figuring out how I could improve upon the place. Somehow, despite the circumstances, I had to impress the propriety of my situation upon Mrs. Thielsen.

By the time I reached our tent I was mentally trying out menus that would impress her with my cooking abilities in spite of the limited range of our supplies. I did not notice Will sitting on his bedroll in our tent at least an hour before his usual quitting time until he said, "Karin, where've you been?"

He did not sound right. I went to him, noticed that even under the beard he did not allow to become unkempt as many of the other men did, and the day's sawdust and dirt, he looked pale. He was cradling one mittened hand in the other.

"What did you do to yourself?"

"Nothing."

"Then why are you holding your hand that way?"

He immediately let go of it, and winced.

I leaned towards him. "Let me see."

He didn't resist. More worried than I dared let on, I took his hand, which was hot even through his mitten, and tugged the mitten off. I drew in my breath.

"It's not that bad." He tried to pull it back, but when I held on gently, he winced again and gave up.

"What did you do to it?" One whole side, the outer edge opposite his thumb, was red and swollen, but as I gently tested each finger, none of them felt broken. His ring finger and pinky might as well have been, though, for all the use they were giving him at the moment.

"I fell off the damned sawpit." His words were coming out strained. "Put out my hands to keep from landing on my head, and that one landed on a rock."

I turned his hand over, and could see exactly where it had hit. A large splotch, roughly triangular-shaped, on the outside edge of his palm near the base of his fingers, was a purple so dark it was almost black. Blood was oozing from two breaks in his skin. When I touched it feather-lightly, he flinched hard enough to almost jerk his hand out of mine.

"It's just a bruise. It'll be fine in the morning. That'll teach me to stay on the bottom, but I was tired of eating sawdust."

"It obviously did not keep you from hitting your head," I said tartly. "You are lucky you did not break any bones. At least I don't think you did." I set his hand back down on his lap and went to fetch cloth and hot water from the pot on the fire. "Can you move all of your fingers?"

"No, I didn't hit my head." He scowled as I came back with the supplies. "I landed on all fours, and if it hadn't been for that rock – you're not wrapping it up so I can't use it. I have to get back to work tomorrow. I shouldn't have stopped today, except I couldn't make my hand hold the saw."

"What makes you think it will be healed enough tomorrow to do so? Hold still. I am going to clean it and put something on it to protect it and keep it that way for tonight. You do not object to that, I suppose?"

He sighed and held it out. "It'll have to come off in the morning. Lawson will be back. He was pretty put out at me for stopping after I fell."

This did not surprise me. "Did he not see your hand?"

"No." This did not surprise me, either. "But at least he yanked the saw out of the way so I didn't land on *it*."

"He is not waiting for you, is he?"

"No." He sounded angry now.

At least he'd had that much sense. I decided to change the subject. Might as well get it over with. "I have invited Mrs. Thielsen to supper tomorrow night."

He'd been watching me clean his hand as if he was afraid I would cut it off at the wrist, but that brought his gaze up. "I didn't think that was allowed unless we both agreed."

"No. It was not allowed unless the cook was given enough advance notice to prepare more food. Since you do not do the cooking, I was not aware you needed advance notice as well." I finished the wrapping, which did immobilize him somewhat whether he liked it or not, with a knot at both ends of the muslin.

He winced again, but flexed his fingers to the limit of the bandage and looked surprised. "I guess that'll do for tonight."

I nodded. "I will look at it again in the morning." It was not a question, and I waited for him to object, but he did not. It was not that I cared if he broke every bone in his body, I told myself. He could do all the damage he wished to himself. But not until we reached the Klondike and went our separate ways.

He leaned back on the sack containing his clothing. I stood, ducking my head automatically to keep from brushing up against the too-low canvas roof of our tent. I was about to leave the tent to start our supper when he said, casually, "Since you've already invited company, why don't I ask Lawson, too? Get all the hospitality over with at once?"

I was glad he could not see my face. I had been willing to reciprocate, but not at the same time. I suspected Mr. Lawson's presence would not help my campaign to prove the propriety of my situation to Mrs. Thielsen. But I could hardly explain that to Will without him poking fun at me. He claimed to understand the precariousness of my reputation and my need to protect it, but he most emphatically did not.

Apparently I was failing to answer him as promptly as he wished. "What? You're not still scared of him, are you?"

"No, of course not."

Something in my voice must have given me away, because his went gruff as he asked, "You are, aren't you? Why? He hasn't bothered you, has he?"

No, he had not. At least not in the sense Will meant. Mr. Lawson had not so much as approached me since our first meeting. I don't know what, if anything, Will told him about me, but, except for his gaze following me at a distance from the sawpit as I went about my daily duties, I would not have known he was there. Except that it did follow me. And I did know.

"He's an all right fellow once you get to know him."

"I am sure he is."

"No, you're not." But his voice had no heat in it.

"Go ahead and invite him." Somehow I knew my cause was already lost, with or without him. Mrs. Thielsen was going to read the worst into my situation, anyway. She would want to, to keep her own situation respectably above mine, since she had to know I harbored doubts about what I was quite sure was a non-existent Mr. Thielsen. She would probably be glad to meet Mr. Lawson on that account alone, to add to her doubts about me.

"You sure?" Will did not sound as if he thought I was.

I was. I was not. I wanted to take a sharp stick to him, since he did not seem to understand anything less subtle. "Do not give me a chance to change my mind," I said lightly, and ducked out of the tent.

I had expected some sort of bantering reply to follow me, but it did not. The silence that did was much more unnerving.

* * *

I could not concentrate on my sewing the next day, and gave it up after the noon meal as a lost cause. I would work twice as hard the next day to catch up. I had nothing promised in the next several days at any rate, even if my customers cared whether I met my self-imposed deadlines, which they did not.

I stretched the kinks out of my back as I took an assessing look around our camp, trying to see it as Mrs. Thielsen would.

I could not do a thing about the tent. It was one tent. We were two unrelated people of opposite sexes, and we were sharing it. Never mind that I had arranged things so my bedroll was at one end, our supplies were arranged in a mountain in the middle so standing by my bedroll I could not see Will's and vice versa – most definitely vice versa – and his bedroll was at the other end. We were still sharing a tent, an unmarried, unrelated couple, and there was no excuse for it, even though there was good reason.

I had done all I could there, and I had done it all long before I met Mrs. Thielsen, for my own reasons, and my own sense of propriety.

I could have moved out under the stretch of canvas covering my makeshift seamstress shop, I suppose, but I would not have felt safe there. I would have been much colder, too, open to the elements in every direction but up. I did not even leave my sewing machine there overnight, let alone my person.

I am not sure Will would have allowed it, either. He might not have been a 'protector' in the only sense of the term Mrs. Thielsen understood, but he did protect me. We did not speak of it, but he did.

I did not give him enough credit for that.

And so. On to the rest of our camp. I could, and had, let things get a bit untidy. It hadn't seemed to matter. No one saw it but us. It was impossible to have a place for everything and everything in its place in such a cramped spot.

Will's end of the tent, in particular, I had all but given up on. He insisted he had an order and a system, but if he did I could not see it. I supposed he would object to my straightening it up, but he would have to understand.

I rolled up my sleeves, figuratively speaking since it was too cold to do it literally, and went to work.

* * *

I had decided to cook the last of Will's moose, which I had been doling out bit by bit since Will had not deemed it worth his time to do any more hunting. To go with it I cooked more of the ubiquitous beans and rehydrated some dried peaches and plums, which would make as much of a salad as was possible in this benighted place.

The last of the goats had long since quit giving milk, or I would have poured some cream over the top of the fruit. But it was the best I could do. A piece of real meat that had not been dried or smoked and carried in from Outside was about as exotic a treat as existed here, and should impress Mrs. Thielsen.

Most of the argonauts were city men for whom hunting was not an everyday skill. I would never tell Will, but I was extremely pleased with my acumen in becoming the partner of one of the few here who knew what he was doing in the wilderness.

I had begun the meal's preparation last night by setting the frozen block of meat next to the fire to thaw, and soaking the beans. I rinsed them and set them to simmer at the edge of the fire with a bit of my precious molasses and some bacon, then checked the meat's condition, which was almost thawed.

I added water to the moose meat in its pot, and from my little hoard of spices, thyme and sage and dried onions, then hung it directly above the fire. And mentally thanked that prissy man in Dyea who had sold those spices to me along with the the clothes on my back. It wasn't my mother's flavorful Scandinavian cooking, but it was the best I could do.

By late in the afternoon I was more than pleased with the results of my work. My table, several crates pushed together under the tent, did not allow for knee room underneath, but it looked respectable, covered with a piece of cloth from my stores. It was blue, figured in green and white, and I had scavenged it from among the piles of goods at the foot of the Golden Staircase, now several months ago, without a thought as to what use I would put it. It had simply been too pretty to leave behind.

Now I was glad I'd brought it. I set it with all of the dishes and cutlery at my disposal, and thought it made the tin plates and wooden-handled knives look at least a bit more respectable than they would have otherwise. I cut and hemmed napkins from the same stores, folded them neatly, and set both of our lamps in the center. More packing crates draped with cloth provided seating, and I only wished I had the means to create cushions. Still, it looked, well, respectable. And pretty. Pretty was not something to take for granted here. Neither was civilized.

All in all, I was more than pleased with myself when Mrs. Thielsen arrived. It was the first time I had ever seen her without her apron, but these were not her everyday clothes, either. She wore a dress of black wool sateen that made my poor tablecloth look dingy, and me look like a drudge. The dress was plain, long-sleeved, and missed the ground by bare inches, the short hem and her sturdy boots the only concessions I could see to our less than civilized surroundings. The fabric shone in the lamplight and the shawl she wore with it was of vivid, heavy wool plaid.

Her bright smile and greeting as she hustled towards the fire did not make me feel any better about how I looked. I had put all of my attention towards my table and the meal because there had been nothing I could do about my own appearance. Oh, I was as clean as I could be, and I had even washed my hair that morning before I retwined my braids and wrapped them into a roll at the back of my head.

But the dress I had been wearing when I stowed away all those months ago had only been workaday calico to begin with, and fairly worn already. It had been stained and torn to the point of ruination by the time we arrived at Dyea, and damaged beyond all repair by the time I had earned the money to buy my outfit.

I had, quite without regret, consigned it to rags and packed my corset away the moment I purchased clothing to replace the dress. None of which had been created with a woman's tastes or modesty in mind. At the time it had not mattered one whit. I had been happy to abandon all unnecessary encumbrances.

But I quite heartily wished now that I had taken the time to sew myself one dress. One skirt. Even one shirtwaist with a bit of lace on it.

I could do nothing about it, however. I knew my smile was not what it should have been as I welcomed her, but I did my best.

"What a lovely table you set," she said, running a hand over my makeshift tablecloth. I could not help but add the 'you poor thing' even if she hadn't said it out loud. "This could make lovely curtains when you have a home of your own someday."

I doubted she thought I would ever reach that stage of respectability, but I nodded, anyway.

She glanced up at me. "Are you expecting someone else tonight as well?"

I let out a breath. "Yes. Will's partner at the sawpit, Mr. Lawson." I don't know why I felt as if I needed to explain further, but I was about to, when both men strolled around the corner of the tent and came to a stop.

CHAPTER 15

"Well, hello, Mamie." Mr. Lawson's no-longer-so-cultured voice boomed out into the silence. Will dropped the tent flap and we were plunged into semi-darkness, illuminated only by the shifting shadows of the lamplight against the canvas. "I never expected to see you here. I thought business was pretty good in San Francisco."

I turned to Mrs. Thielsen in surprise. He was the last person with whom I expected her to be on a first-name basis. "You know each other?"

Her face was working as if she was about to cry. She made as if to head for the tent flap, but her legs gave way under her, and she sank onto one of my crate-seats. Her head resting splat in the middle of one of my carefully arranged place settings, she waved an arm at all three of us. Warding us away? Probably.

I sank down beside her, anyway. "Fellows, go away. Can't you see that something has upset her?" I glared at the odious Mr. Lawson

Instead, he plunked himself down on another crate. "I'm hungry. You promised me a meal."

I shot Will a desperate glance. He just stood there looking baffled, drat him, then, drat him even more, he said, "So'm I. I'll dish it up. You ladies just go ahead, and, " he faltered. "Do whatever it is you're doing."

"Ladies?" Mr. Lawson laughed. "I don't know what that one's been telling you, but she's no lady."

Mrs. Thielsen lifted her head. "You would not know a lady if you stepped on one. As you have done, many times."

"I only took what you and your kind were selling. Where's your 'shop', Mamie? I'd like to come see you again."

I stood up. Will, in spite of what he'd said, had made no move towards my cookpots. "Both of you will leave this tent at once."

Will stared at me, but started to leave. *Mr.* Lawson planted his feet and smiled. It was one of the ugliest smiles I've ever seen.

"Will." I did not say it as a question.

"Come on, Lawson." Will lifted the tent flap and waited, pointedly.

"Why? I just want what I came for. And maybe a little more, now that I know what's on offer." Lawson stepped forward.

Mrs. Thielsen's head came up. "Do not touch me. I am not in that business anymore."

"Once a whore, always a whore." He turned his nasty gaze on me. "Both of you."

And that, bless Will, was when his fist met Lawson's face, hard enough to knock that, that *barbarian* flat on his back.

* * *

We did end up eating at least part of my fancy supper that night, Will and I. Mrs. Thielsen pleaded a loss of appetite, and I could not blame her. She was gone, without saying another word, by the time Will came back from dragging *Mr.* Lawson away, I know not where. Nor did I much care.

Her eyes had said enough. So had Mr. Lawson.

Will's punch had knocked the horrible man out cold, or perhaps it was the corner of the crate his head banged against with enough force to for it to hit one of our tent poles and knock everything cattywampus. The tent pole mattered much more to me, frankly. I set about straightening it up, and had long since succeeded when Will finally stuck his head back into the tent.

"All clear?"

"I suppose."

He came the rest of the way in, looking relieved. "I'm sorry."

That startled me. "What have you to be sorry for?"

"Not paying attention when you told me he bothered you."

The lack of attention had been no more than I had expected of him. I was much more impressed with his efficient treatment of the odious man when it came right down to it.

"I am sorry as well."

"What for?"

"I did not mean to bring a woman like that into our —" I did not choke on the word, not quite. "Home."

He looked around the tent, his eyes evidently taking in my attempt at a civilized supper table for the first time. He didn't smile, but he looked as if he wanted to. "You didn't know. Besides, according to everything I've seen of her, she's not a woman like that anymore. Lawson shouldn't have —" He let the sentence hang. "Well, I knew the man was obnoxious, as my Dad would say. I just didn't realize how far he'd go beyond obnoxious."

He looked at me, and obviously saw more than I wanted him to. I couldn't help letting him. It was equally obvious he had been going to say more, but instead he changed the subject. "We shouldn't waste your pretty table. Or what you've got that's smelling so good in those pots."

So Will and I dined, with cloth napkins and by lamplight, on the last of his moose, stewed with onions and herbs, baked beans with molasses, and dried fruit salad, and chatted about inconsequentialities as if nothing had happened.

At last, Will pushed his crate-stool back so that he could lean against the pile of our baggage. "That was the best meal I've had since leaving home, and that's saying something."

I could not help smiling. Since I had been cooking for four, I'd thought we would have more leftovers than we did, but it did not bother me. I pushed my crate back as well, and wiggled until I found a comfortable spot to lean into, next to Will.

He glanced down at me. "The company you keep doesn't say who you are, you know. Besides, nobody else knows about Mrs. Thielsen's past. If they did, it would have come out by now and she'd have been out of business."

I pulled in a breath. "They will now."

"Not for a while, I bet." I glanced up at him. He grinned down at me, and suddenly I realized his arm was about my shoulders, resting lightly as if he would pull it back at the slightest indication from me. I found I did not want him to pull it back. I leaned into him, just as cautiously.

"Why do you say that?" I asked, although I was not sure I wanted the answer.

"Let's just say that when he wakes up he's going to have a hard time doing much of anything besides going back to the hole he crawled out of."

"What did you –" I stopped. I suspected I really did not want to know. "Never mind. I am sorry you lost your partner."

"I'm not. I don't need him anymore."

"You don't?"

We both started as the tent flap moved. It was not the wind. Surely it was not the odious Lawson. It would not be Mrs. Thiel – Mamie. I jerked out from under Will's arm and we both leaped to our feet as the flap rose to admit – Eric.

"Where the hell have you been?" The words were Will's. I admit I was stunned speechless. I had long since assumed Eric had abandoned us for good.

Eric shrugged his pack off into the middle of my table. Before I could object, he said, "Taking photographs. Many, many photographs, more than I ever dreamed. The Klondike truly is a gold mine, even if it cost most of what I made to ship the finished plates home. When I return I will be able to make my fortune on those plates, and even now I have enough to buy the lumber for our boat.

"Although," he added, a pleased look on his face, "judging from the pile of planks outside, it does not look as if I will have to spend it."

"No thanks to you," Will all but snarled. "How was I supposed to know you'd even come back?"

I found my voice as well. "You just – left. And you didn't come back, and didn't come back."

Eric looked puzzled. "Of course I was coming back. The rest of my plates are here. And the goats."

"Oh, of course," Will said. "You weren't going to abandon the *goats*."

"Of course not. Nor you." He ignored both my snort and Will's outraged expression. "I brought mail from Skaguay." He rummaged in his pack. "Several letters from your family, Will."

"Well, that's something at least." Will snatched the letters from Eric's outstretched hand, and carried them and one of the lamps over to his bedroll.

Eric glanced at the remains of my supper table. "That is pretty," he said mildly. "Did it taste as good as it smells? I have not had cooking as good as yours since I left here."

I sighed and gave up. "Move your pack out of the way and sit down."

* * *

As he wolfed down the last of my aborted supper party's leftovers, I looked him over. He did look as if he had not eaten well in a while. Or washed himself or his clothing. Even his formerly clean-shaven face had several inches of blond hair sprouting from it. Now that I had a chance to observe him, in fact, he looked exhausted.

But he had more to tell me between bites than I had heard him say during the last week before he left us.

"The White Pass Trail from Skaguay is horrible, worse than anyone said it would be."

"I saw some of the horses that had traveled that trail," I said as he plunked another bite of moose meat in his mouth and chewed, a blissful expression briefly chasing over his face before it disappeared again into, was that disgust? It had better not be from my cooking. "I have never seen such miserable-looking creatures."

"You saw the ones who survived. Hundreds did not." He swallowed. "And no one cares. The ones who come after trample over them until they become part of the mud and the rocks. Men beat animals that can go no farther until they drop dead in their tracks, then they curse and beat them some more. I heard tell of one that men swear committed suicide by leaping over the cliff. It would not have been hard for it to find such a place. That trail should never have been advertised the way it was.

"Cheechakos" he glanced at me and I nodded. I knew the word. It was what the Chilkoot Indians on the pass called all of us newcomers. "Cheechakos think that it will be like riding down the streets of Seattle, when in reality it is not even a trail at all."

"Surely it is more of a trail than Chilkoot Pass," I said as he took a mouthful of peach.

"At least no one expects to take a horse over the Golden Staircase." He shook his head, swallowed and scooped up a spoonful of beans. That pleased expression fleeted over his face again. "I did not realize how much I missed your cooking, Karin."

"Then you should not have stayed away so long," I told him tartly. I glanced over at Will, who was still head down in his letters, trying not to envy him.

"I am sorry not to have any letters for you," Eric said. "I know you are not expecting any," he added as I opened my mouth, "But that does not make me any less regretful."

I shrugged. "Have you had enough?"

He smiled. It was hard not to forgive that smile. "Yes. Thank you."

I gestured at the pot of wash water simmering on the fire. "Would you like to use that? I can heat more." It was for me as much as it was for him, I told myself. He smelled about as bad as he looked.

"Thank you, Karin. Yes, I would."

"Leave me your clothes as well, and I will take care of them," I heard myself say.

"No, you will not," he said firmly, removing his coat. "Unless they need mending, which I do not think they do. I am quite capable of washing them myself."

"Here is the soap, then," I said, fetching it from the sack I kept it in and handing it to him.

He accepted it. "Thank you."

"The sooner you clean your reeking self up, Eric, the happier we will all be." With that, I retreated to my bedroll and rolled to face the canvas wall. For once, the dishes could wait until tomorrow. I had had a long enough day already.

CHAPTER 16

The next morning Eric inspected the goats and tended them himself, coming back to tell me as I began catching up on my work that I had dealt with them to his satisfaction. As if his satifaction mattered. When I stopped for food at noon, I found the men at the crate table poring over a piece of paper by lamplight.

Yes, it was the middle of the day and it should have been bright enough, at least in theory, to examine whatever one wanted to examine by daylight. Daylight is not very useful for examining anything in detail when it is shrouded in damp and fog, however. I pushed my hood back and went to join them.

The piece of paper was covered in drawings, or, rather, in one large drawing that looked recognizably like a boat, and a number of smaller, more detailed drawings of what I presumed were parts of the boat. It looked to have two prows, so that I could not tell which was the front and which the back, and it was relatively flat-bottomed, presumably to handle better in shallow water.

It looked riverworthy enough to me, though not like anything I had ever seen on Puget Sound. Or like anything else I had seen under construction in my brief and infrequent forays along the shore. Nor did it look even remotely like the drawings in Will's book.

This, it seemed, was Will's main, I will not call it an objection, perhaps just a dubiousness. It was not until I realized he was the one peppering Eric with questions and not vice versa on details I could not even discern that I grew bored and started putting a meal together.

They kept the discussion up while they ate, and I went back to my sewing machine.

I am not sure when it was I had decided I could entrust some things, including Eric, to Will. He did, after all, trust me to keep him fed and his clothing in good order, and to husband our supplies carefully, which were every bit as important to our immediate survival as his share of the work. If we were to arrive safely in Dawson City to make our fortunes, we needed to work together. Time enough once we arrived to go our separate ways.

Although I did wonder if Will would be as eager to go his own way once we got there as I know Eric and I were. And if I would mind if he was not.

I picked up another pair of trousers, and thought some of my Norwegian curse words at a particular Seattle merchant whose "Klondyke all-weather trousers" had been sewn with such poor thread it seemed every pair they sold had passed through my hands at one time or another. Then again, perhaps I should not have been cursing them, because they kept my hands busy and filled my purse. Even if the fabric they were made from was not much better than the thread, much less "all-weather." This I had first-hand from the men who brought them in.

A shadow crossed my lap again. I looked up to see both men gazing down at me. "What do you want?"

"You have nothing to say about this?" Eric asked, gesturing with the drawing.

My foot stopped on the treadle. "I know less about boats than either of you."

"That's not what you were saying a couple of months ago," Will told me.

"Yes, but that was when you were insisting your book was the Bible, and unwilling to listen to any other authority. You have become much wiser since then."

Eric grinned. "She has you there, my friend."

They watched me put a few more stitches into those wretched trousers. It made me self-conscious, and I looked up again. "Is there something you need from me?"

"Just your curiosity," Will said. "Your stamp of approval."

I could not help feeling pleased, even as I wondered if my disapproval would make any difference whatsoever. "Will it be large enough to take all of our goods in one trip?"

"Yes," Eric said.

"Including your cameras, my sewing machine, and Will's book?"

They both laughed, and Will said, "Yes. We know better now."

"Then I approve. Or I will once you have it built." I put my foot back on the treadle.

"Well," said Will, "If that's the best she's going to give us, I guess we'd better have at it."

* * *

And so the long hours of sawing and hammering, argument and resolution, and frustration and satisfaction began. Eric complained about the quality of the boards. Will showed him the small crooked spruce trees that were all that was available to cut them from and challenged him to do better. Will complained about some detail or other of the plans, and Eric mentioned the quality of the boards and asked him to create something better with them. I complained about how it seemed as if most of the pieces of the boat were being built inside our tent, and both men dragged me out into the snow and challenged me to wield saw and hammer in the occasional blizzards that still roared through even as the days grew longer and the ground began to thaw.

But somehow we managed to keep from murdering each other. I'm still not sure how, especially when we heard about the partners who split up, literally, each taking half of every item they had brought along, including a sack of flour they cut down the middle.

As it turned out, watching partnership after partnership break down over those godforsaken sawpits, perhaps Eric had been right in escaping with his cameras and leaving Will to manage that part of the affair. And as Will told me, sitting down on his crate to yet another meal of beans and bacon, yet more partnerships had broken up because there was no one to "keep camp," and more blame was thrown by men who came back to their tents hungry at mealtime and no one to cook.

This place was getting to us all. I always thought spring took too long to come in Ballard each year, the cold rain returning over and over when we'd thought it gone at last, but that winter made me add yet another item to my list for when I became rich. Wherever I built my mansion and planted my gardens, it was going to be somewhere warm. And not just in the summertime. I was going to be able to go outdoors in January, let alone April, without wearing long underwear, thick stockings, wool trousers, heavy coat, muffler, cap, hood, mittens, and boots.

Honestly, that winter I would have been happy to be somewhere where I only had to put on heavy clothing to go outdoors. A tent, even one with a red hot fire in it, is never warm, especially when the temperature is cold enough for your breath to form ice crystals in front of your face when you let it out, and inhaling is like swallowing glass shards. I was going to live somewhere where I could go outdoors in a cotton dress in the dead of winter. Surely I could find somewhere like that. California, perhaps.

'Mrs.' Thielsen had been from California, at least according to Mr. Lawson. We had not seen either one of them since that awful night, and from what I heard from my disappointed customers, the lefse tent was no more. I did not go looking for it. Or her. She'd not only misled me, but she'd made me out to be something I should not be merely because of my circumstances. Made me out to be less than she was, when she – until that day I had thought she and I were becoming friends, and I had enjoyed her company. I put her firmly out of my mind.

* * *

The daylight, such as it was, did lengthen as time went on, as the construction of our boat progressed. I developed the habit of stepping out to take a look at it once or twice a day, watching as it slowly took shape. The men seemed to enjoy pointing out this and that new part, and I had to admit ours looked much better than most of them.

Even Will came back from a reconnaissance down the shore and told us he'd seen a boat that its owner proudly claimed was built from the plans in a copy of the same guidebook Will had once brandished at us. "I wouldn't cross a puddle in that thing. It's topheavy and has too deep a draft. It's going to get hung up on every sandbar on the Yukon River, if it doesn't turn turtle the moment he launches it.

"Go ahead and say I told you so," he added to Eric, who, to his credit, only smiled and shook his head in refusal.

The weather finally began to grow warmer, and even threw out sunny hours and sometimes whole days. We all watched the ice on the lake as if it held our destiny, which I suppose it did. These days it never looked the same for two days running. The wind pushed the floes into small mountains and then bashed them against each other until they disintegrated. The nights were still too cold for even a small patch of open water to last till morning.

At last the ice grew spongy and gray. The snow on the ground had long since begun to melt, and the goats, which had been subsisting on small rations of grain and whatever twigs and branches we could find to cut and bring back to them, enjoyed their first taste of grass since we left Dyea. Even a few wildflowers poked their heads up on the hillsides above the tent city.

I was standing outside our tent, breathing air that did not slice at my lungs and wondering if unbuttoning my coat would be too rash, when I heard the shouting.

"There's a man come upriver from Dawson! From Dawson!"

"Where?" I asked, my heart in my throat, but the man did not stop. Men went back and forth regularly over the passes to Skaguay and Dyea, giving us contact Outside, but this was the first news of the Klondike we'd had since the river froze over.

He shouted back. "He's at the Grand Hotel," and dashed on.

The grossly-overnamed Grand Hotel was like similar hostelries I'd seen in the temporary communities on the trail up to Chilkoot Pass the previous fall. It was not what the word implies, but simply a board structure with a canvas roof where, for an exorbitant fee, one was allowed to roll out one's bedroll on the floor wherever space could be found. One could buy liquor there as well when the saloon was not being used as sleeping quarters.

Eric and Will, having heard the excitement in the man's voice, if not the sense of his words over their hammers, came running up. Will asked, "What's going on?"

To which another man in the ever-growing stream of men yelled back, "A fellow. From Dawson! He sledded the full 600 miles with the most ornery-looking set of dogs I've ever seen. He says the river's still full frozen, but ought to be breaking up any day now."

Will said, "I'm going to see. You two coming with me?"

It appeared we were. Eric and Will threw down their tools, and I followed. The closer we got to the hotel, the thicker the crowd became. We were all so hungry for any information I would be surprised if anyone on all of Lake Bennett was still at work or even at his camp. I even saw 'Mrs.' Thielsen, who I had thought long gone, perched on a tree stump, and by perched I mean she was standing on her tiptoes on it so she could see above the men's heads. She looked anxious. As well she ought, I thought spitefully.

All of a sudden I felt hands at my waist and a pair of shoulders pushing at the back of my legs, and the next thing I knew I was up above the crowds, too. "Can you see better now?" came Will's muffled voice. I reached down and scooped my coat out of the way.

The green cap I had mended at least twice over the winter poked between my legs, and my feet draped over his chest where he held them. I said, "Will, what on earth?"

His voice was clearer when he answered, "I figured one of us ought to get a good view and you're the lightest. What's going on?"

Nothing, at least so far as I could tell. I leaned forward, hoping to get a better look. Will staggered a bit, and yelped when I grabbed his head but hung on tightly to my ankles.

It was all I could do to keep from squeaking. "Put me down!"

"In a minute."

But then someone shoved out through the door and stood on the planks doing service as a stoop. "Wait," I said.

"Just stay still," Will replied, and Eric laughed.

"Hush," I told him, but the entire mob had gone quiet.

The man on the stoop stared around at the crowd and shook his head. "You're too late!" he called out. "All the good claims have been taken!"

That caused a rumbling, I can tell you. Not that I believed it for an instant. In a country this large, there would always be more gold to discover. I could feel more than hear the vibration as Will growled in frustration.

"And if you've spent this winter eating all your supplies, don't think you can buy more when you get there, either. There's barely enough food in Dawson to feed them that's already there."

Well, and we still had enough food to last us a good long time, and we had the goats, and surely the hunting and fishing would be better once we were out on the river, and of course the steamboats would bring plenty of supplies to Dawson once the ice melted.

"That's all I have to say."

"All!" yelled somebody. "You better tell us more than that. What about the gold?"

"There's them who's dug out fortunes, and them who's dug 'em out and lost 'em," the man replied. "It's damned hard work, though."

The incredulity went through the crowd like butter on hotcakes, and someone shouted, "Tell us somethin' we don't know!"

"How much are you bringin' out?" That voice piped above the racket, sounding young enough that it hadn't even broken yet.

The man shook his head and went back inside the hotel. I think half the crowd would have followed him, and too bad for the woman who guarded the door, but she'd apparently taken the precaution of hiring herself a couple of bruisers who stood one on either side of it. They blocked the crowd from knocking the place down trying to get in.

The throng began to break up and head back where they'd come from. "Put me down," I told Will.

"You'd just get trampled." He struck off down the beach with me hanging on to his head for all I was worth. We acquired a few ribald comments and some rude laughter along the way, and as soon as we had outdistanced the bulk of the crowd I said, "Take me over to that rock."

He did, and I climbed down. He straightened, rubbed the back of his neck, grinned, and said, "You're heavier than you look."

I glanced heavenward. "God save me from ill-mannered men." I sobered as we continued back to our camp. "Where's Eric?"

"You need to ask? He's probably talking the fellow into having his portrait taken, and paying handsomely for the privilege while he tells him everything he didn't want to yell to a crowd."

"Perhaps I should have asked him if his clothes needed mending?" I asked, looking up at Will slyly.

His lips quirked. "I don't see why not."

Abruptly I turned and headed back the other way. Will followed me, our footsteps crunching on the pebbles.

There was barely enough room to edge into the place sideways, in spite of the best efforts of the guards at the door. They took one look at us, however, and apparently decided throwing a female out on her ear probably wasn't a good idea.

I wanted to hold my breath. I thought I was used to the smells of unwashed bodies, including my own. Not to mention cooking smells and heaven knows what else. I'd long since become used to the trench draped with canvas we used as a latrine, sans lime or anything else to knock the stench. It was still better than finding nonexistent privacy in the spruce scrub. But I had utterly forgotten what the reek of alcohol did to magnify the rest.

Holding my breath would be counterproductive. Instead I nudged my way past and around and through the crowd to where, yes, indeed, Eric was holding forth with the new arrival. He held onto his camera on its tripod in one hand, and the magnesium powder flash in the other. A grateful smile lit his face when he saw me, and he handed me the flash.

"Pretty assistant you have there," said our subject.

"Only when I'm shanghaied into it," I said, but I accepted the flash, and waited patiently while Eric took several exposures, then told the man he would have the developed prints back to him early the next morning. I groaned inwardly. Eric had the materials with him to take prints from his glass negatives, but on the few occasions he went through the process to sell the prints before he and his customers parted ways, he had taken over most of the tent including my cookstove. I had no idea how he'd done it while he was gone.

Concentrate, I told myself. You want to learn, not get wrapped up in your own private complaints. I smiled at the newcomer. "I am a photographer's assistant only when called upon. I am a seamstress by trade. Surely your clothing and other gear have taken hard wear in the last few weeks."

"Miss," he replied, his tone and vocabulary in marked contrast to his earlier shouted comments, "everything I own has been through enough to disintegrate it in the last six months. I think it will last me until I get back to civilization, however. My name is James Marsh." He smiled at me, then glanced around the crowded room and his nose wrinkled.

I ignored the invitation to reciprocate, but smiled back at him. "You are going back all the way to Seattle, then?" I asked. "You won't find civilization any closer than that."

He laughed. "No. Just Skaguay." He took a swallow from the brown liquid in his smudged glass and grimaced. "I hope the he – Pardon me, I hope they've got real whiskey there."

I remembered Dyea. "Oh, I'm sure you'll find better."

A feminine voice behind me said indignantly, "That's good Canadian whiskey!"

He grimaced again. Eric, who had been watching the conversation, leaned his equipment against the bar, such as it was, and set down a coin. The woman took it and handed him a glass. I blinked. It was the first time I had ever seen Eric take up spirits, but he raised the glass to Mr. Marsh. "To good whiskey."

Mr. Marsh tapped his glass to Eric's. "I can drink to that."

CHAPTER 17

All in all, we really didn't learn much from Mr. Marsh. For one thing, it was almost impossible to carry on a decent conversation under the circumstances, and for another, if the proprietor herself had not been a woman I would not have lasted five minutes in that establishment.

As it was, I was the recipient of enough speculative glances from her and the men crowding the place, even those who were my customers, to make me uncomfortable. Not to mention from Mr. Marsh himself.

When Will shouldered us a path through the mob, Eric finished his drink and picked up the tools of his trade. I made my farewells to Mr. Marsh, wished him a good journey the rest of the way, and allowed my partners to finish parting a path through the crowd and out of that nasty place.

The first thing I did was take a good, deep breath and ask Eric, "Will that vile liquid make you sick?"

He laughed. "I have had worse." He paused. "But not much, and, thank God, not often."

"Good Canadian whiskey my foot," added Will. "Unless she's got a supplier none of us knows about, she's making that stuff on the premises."

"She could be getting it from Skaguay," I said.

"Not unless she's bribing the Mounties," Will said firmly. "And I doubt she'd find it worth her while to try."

I bit my lip. "If she is making it on the premises, it is Canadian." I looked at Eric, then at Will, and we all burst out laughing.

"Canadian, maybe, but that's not whiskey," Will gasped, and set us all off again.

* * *

I was staring around the tent after we got back, contemplating the boat packing considerations again, when the tent flap lifted, and Will stuck his head in. He had a very odd expression on his face. "There's somebody here to see you," he said in a voice to match his expression.

"A customer?" I asked.

"No." He ducked back, the flap flopping closed, before I could reply.

Somebody? Who? Surely not – Well, I was busy. If I didn't come out, surely they'd go away. Especially if – A sense of panic I hadn't felt in months came rushing back over me.

It had been over six months since I'd left Ballard. I never really expected anyone to come after me, not even in the beginning, and the only thing I had ever been careful about was my name, which had become more of a habit than anything else.

Will would not have betrayed me to anyone. I knew it as well as I knew my own name. Surely Eric would not have. Unless he wanted to rid himself of me before they headed north. But why? I had done everything he asked of me, and more. I had not abandoned his goods and his livestock, but cared for them as if they were my own. No. He would not –

The tent flap lifted again. This time it stayed up, held by a hand I recognized as Will's. "Since she won't come out, you go on in."

"Thank you."

The breath blew out of me in a great sigh of relief. The next one I drew was as full of irritation. "What do *you* want?"

Mrs. – Mamie straightened as she yanked her skirt through the tent hole. "I wished to see you before you leave."

"I do not wish to see you. You misled me and condemned me when your own past was worse."

She did not deny Mr. Lawson's accusations that long ago day. "I am trying to save you from my fate."

"Do not worry. I have no intentions of succumbing to your fate."

154

The look on her face was sad. "Did Mr. Lawson not convince you that truth is less important than appearances?"

I did not want or need her pity. "I cannot think of anything I care less about than Mr. Lawson's opinions. Except perhaps yours."

She nodded acceptance. "Yet it is what others will think as well."

I knew she was right about that. Until she came along, however, I had been able to convince myself it did not matter. "Because you told them."

She had the gall to look shocked. "No!" But she went on. "I do not have to. Mr. Lawson will. Believe it or not, that man has friends, or at least others he has gotten drunk with. And so do they."

"Gossip. I have no proof you did not start it." I turned away and picked up something at random. "I am busy. We only have a few more days before the ice breaks up."

She took a deep breath. "I apologize."

I could feel nothing but disdain for her. "For what? Lying to me?"

She drew herself up. "I knew no more about your past than you did about mine, and your present circumstances –"

"Yet you condemned me out of hand. Made the worst assumptions about me."

"I was trying to warn you."

"I consider myself warned."

Silence. But she did not leave. Finally I burst out, "What do you want from me? If I give it to you will you go?"

She sighed. "Perhaps we will meet again in Dawson."

"I thought you were going back Outside." It was one thing I was happy about, that I would never see her again.

"Lake Bennett will be all but deserted in a few weeks. I had hoped to make enough money to go elsewhere and open a real bakery, but as it turns out I did not. I thought I might as well keep heading north. I am sure there will be a need for baked goods in the Klondike, if my recent experience is any guide."

"Good luck." My feelings made a mockery of the words.

Which she seemed to understand. "And you." She lifted the tent flap, then, with her back to me, added, at a volume loud enough to be heard yards away, "I like your young man. The older one, he is irresponsible, but your Will is a good man. You should marry him if he will have you."

"You – you –" I could not catch my breath. The lamp I held in my hands fell to the ground with a clatter, chimney end up, thank goodness. *Marry* Will? Was the woman mad?

* * *

Mr. Marsh was gone, Eric informed us when he came back from delivering the photographs early the next morning. He had been hitching his dog team when Eric arrived. "Your Mrs. Thielsen," he told me, "was talking with him. No, I do not know about what." He shook his head at my scowl, but it was no use telling him to quit talking about her as if I owned her. He had tried to quiz me about her, and failing, he had turned to Will, who, as forthcoming about her as he was about everything else, made me wish I had a way to quiet him.

The men both worked feverishly to finish the boat. It seemed as if the final stage consisted of a hundred little details, and each one essential to its riverworthiness. The days grew warmer still, the mosquitoes came out in droves, and, something that raised my spirits in spite of everything, the few wildflowers turned into thousands, bursting out everywhere to cover the denuded mountainsides in pink and blue and gold in spite of hundreds of trampling boots.

I wished I had time to examine them more closely, but with the breakup of the ice coming any day, I had no time even to take in more business, let alone go strolling amongst the blossoms.

Everything had to be organized and repacked, and not in the sled portions of the previous fall, but in such a way as to ballast the boat in a balanced way.

The goats, several of whom were increasing much to Eric's pleasure, ate every green shoot they could reach, then tried to escape their corral to find more. Since their corral was made partly of our outfits, Eric finally resorted to tying them to a tree. Samson in particular complained bitterly about this twenty-four hours a day.

* * *

The next afternoon I looked up to find myself face to face with one of the Mounties from the post at the head of the lake, and nearly swallowed my tongue. He doesn't know you from Eve, I told myself. He held a can of paint in one hand and a brush in the other. "Boat, miss?" he asked politely.

I pointed, and followed him down to the shore where Will and Eric were, of course, 'discussing' the placement of this or that.

The Mountie cleared his throat, went directly to the bow of the boat, took his brush, dipped it in the black paint, and carefully began to draw a number right on the end of the bow.

"Hey!" said Will.

"It is the law," said the Mountie. "Every boat must have a number, and every person who means to travel in that boat must tell me his name and the name and address of the next of kin so we may send notice if he doesn't survive the trip downriver. You must report in at every checkpoint as well."

I blanched, and not out of fear of drowning, but Eric was already giving the man his name and that of his wife back in Tacoma. Will glanced over at me and, evidently seeing my reaction, raised his eyebrows. I dropped my gaze to my boots.

When Eric was done, Will said, "William McManis. My father is Charles McManis of Helena, Montana, and Yellowstone National Park, Wyoming. I don't know which place my parents might be this time of year if you do need to contact them, but my uncle tends to stay put. His name is Martin Cooper of Helena." He recited a street address, and added, as if in afterthought, "Oh, and this is my wife."

The Mountie nodded. "Mrs. McManis," and wrote the information down.

I watched the Mountie's back as he went on to the next boat. Eric went back to ours and to work without comment. I'd have sunk to the ground if it hadn't been sopping wet.

"You know," said Will, casually, as he turned to follow Eric, "if something does happen to us now, your family will never know."

I nodded, then headed back up the shingle to the tent before he could say more. Had Mamie put him up to the deception? We had not seen her since she made that ridiculous parting shot over a week ago. I was sure Will had heard her, but not that the foolish man would take her seriously even to that degree. But if she had put the thought into his mind, I was grateful to her. Reluctantly.

"Thank God," I said fervently. But I waited until I was almost back to the tent and both men were well out of earshot before I said it.

* * *

The breaking of the ice came in the middle of the night, such
as night was that late in the season that far north, on May 29, 1898.
We were all lying in our bedrolls in the tent, closed up in an attempt
to thwart the mosquitoes. I could tell by their breathing that the men
were as awake as I was. The air was close and still and even warm, and
I felt as if I wanted to crawl out of my skin with it all.

The noise wasn't all that loud at first, sort of a squeaking that
sounded vaguely like two branches rubbing together up in a tree. Or
faintly like the creaking of the boat from where I had sat trapped in the
hold on my way north from Seattle. Or like nothing at all.

"Will?" I said softly. "Eric? Do you hear that?"

"Yes," Eric said. "It is time."

"Finally," Will said in a tone of satisfaction. We all rose and went
outside, and walked the few feet down to the lake. All up and down the
shore people were doing the same thing, staring out through the silver
twilight at the surface of Lake Bennett.

It was no longer solid. A spring wind blew over the ice to us,
stinging cheeks and watering eyes, but the ice itself was cracked and
splintered, strips of gray water in a pattern like crazed pottery widening
even as we watched. One chunk, then another and another, bashed into
each other and broke into ever smaller chunks, which bobbed like small
rafts in the ever spreading channels.

It was eerily quiet, except for the noise of the ice. No running, no
yelling, no cheers or huzzahs at the sight we had all been anticipating
for weeks. Even the goats stopped their incessant bleating. I stared
up and down the lakeshore at all the other people watching as if
mesmerized at the breakup of the ice.

"Time to finish packing," Eric said, and turned back towards the
tent. It broke the spell, for us at least. I had the tent emptied of our last
few possessions in the amount of time it took Will and Eric to herd the
goats on board, then Will tore down the tent while Eric and I carried
the last of our goods on board. The last step was to set the sail and we
cast off, bobbing among the ice floes until Eric could catch the wind
with it, and then, as if the long winter had never happened, we were
moving again.

* * *

Moving again. Mere words do not convey the sheer joy of the act. The wind, a nuisance at best for the last five months, caught my hair and swirled it around my head. I laughed and swiped it out of my face. My shirt clung to me, then billowed out, then clung again. Eric shouted at me to help him with the sail, while Will, who had somehow learned more than I thought, used the sweeping oar to guide us out among the hundreds, no, thousands of boats of all kinds swarming the lake, all headed in the same direction. North. On to the Klondike again.

I knew this was history, that someday when I was living in that mansion in California, sitting out in my warm sunny garden watching my grandchildren play around me, I would tell them the story of how Grandmother sailed down the Yukon River to the Klondike to make her fortune. What it was like, the exhilaration and frustration and hard work, what the wind tasted like and how the sky looked and –

"Hey!" I yelled, as some numskull in a topheavy, ill-loaded craft nearly rammed us, "Watch where you're going!"

I could hear Will's laugh being whipped away by the wind as we left that bucket behind. "You tell 'em, Karin!"

It really was something like a race, as we all sped down the lake towards the next channel, between it and yet another lake and another, until we would finally reach the river itself.

Lake Bennett is larger than it looks, however, and by the time the evening came and the wind dropped, we were still some distance from the other end.

The canvas drooped and the boat rocked. Into the sudden silence Samson's bleated bellows and those of his harem sounded as if their calls would bounce off the mountaintops. Eric rolled and tied the sail securely for the first time, then sank down onto a canvas sack and leaned back on another one. Will secured the sweep and relaxed as well.

I stared at both of them. "Are you just going to sit there?" I demanded.

"Not much to do until the wind picks up again," Will said.

Eric smiled, but didn't say anything.

"But we just got started!" I wanted to stamp my foot, but I was afraid I would upset something. Maybe me. The ice was broken, we were on the water, we'd traveled halfway down the lake, all this, only to stop? "We could row –"

"You did not sleep tonight," Eric said. "Sit down."

I glared at him, then stared around. All around us boats of all descriptions, from a three-log raft to an enormous barge, bobbed in the still water. Some were long and narrow, some were round like a teacup. Some sank low in the water, and some bounced almost on its surface. A few looked as if they had been packed over the summit in pieces and assembled like puzzles, but most bore the stamp of the same spruce log construction materials as ours, sap oozing and boards curved.

None of them were going anywhere until the breeze picked up again. I sighed and sank onto one of the sacks serving as goat corral wall, and leaned over to pet Samson, who had learned over the winter not to bite the hand that fed him. He butted my fingers, and a couple of his ladies, who were still, I think, in shock at their new fortunes, sidled up to look for reassurance.

I knew how they felt. I slid down the sack and leaned back. Looked at both Eric and Will, both of whom appeared more at ease than I had seen either of them in weeks.

"I suppose," I said dryly, "a few becalmed hours will not make much difference one way or the other. The boat does not appear to have sinking underneath us in mind, at any rate."

CHAPTER 18

We lay becalmed most of the short night, watching the light fade and the sun perform its brief disappearing act behind the mountains. One true advantage to spending the night on the water – it thwarted the mosquitoes. I wondered if the tiny beasts were baffled as to where their smorgasbord had disappeared to so suddenly, as I dozed off to of all things the sound of singing, drifting across the water from all around us. It was as if the very mountains were making music. The last thing I heard was Will's rich baritone. I believe the words had something to do with someone called Peggy Sue.

I woke to a freshening breeze and Will's hand on my shoulder, shaking me. "Time to go, sleepyhead," he told me, grinning. "I thought you couldn't wait."

I popped up, then almost lost my balance as the boat shifted beneath my feet. The sail was up and the sun was high and I could already see the shore passing by. Along with a good many other boats, I noted with satisfaction. Will's hand steadied me at my elbow, then let go. "Got it?"

"Of course."

"Good. I'm starving. I bet Eric is, too."

I had planned for this. "You won't be for long. Give me a few minutes."

He nodded and went to relieve Eric at the sweep.

Already we had determined that Eric was our expert at the sail. He had made it obvious last winter as we'd skimmed across the ice. We wouldn't always need the sail. Once we were on the Yukon River proper we could count on the current to carry us, but while we were still on the lakes we must depend on the wind.

As I watched him skillfully tacking the boat in and out of the breeze, I almost forgave him for abandoning us most of the winter. We passed boat after boat, some I doubted would make it to the end of the lake let alone to the Klondike, but some that but for their inexpert handling could have passed us.

The scowls on the men's faces as we slid past them warmed my heart. We would arrive first. We would stake claims. And we would become rich. Not them. Not them.

* * *

I made sure both my partners and the goats, who had also awakened and were telling the world about it in raucous tones, were fed as best I could. The men ate the cold food I had prepared and stored in the last few days while we watched the slush grow like fur on the ice. The goats ate grain and still green grass. Then I sat down with my own bread and bacon, and watched in utter exhilaration my world moving past as the wind blew us along.

And watched the men. Will and Eric handled the boat as if they had been doing so all their lives. I wondered at that, then shrugged. Perhaps Will's book had discussed how to steer a boat. Or perhaps Eric had devised a way to teach him on dry land. All I knew was that he seemed far more capable than I would have expected, at least out on the wide open spaces of the lake.

Then a gust of wind harder than the rest hit us, and the sail whipped around, but instead of grabbing it Eric leaped to the back of the boat and yanked the sweep from Will's hands. His mouth was open, obviously yelling, but I could not hear him for the wind.

Will yelled back, then headed towards me. I wanted to strangle the man. The boat was tipping and the sail was flapping. We could go over at any moment. I had no idea how to bring it back to where we needed it to be, nor did I have the strength to do so even if I knew what I was doing.

He was still yelling as he came closer, but his words now appeared to be aimed at me. "Get over here!" I had no idea what he thought I could do. But when I tried to stand up I could not keep my footing and I landed on my backside hard enough to jar my teeth.

For once, he did not behave like a gentleman. "Fine," he all but growled, and shoved a rope into my outstretched hands. It turned out to be fastened to the bottom part of the sail. "Hang onto that, will you?"

He did not wait to see if I would, but went back to the sweep and gestured angrily at Eric, who gave up his place, but not without what looked like instruction Will did not want to take.

Under Eric's guidance and Will's effort both sweep and sail settled down. Eric came to take the rope from my clenched fingers. I was still holding it as if my life depended on it, which I supposed it had. "Are you hurt?" he asked me.

"N-No," I said, opening and closing my hands to unstiffen them. "But may we please not do that again?"

We had slowed down considerably, which, I decided, was not such a bad thing after all. But the shore still slid by even if we were no longer passing other boats.

The lake narrowed as it reached its outlet, and on the far shore I could see a bear wandering along the water's edge, intent on something. He was the first bear I had seen since the last time we had been on the water, and I watched him as long as I could see him. Will, from the stern, pointed and grinned as well.

That day we were among the first to reach the end of Lake Bennett. The passage to the next lake was called Caribou Crossing. Will's book said caribou were another name for reindeer, not that we saw a single animal there.

It led to what Will's book labeled Lake Tagish, and was shallow, almost marshy, with but one channel deep enough to take a boat, so narrow that no more than one could pass through at a time. We impatiently awaited our turn, then, sail furled to its pole, Eric at the sweep and Will and I at the bow on either side with poles of our own to push us away from the shallows, we passed through into open water again.

The shore of Lake Tagish looked like the shore of Lake Bennett as we had left it, trampled flat and denuded of most of its trees, but it appeared we had left the mountains behind. The country was much more open here, and the wind, as if grateful to have more room to spread out, calmed from a gale to barely enough to push us along briskly.

All of the lakes in this northern country are long and narrow, and there is no clear demarcation line between lake and river, the one becoming the other and the other changing back into the one with great ease. The wind died down again late in the afternoon, as seemed to be normal in this country, and this time Eric broke out the oars he had whittled from two of Will's planks.

This did not seem to be a skill he had been able to teach Will while still on dry land. I think they would have come to blows, or perhaps breaking the oars over each other's heads, if I had not been there.

It was not the first argument I had broken up by my mere presence, although I am still not sure why at this late date I inhibited them from the full expression of their opinions. I did not scruple to use my influence for the purpose of setting our little ship to rights again.

At any rate, the men did eventually manage to pull together and keep the boat moving forward down the lake instead of in circles or zigzags, as creative as those might have been.

They were both sweating and exhausted by the time we reached a point above the lower end of the lake, when Eric decided we should spend the night on land.

And so we had our first experience of pulling in to the shore and landing the fully-loaded boat. It required much commentary from men and goats, a great deal of splashing, and a dunking for Samson, who had managed to get out of his tether yet again.

"I don't think we ought to do more than cook here," Will said, swatting at a dozen or so of the ubiquitous mosquitoes. "We slept fine out in the lake last night."

Eric shook his head. "We should set up the tent. That will keep the mosquitoes away. Besides, we should check to make sure nothing is leaking."

Will opened his mouth again and I said quickly, "I would prefer to spend the night on dry land." I did not, actually, and I think both men knew it, but Will clamped his mouth shut and only glowered at me.

He grabbed the bag with the tent canvas in it, and hefted it over one shoulder. "If we do this every night, we'll lose precious time." He gestured out towards the lake, where two boats, one full of barking dogs and another piled high with wooden crates, went by without stopping.

I shrugged, jumped off the prow onto the muddy shore and scrambled up the bank, slapping at mosquitoes with one hand and breaking off likely looking goat fodder with the other. When I had a bag stuffed full, I threw it down onto the deck for Eric to dispense after he finished throwing the results of prior feedings overboard.

Even after only two days, solid ground felt strange under my feet. In the long twilight I fetched food and cooking gear from where Eric had tossed it up on shore for me, and lit a fire with the first of the wood Will had gathered. It was green and smoked terribly, but I had dealt with worse, and the smoke did keep the mosquitoes at bay.

Before long, we were sitting around the campfire devouring good hot food as the light finally faded into what little darkness we would have, turning the lake silver with shadow.

"I still think we ought to skip setting up the tent and sleep on the boat," Will said.

Neither Eric nor I bothered to reply, and Will sighed as Eric got up, and followed suit himself.

But they were only halfway finished spreading the canvas over the poles, and I was fetching the bedrolls off of the boat when I glanced up to see another boat out in the lake.

It did not appear to be moving, nor did I see anything moving on it, either. I supposed the people on it could be doing what Will had wanted us to do, but something seemed odd...

"Will! Eric!"

I guess my voice must have seemed odd to them, too, because both men dropped what they were doing and came to me where I stood on the edge of the bank with my arms full of bedroll. I snaked a hand free and pointed. "Does that not look strange to you?"

They peered out into the gloaming. Will sighed and said, "Looks like they're not wasting any time setting up camp."

But Eric, who was gazing into the dimness as if he could part the shadows with his eyes, said, "No, look."

And we all watched as something, the current? the wind? began pushing that boat round and round and downstream with no more consequence than if it had been a cork in a bowlful of water.

Before long it was out of sight, and we got back to work, Will taking the bedroll I had been carrying, and another as well. I brought up the rear with the third.

The fire had died down to red coals by the time we were settled in for the night, and the sky was already beginning to lighten again. I was no longer wishing we had slept on the boat, as my thoughts kept going back to that helplessly bobbing, circling craft. I wondered if its passengers would wake in the morning and wonder where they were. Or if they would wake to find themselves awash. Or aground.

The earth felt very good and solid under my bedroll, and even the mosquitoes fruitlessly whining their way around and over our tent looking for a way in sounded comforting.

* * *

As we were eating breakfast the next morning, and I was cooking the extras for our noon meal, two damp, bedraggled scarecrows stumbled up to our camp.

All three of us stood up as they approached us, and Will and Eric moved one to either side of me, although I can't say either of the strangers looked threatening in the least.

Drowned rats was a better description, their beards tangled and their clothing obviously still in the process of drying from what must have been full immersion. I've never been all that fond of a beard on a man, but at least the ones Will and Eric had grown over the winter did not look as if they belonged on wild animals.

"Gentlemen," Eric said, "may we help you?"

It was the tone he reserved for people he did not approve of. Although why he disapproved of the victims of an accident, I could not say.

One of them stepped forward, squatted, and put his hands, one of which was bleeding from a cut on the palm, out to the fire.

"Let me see that," I said.

"It's nothin', ma'am." He lifted his face up to me, then rose. "Sorry. It's been a long night. I'm Johnny, and this here's Clint. Our boat went down with everything in it but us."

"Oh," I said. It seemed horribly inadequate, but then so did anything else I could think of. I poured more coffee instead, and handed the cups round.

"Thank you, ma'am," they each said in turn, and took long swallows.

What else could I do? "Sit down and eat something." There was still some oatmeal in the pot, and I could cook more bacon for lunch. They accepted the food just as politely, and sat on the ground to eat it.

"What are you going to do?" asked Eric. Will was an oddly silent presence beside me still. I spared a glance in his direction, but he looked away, and I could not read his expression.

The man shrugged. "Our trip's over unless we can figger out a way to earn another outfit."

The other man spoke for the first time. "My trip's over even if I can."

His partner glared at him. "Clint's had enough Klondike." His expression went wistful. "I ain't. But I gotta go back at least as far as Dyea, I guess, before I can go on agin."

"You might," Will said slowly, "be able to put something together again closer than that. Lot of people left a lot of stuff on the trail when they saw the elephant and headed back down."

The man who had introduced himself as Johnny brightened. "Maybe we could at that." His partner only shook his head.

Having wolfed the oatmeal and bacon, they stood again, and Will and Eric stood with them. I, preoccupied with cooking more bacon so we would have something to eat out on the water, nodded acknowledgement of their repeated thanks, and their footsteps faded into the distance under the everpresent bleating of goats.

"Poor bastards," Will said. "Okay, Eric, you win. No more sleeping on board."

"You think that was their boat last night?" I asked, dipping a plate into the fireheated wash water.

"Most likely," Will said. "Makes as much sense as anything else." He shrugged and began breaking camp.

We sailed downstream all day, Eric giving more lessons to Will on how to man the sweep, which caused a great deal of lurching back and forth across the lake, especially when Eric also had to dash forward to move the sail about. When I volunteered for the same job, they both said no, or rather no!

"Why not?"

"You do enough," Will said.

"Plenty," Eric agreed.

"But what if the two of you were swept overboard and I was the only one left on board? Would you leave me to be swept downstream alone?"

The men glanced at each other. Will said, "If we're both swept overboard, what makes you think you won't be in the water with us?"

"You are lighter than we are," Eric added.

"Oh, nonsense." I turned to go back to the bow of the boat, where the voices of men and goats, which at that moment sounded much the same to my ears, would be blown astern where I did not have to listen to them. Thanks to the small boxlike enclosure perched in the middle of the boat where Eric developed his photographs, I would not have to look at them, either.

It was not easy, however, to navigate even the few feet over bags and crates stacked till there was nothing between me and the water but two inches of freeboard around the goat pen. I had to go down on hands and knees to keep from knocking the sail out of kilter. I was just standing up again when it suddenly billowed out and struck me square in the back, knocking me off my feet and down.

CHAPTER 19

I hit what felt like liquid ice, which illogically felt even colder than the worst days of the past winter. It literally stole my breath and seemed to freeze every square inch of skin I possessed. I flailed and gasped as I managed to break the surface, then the water dragged me under a second time, a third time...

Two strong hands caught me by the wrists and hauled. I heard cursing as I banged into something hard, then another pair of hands caught me around the waist and swung me high. Somehow I didn't fall again, but I couldn't hang on as whoever had me, Eric? Will? sank down suddenly with a thud and an "oof!" I could hear the tinkle of glass and swearwords in Norwegian. I curled up, shivers wracking me, rapidly becoming shudders I could not control.

A blanket dropped down on top of me. I tried to grasp it and pull it round me, but my fingers would not work. Hands came down and did it for me, swaddling me in it like a baby. Arms lifted me, and settled me more firmly against a warm chest.

I peered up, could not see a thing, tried to free a hand to push my sopping hair out of my face. Gentle fingers did it for me. "I'm getting you wet," I said weakly.

"Don't worry about it." The voice was Will's. It was Will's lap I was sitting on, Will's arms around me. They felt far better, more secure, safer than they should have. It was not proper for me to be sitting here. It was too familiar of him. Of me. I stiffened. His arms tightened around me, and I felt his breath through my wet hair.

I should, I should – I couldn't. I felt the boat jolt, and my body jerked.

"It's all right." Will stood as the boat rocked, banging up against something. He was still carrying me. "We need to get you on shore. You need a fire, and dry clothes."

"Coffee?" My voice sounded like a thread about to break.

"You can't be in too bad a shape," he said with, was that relief in his voice? "Coffee, too." He hefted me, getting a better grip, I supposed, and stepped off the boat.

"I will get wood," Eric said. "Here."

"Wait a minute." Will set me down on the ground, which felt wonderfully solid beneath my feet, then stepped away, and back. I grabbed at the blanket as it threatened to slide off of my shoulders. A canvas bag plopped next to me. "You need some help?"

I tried to bend down to get into the bag, but my legs were too wobbly. "If you could –"

"Sure." He dug through the bag in a manner which made me wince, but I was not about to complain. "What the –?"

How that man managed to get hold of one particular item of clothing – I reached for the corset. "Give me that." And somehow found the strength to push him away from the canvas bag.

He let me have the corset, but he shoved a crate up against the back of my knees until I had no choice but to sit on it. Not that I would have chosen otherwise. I sank onto it gratefully. He lifted the sack and held it where I could reach easily. I stuffed the corset back into the bottommost corner and pulled out trousers, shirt, socks, and underthings.

An armload of spruce deadfall dropped down next to us, and Eric bent to arrange and light it. "Will, string a piece of rope," he said as he worked.

"Huh?" He stared for a second at me, as I held my dry clothing out away from my body.

"And throw a blanket over it. Give the poor girl some privacy."

"Oh." He headed down to the boat.

"Can you manage?" Eric asked.

I stared around blankly: at him, at the fire leaping up to consume the branches he had collected, at Will striding back with another blanket and some rope. The dratted boat bobbed innocently tied to a tree a few feet away. "Yes, yes, I think so."

The rope went up, and the blanket, then they both went back to the boat. Apparently that was all the privacy they could manage for me. It was all I needed, or wanted, right that moment. I was hidden from the river, at least, and anyone floating by.

Quickly I stripped down, dried myself and my hair as best I could on the blanket I'd been wrapped in, and dressed in my dry clothing. Let out a sigh of pure relief as I put my shaking red hands out to the fire.

After a few moments, considerably less than a decent interval but long enough, both men came back. "You said something about coffee," Will reminded me, and plunked the pot into the fire.

I could hear it sloshing, but I'd tasted Will's excuse for coffee before, and said hopefully, "Beans?"

"Not yet," Will said.

Eric handed me the grinder. I looked inside the empty little hopper, then pulled out the drawer full of grounds. I smiled up at him. "So you can do this for yourself."

"If I must." Eric smiled down at me.

I don't think it has ever taken so long for water to boil, or coffee to brew. Finally Will poured it into our cups and I took a long swallow. I felt it go down my throat and into my stomach, and the warmth spread out all the way to my fingers and toes. "Ohhh..." I was almost embarrassed by that moan, but I couldn't help it. It felt too good.

"I think she's going to make it." Will took another swig from his own cup. "I think I might now, too."

Eric drank deeply, then looked straight at me, an expression in his sharp, pale blue eyes I had not seen since I had reached the top of the Chilkoot Pass with my sewing machine strapped to my back. Come to think of it, I am not sure that is what I saw then. It was intimidating, to say the least. "Please have the courtesy not to do that again."

"I didn't do it on purpose," I began, but Will broke in.

"For pete's sake, Eric, it was an accident. You think she would have done something that stupid on purpose?"

I could feel myself going scarlet. With rage, not embarrassment. I turned on Will. "You both saw me going forward. The least you could have done was keep better control over the boat when people are moving about on it!'"

"I can't control the wind, you little fool!"

I jumped to my feet. "If you can't control the boat, then you are no more capable of manning that sweep than you say I am!"

He thumped to his. "I am perfectly capable of manning the sweep, and if you hadn't gone stalking off in a snit without watching where you were going, it's not my fault!"

"I *was* watching where I was going!" We were toe to toe now.

"Didn't look like it to me."

I could see every lash around his angry brown eyes. "So that's why you didn't have control of the sail. You were watching me instead of paying attention."

Will inhaled, but Eric broke in. "Children. Children."

Will and I both turned on him. "I am not a child," I said indignantly, at the same time Will said, "Watch who you're calling a child, Hoel."

"I am only describing what I see," Eric said mildly.

"Have you, " I asked, with as much dignity as I could muster, "never seen two adults have an argument?"

"Two adults? I didn't think I was arguing with Eric."

I rounded on Will again. "Oh, you. Hush until you have something sensible to say." I poured a second round of coffee into our cups, and dumped the pot over the fire, which went a small way to putting it out. Will took the pot and filled it from the lake, then poured it over the fire as well.

As we all climbed back aboard the boat and prepared to cast off again, Will said, "Well, at least your dunking didn't put your fire out."

I glanced back at him as I seated myself carefully in the bow. "It takes more than soaking me to accomplish that."

"Yeah. So I've noticed over the last few months." He paused, then untied the rope from the tree Eric had fastened it to. "Don't let it give you a swelled head, but I don't think that's such a bad thing."

I was still thinking about his comment as we started down the lake again.

* * *

We went from lake to river to lake again, heading ever downstream and ever farther north. Lake Tagish widened out as we crossed its Windy Arm, which more than lived up to its name as the whitecaps roiled around us and the cold breeze swept down off the still-snowy mountaintops. We were all glad to see the far shore, and better yet, to reach it, that day. Lake Marsh, with its swampy inlet, almost caused us to run aground.

All three of us liked the river better than the lakes, but I was in favor of anything that kept us from having to use the oars, or, worse after my experience, the sail. The lakes must have had something of a current to keep the water moving, but it was only as we approached each successive outlet that we could feel it pulling the boat along.

Most of the channels between the lakes were either marshy or rocky. It wasn't until we reached the first of the rapids that we saw the sheer power of the river we proposed to travel down for several hundred miles.

"It's called Miles Canyon," Will said. "After General Miles. My dad met him once in Montana when I was a kid." He sounded proud. I could not see why it was useful information.

The hand-lettered sign, reading "Cannon," was almost redundant. The Mounties' cabin, the dozen or so boats tied up at the bank, the men milling about on shore, all would have told us something was ahead to beware of. Not to mention the acceleration of the current.

Eric guided our boat neatly in between a barge loaded with wooden crates that made our bateau look small, and an odd-looking little boat he called a wherry, and Will jumped out to tie us up.

I elected to stay on board. The Mounties still made me uneasy. I knew it was a ridiculous fear. I had made it this far with Will's deception, so I would most likely make it clean all the way to Dawson. No one here cared if I was a runaway. But the law, no matter whose or where it was, still made me uncomfortable. I wondered if I would ever get past starting this journey as a stowaway.

At any rate, Will and Eric were back sooner than I expected. They were, as I should have known they would be, arguing.

It wasn't until Will said, "She's not going to like it," that I started paying attention.

"I'm not going to like what?"

"The Mounties say no women or children are allowed to ride through the canyon. It is too dangerous." Eric spread his hands. "There is a portage. It runs along the edge of the cliff."

"So I guess we'll take the boat down, you walk around, and we'll meet you at the other end." Will smiled at me, but I could see him bracing for a fight.

"The Mounties say it is safer for me to walk around the canyon alone than it is to ride through it on the boat I have been traveling aboard since we left Lake Bennett?"

"You've already fallen in once," Eric commented.

Will and I both turned to glare at him. "Through no fault of my own!" I said indignantly.

"Hoel, you idiot, shut up. You won't be alone," Will assured me. "There's lots of people doing the same thing, not just women. Some of 'em are portaging everything but their boats, and lining those through." At my sour expression, he added, "I guess one of us could walk you down, then come back and run the boat through."

I simply looked at him.

"I knew that would not help," said Eric. "You will bring attention to yourself if you attempt to break the Mounties' rules."

I turned the look on him. He shut his mouth.

"Have you two reconnoitered the canyon yet?" I asked.

"No."

"Not yet."

"Hadn't you better, then? Or is it not possible to do from the shore?"

Will, poor fellow, looked relieved. Did he honestly think I had given up so easily? He should have known me better by now. Eric, on the other hand... Well. He did not look relieved. He looked suspicious. But he only shrugged and led the way off. Will glanced back at me as they headed downriver along the bank. I waved. He said something to Eric, who did not look back at me. They both trudged on.

I did not know how much time I would have before they returned, so I got right to work. The first thing I did was find a scrap of paper and a pencil to write a note. I needed to make them believe I had taken the portage trail before they returned. I stuck it to the handle end of the sweep with a small splinter.

The second thing I did was make a space for myself inside the small, windowless cabin Eric used to develop his plates. This was not easy. I had to rearrange things more drastically than I intended, and when I was done one crate still sat out on the deck, looking about as innocuous as the Union Jack atop the Mounties' guard post.

I was still trying to figure out what to do with it when a voice behind me said, "Need some help, miss?"

I about jumped out of my skin, but I turned around. Oh, dear, I thought. Speak of the devil. The mountie smiled at me. I swallowed. "No, thank you."

"Where are your menfolk?"

"Off to look at the canyon."

"You know the law." It was not a question.

"Yes, sir."

He gave a bemused glance to Samson and his ladies, raising their usual ruckus. Some of the nannies were getting quite large. We were all devoutly hoping they waited to drop their kids until we arrived in Dawson.

"Surely you don't mean all female creatures," I said.

He chuckled. I suppose it should have sounded cheerful, but all I wanted was for him to go away.

"No, certainly not."

"Thank you."

He nodded, and went on to the next boat. I let out my breath. Gave Samson and the nannies – and the space their pen occupied – another glance. Picked up the crate, fortunately not one filled with glass plates, and deposited it inside their pen. Then, elbowing goats out of my way, I shoved it into the corner, strewing branches I had gathered for their feed over it. All of them tucked in immediately. I hoped sincerely they would not eat all of the camouflage before it had a chance to do its job.

The door to the cabin had a latch on the inside as well as the outside, so Eric could use it for its intended purpose. I ducked inside and pulled the door closed behind me.

Pitch black engulfed me. I crouched stock still as I waited for my eyes to adjust. It wasn't 'can't see your hand in front of your face' dark, not truly. Eric draped a sheet of rubberized canvas over the plates when he was working on them to further limit the light.

But it was dark enough, and close, and hot as Tophet in spite of the comfortable temperature of the day outside. Sweat beaded on my forehead and dripped down my hairline to my neck. I felt my way to a crate and sat down, my head barely clearing the planks constituting the roof, and waited.

CHAPTER 20

I don't know how long I waited for the men to come back. I am sure it seemed much longer than it really was. It *seemed* long enough for them to have walked to Dawson City and back. But at last I heard familiar human voices, pitched above Samson's bellowing. I grasped the edges of my crate with both hands to keep from moving and making any noise as the boat shifted when the men stepped aboard.

Will called my name. I remained still and quiet, breathing as softly as I could, even though I knew he could not hear me over the sloshing of the water, the creaking of the boards, the wailing of the goats. "Karin? Where are you?"

Eric's voice. "She left a note."

"What the hell? Let me see." I could not hear Eric hand Will the paper, but I heard the results. "So she's gone on around? Good. We'd better get going, too."

Eric did not answer. I heard footsteps go past the door to the darkroom cabin. They paused. I held my breath. He did not try to open the door.

A few moments later, I could feel the motion as the boat left shore and moved out into the current. Since I could not see, my other senses became much stronger. The boat's wooden structure creaked a symphony and we seemed to be picking up speed at an alarming rate. Worst of all, the goats' bleating took on a note of panic I had not heard since Eric almost spilled us onto frozen Crater Lake ice-sailing months before.

I kept catching myself holding my breath, and I gave up holding onto the crate, stretching my arms out with my elbows locked, bracing myself on whatever I could reach. One of the crates in my grip slid; I completely lost my balance and landed on the floor with a thud. I hoped they didn't hear it, but I was scrambling to my feet again when someone commenced banging on the cabin door.

"Open up!" Will yelled.

I struggled to the cabin door and unlatched it. It flew open and his hand reached in to yank me out.

I stood, my eyes dazzled by the sunlight, then grabbed for something, anything, to stay on board and keep from landing in the river again. It was like trying to stand on a hammock.

"Thought so," said Will. He all but threw an oar at me. "Get on the other side. If we get too close to a rock, shove us away."

I blinked.

"Go, dammit."

I did not bother to answer. He was already back on his side with an oar ready. As I scrambled over opposite him, I spared a glance back at Eric, manning the sweep. His face was fierce with concentration and did not acknowledge me. The sail was rolled down and tied in place, so at the very least I did not have to worry about the boom. I planted my feet apart for balance, and lifted my oar.

* * *

It was not terribly difficult, once I got the hang of it. Maybe for an ordinary woman, in her long skirts and corsets, relieved because the Mounties took her choice from her, but not for *me*. I had made it this far, done things I could never have dreamed of doing back in Ballard, and this wasn't hard. It was *exhilarating*.

The canyon walls closed in around us and the water rose, roaring down through the chute like a team, no, a veritable herd, of runaway horses. It pounded under our boat like hoofbeats, yanking us along like a stagecoach over rougher ground than I had ever experienced.

The boat sluiced down the main channel, enormous billows of white water splashing over the gunwales. I was soon as soaked as I had been after my dunking, the wind trying to whip me dry and failing utterly. It didn't matter.

Rock after enormous boulder waited in ambush to smash us to smithereens, but they did not. Not on *my* watch. I fought with them as if my oar was a sword and they were warriors worthy of my steel.

I was too busy to look up, or forward, or in any other direction except a few feet directly in front of me, which was off-sides with regard to the boat, when suddenly the current caught Eric unprepared and swung us sideways.

I found myself staring straight down the canyon. Then at the other side. Then of all things, up the canyon, as we went broadside again, this time in the opposite direction. I did not dare look up as I jabbed my oar into the canyon wall itself. I could not hear anything over the roar of the whirlpool that had caught us in its grasp.

I don't know how many times we went round before something Eric did freed us from that dizzying, bounding merry-go-round, or perhaps the whirlpool itself tired of us and spat us out. I suspect not nearly as many times as it seemed.

Dizzily I shook myself, but there was no time. The water flung us out and down the canyon, and if I had not recovered myself, heaven only knows what would have happened. As it was, the water continually slapped me in the face, the wind howled, and I could not see more than a few feet in front of me.

Then, inexplicably, the water calmed for a bit, and I finally had a chance to draw breath. It was at that exact moment I heard Will for the first time since we dropped into the maelstrom – "Karin, watch out!"

What did the man think I had been doing for the last – *gode Gud*.

It wasn't a rock. It was a tree. Or an entire forest, growing out sideways from the wall of the canyon, directly in our path. If such a tree as this had been within Will's grasp last winter, half our boat would be made from it. I could not, I could not – I dared not shove my oar into that tangle. I would never get it back out again.

Instead I reached out, grabbed, and almost before I had the chance to put even half my strength behind my shove, I heard a thud behind me. I felt Will's arms wrap round me with such speed and force that the wind was knocked out of me. The boat swayed wildly, knocking us both off our feet, and we crashed into the side of the cabin.

All the swearwords I knew, both Norwegian and English, were not adequate to the purpose. "William McManis!"

"You know," he said, sounding both amused and breathless from underneath me, "if you get yourself killed you're not going to find any gold." His arms tightened around me and I stared down at him. He shook his soggy head, water spraying into my face.

I blinked. I had seen that expression before, on other men. But not quite like that on other men. I scrambled back, and he let me go, grinning.

"I have no plans to get myself killed."

"Good. Then get back to your post."

* * *

But almost as soon as I did, our boat shot out of the end of the canyon into relatively calm water. As Eric guided it towards the already-crowded shore, I noticed that even the goats had gone silent, piled up together in a corner of their pen. It was as if they were giving thanks they had survived the tumult.

"We need to take stock," Eric said as we tied up. He gave me an approving glance. "You seem to have a talent for stowing away."

Will snorted. "For almost getting herself killed, you mean."

"If it had not been for me, we would still be in the canyon," I retorted.

"The hell —"

"We would," said Eric. "We would have smashed against that tree, and whatever it was hiding, and never have gotten loose again."

"I'd have gotten there in time," Will grumbled.

"But you didn't," I retorted.

"Because I was trying to save you from yourself!"

"I am," Eric said, sounding exasperated for almost the first time, "getting very tired of listening to the two of you. You may fight all you like when we do not have work to do. There is plenty to do, and I must get to my own." He disappeared into the little cabin, and came out with one of his cameras.

"What the hell —" Will said.

But Eric had gone ashore and disappeared onshore into the milling men before either of us could stop him.

I stared at Will in consternation.

He stared at me, then shrugged. "I guess we'd better get to it."

"I guess so."

Of course Eric was not back by suppertime. Will found us a place on shore to set up our tent. Eric was not back by the time we crawled into our bedrolls, either, but I was waked in the middle of the night by his snores, and, relieved we would not be delayed any further here, rolled over and went back to sleep.

* * *

We shoved off again the next morning, and floated into another lake. Lake Laberge, according to Will and his book. It was a wider lake than the ones we had traversed before, and, following advice Eric had acquired the previous day, we clung close to the eastern shore, which was more protected from the squalls which could blow up with unpredictible speed. The winds were brisk. They also kept the everpresent mosquitoes at bay, even when we finally pulled in to shore to sleep that night.

We did not set up the tent, but simply spread our bedrolls out on top of the crates and bags and fell asleep under the long silver twilight. I stared up at it wondering if we would ever see a real night again as my eyes closed almost in spite of myself.

The wind died down towards morning and the mosquitoes came back. I swear the farther north we went, the larger the nasty little beasts became. I began to wonder if they would pick up the goats, or perhaps us, one by one and fly off before we ever reached Dawson.

We had traveled only a few miles that morning when we saw a number of raggedy shelters in a cluster at the edge of the woods, and almost ran into some sort of underwater fishing apparatus. For it was an Indian encampment, the first Indians we had seen since the Chilkats who had worked as hired packers over the pass last autumn.

Several of them were at the shore, and they gesticulated wildly at us to keep us away from their fishing grounds. The apparatus was very odd, almost like a waterwheel with large wooden-slatted baskets, which was almost completely submerged except when one of the baskets rose to the top to be emptied of its catch of shining silver fish.

As we were floating past, two Indian men in a canoe rowed up to us. These Indians were not like the stumpy, sturdy Chilkats. They were wiry and small. They smelled about the same, though, musty and unwashed.

A large basket of fish sat between them, and another smaller one held furs. They offered both to us. We declined the furs, but Eric accepted two of the fish in exchange for some coins, then, just like a man, gave the fish to me to deal with until we went ashore that evening.

We raised the sail again, but the two men kept paddling alongside us, gibbering and gesticulating, and, for some reason, pointing at me. It was extremely disconcerting. I scurried as far away from them as I could get and still stay on the boat.

Then I heard Will shout, "No! She belongs to us!" in a very loud voice, and I peeped over the crates to see the two Indians paddling away back up the lake to their village.

"Should I ask?" I said, fairly sure I did not want the answer, surreptitiously watching the village recede into the distance and expecting a fleet of canoes to come after us at any moment.

Will said, rather indignantly, "Probably not."

But Eric laughed, although his voice sounded strained. "They wished to purchase you, as a gift for their chief, I think. For the basket of furs." He added wistfully, "They were beautiful furs."

"Not nearly beautiful enough," Will said.

"I should think not!" I said.

"We could have made quite a bit of money selling them when we reached home," Eric said.

Will said, "That's not funny, Eric. You're scaring her."

"No," I said slowly. "He is not what's scaring me. What if they come find us tonight and try to kidnap me?"

That sobered Eric up, I must say.

Will said, "The book says —"

"Will, I do not care one particle what that dratted book says about those Indians. It was probably written by a man who has never had to fear kidnapping in his life!"

Eric added, "She is right. We must —"

"The. Book. Says." Will intoned the words loudly. "There's another Mountie cabin halfway down the lake. We can reach it by dusk if the wind keeps up."

I cannot say I would have been able to hear a pin drop. The boat was never silent, the sail snapping and the wood creaking and the cargo shifting, and, of course, Samson chose that particular moment to let out a bellow which made us all jump.

"Oh," I said. "Yes, please."

"Certainly," Eric added. "That is a very sensible idea, Will."

I might not have been overly fond of the Mounties as a species, either as representatives of the law or for their sometimes senseless rules and regulations, but right then near a Mountie cabin seemed like the best place to camp on the entire river.

* * *

We reached the cabin and its attendant cluster of boats as twilight turned into what answered for true night. The days were endless, the only difference being the angle of the sun in the sky, and the almost perpetual golden and pink glow as it sank towards or rose from the horizon, although it never went completely out of sight.

My parents had told wistful stories of the midnight sun back in Norway, but I had never experienced it before. It made everything look different, almost jewel-like, the light bouncing off of Lake Laberge and into the trees, doing odd and beautiful things to the boat and the men's faces. Even Samson's habitual yellow grumpy glare was transmuted, although in his case it was strictly an illusion, obvious as soon as one stepped downwind of him.

Eric rolled the sail as we coasted towards the shore and found an empty spot to tie up the boat. For the first time, I felt no desire to wait at the boat while they went to report our passage to the Mounties.

It was a brief, perfunctory procedure, and I couldn't quite remember why I had been so worried about it. Eric Hoel, William McManis, and 'Mrs. McManis,' of boat #1273, a thirty-two foot bateau labeled Hoel's Photographic Views, were duly reported as all in one piece and still on our way to the Klondike.

As we left the battered and crowded little cabin, Will said, "See, and nobody hauled you away."

I glanced back over my shoulder at the line of men waiting their turns to report in. No one appeared to be paying any attention to us whatsoever, not even me in my trousers, but still. "Hush," I told him.

"You're lucky I didn't tell them you'd ridden the boat through Miles Canyon." He laughed.

Eric said, "Why would you wish to do that?"

"Well, I didn't, did I?" Will eyed me. "I've been darned good about not asking questions, I thought. And not just about being foolhardy."

"Yes." But what could I say to him? Nothing. So I closed my mouth and headed back to the boat. I did not owe them any explanations, any more than they did me. What did I care about where they came from or who they were? If they'd chosen to tell me more than I had them, it had been just that. Their choice.

Neither of them behaved towards me as anything but gentlemen, treating me as an equal partner from almost the very beginning, except when that gentlemanly attitude intervened. I supposed they could not help that.

But Will's sudden expression of a curiosity I had studiously been ignoring until now distracted me as I went through the nightly routine of making sure my partners were fed and the camp tended. By unspoken agreement we slept on board again that night, having paddled down the lake far enough to get out of the thick of the crowds at the checkpoint, but not out of sight.

I was settled down in my spot near the bow, when Will's head popped up on the other side of the darkroom cabin.

"You know, it's not fair of you to keep hogging the best sleeping spot in the boat." He plunked his bedding down a couple of feet from mine. "I'm tired of having Hoel's snoring in my ear all night."

"Suit yourself," I said, too tired to care, and rolled over.

I was half asleep, having pulled my blankets up to protect myself from the wind blowing in off the water, when he said softly, "Look, I'm a patient man. And I won't tell your secrets. But you've trusted your life with me, more than once. Don't you think it's time?"

CHAPTER 21

My eyes snapped right open onto the pale sky. My breath caught. Even after months of traveling so closely together, he couldn't let it go?

"Do you still feel I owe you? Is that the price I must pay for carrying my weight? To tell you my 'secrets'? What makes you think I have any?" I snapped my mouth shut. That was already more than I had intended to say.

A faint sound came from his direction, a cross between a breath and a snort. "I'm not stupid. Everything you've said and done tells me you're running from something. I just want to make sure it doesn't catch you."

I wished I could believe that. I wished it with all my – heart, I thought regretfully. He was a good man, I had seen him demonstrate it over and over. Even back in the days when he was trying to convince me I needed to give up, it had been for my sake, not because he did not want to be saddled with a deadweight.

He had to believe I was not a deadweight now, but an even partner. I did not owe him anything. I earned my own way. Simply because he had chosen to help me conceal my identity did not mean –

His deep, soft voice drifted across to me again. "I just want to help."

Then why did he make me feel so helpless? "You already have. You gave me a name to give the Mounties. That's more than enough."

I did appreciate it. But I did not want any more help from him. I did not want anyone's help. Had I not proved it to him over and over again? Yes, I was caught in a web of dependence for now. It was the only way I could reach the Klondike, and I was glad I realized it before I had attempted the journey on my own. But if they were not as physically dependent on me as I was on them, I did make their lives easier, and that could also mean the difference between life and death.

I had seen the envy other gold-seekers had cast towards Will and Eric because my partners had a woman to do for them and they did not. I had seen the poor excuses for food those men ate. Since it was their own fault, I had easily restrained myself from wanting to give all of them at least one good meal.

No, I was carrying my weight. I did not need any more help.

"It can't be that bad, Karin."

I cleared my throat. "It is not. I appreciate your concern, but it is not necessary."

"Then why do you spend so much time looking over your shoulder? You've been doing it ever since I hauled you out of the *Tacoma Belle*'s hold."

I had not realized I was so obvious about it, I thought with chagrin. I deliberately misunderstood him. "You did not haul me out, I climbed out. And I have been looking. Over my shoulder and up and around and everywhere. This is a beautiful country. And a dangerous one."

He sighed. His silence lasted long enough I thought he'd given up, and was congratulating myself and settling in to sleep again, when he said, "It's not as pretty as Yellowstone."

I knew better than to encourage him, but I couldn't help myself. "Yellowstone must be beautiful indeed."

"Oh, it is." I could almost hear the wistful smile in his voice. "Have you ever seen a geyser?"

The word sounded almost Norwegian. "A what?"

He laughed. "A geyser. It's what Wonderland is famous for. Hot water, squirting up out of the ground in great fountains."

I sat up and stared over at him in the faint light. "Why would anyone build such a thing?"

"Nobody built them," he said indignantly, sitting up in his turn. "They've been there for thousands of years, my dad says. There's a dying volcano underground, and it heats the water, and when it gets hot enough it boils over and sprays water all over the place. There's one that goes off every hour or so, even. It's called Old Faithful."

So. He was angry with me still, did not like me lying to him, and so he was telling me lies in his turn. I supposed it was better than his curiosity.

He reached over and started pawing through his canvas clothes duffel he'd been using as a pillow. "I'll show you." After some time he yanked something out, a small leather photograph case. "Ha!" And opened it, sorting through till he found the one he was looking for. He thrust it at me. "Here."

I peered at it. "I can't see it. There's not enough light."

"Fine. Hang on." He got up. "Where's the matches?" He headed towards my cooking gear.

"You hold on," I said in turn, and reached for the bag I carried with a few necessaries in it, including some matches. I struck one. It was a large wooden match, and would take more than a few seconds to burn to my fingertips. I held it closer to the photograph.

"Hey! Be careful!" He made to take the photo from me, but I pulled back out of his reach.

"I am."

The photograph was indeed beautiful. Taken from some point far above its subject, it did depict a fountain of water shooting up into a clear sky dotted with small clouds. The fountain generated a cloud of its own, hundreds of feet tall. Behind and around it stood a small crowd of tiny figures, and behind that a ramshackle building and some striped tents, dwarfed by the geyser. Beyond that was nothing but an endless forest looking much like what we had been traveling through since Lake Bennett.

The fountain did not look manmade. In the first place, where was the steam plant? It was obvious that this was not anywhere near civilization in spite of the twenty or so people in the photo.

The match had burned down without my noticing. "Ow," I said, and absently tossed it overboard where it disappeared with a tiny hiss.

"Did you burn yourself?"

"Not to notice." I glanced over at the little leather case. "Are there more?"

He grinned. "I'll get a candle."

* * *

I stayed up far too late looking at Will's photographs and listening to the stories he told me about them.

"That's my dad," he told me, pointing to a lanky light-haired man wearing spectacles, his arm over the shoulders of a shorter, rounder, darker-haired woman. Will looked like his father except for his coloring, which was obviously his mother's. "And my mom." Both of them were smiling at the camera, standing in front of a two-story building which in turn stood before an odd bit of scenery.

"What is that behind them?"

"The photography shop. My dad is, was, partners with Bird Calfee the photographer. I'm not sure if they are still, since Mr. Calfee went back east after he got hurt not long before I left. To Minneapolis. Have you ever been to Minneapolis?" His expression was innocent, but his eyes were not.

"No," I said, ignoring the question, "I meant behind the shop."

His disappointed look fled quickly, but it was unmistakable while it lasted. "Oh. That's Minerva Terrace. Part of the Mammoth Springs. That photo was taken in Yellowstone, too."

"Is that a geyser?" It certainly did not look like the one in the other photograph.

"No. It's a bunch of limestone hot springs. The chemicals in the water melt the limestone, I guess you'd say, and bring it up to the surface, where it, well, falls out of the water and hardens again. Some of the old timers say the mountain is turning itself inside out."

"Now I know you're making fun of me," I said, and handed the photo back to him.

"No, really," he said earnestly. "I could show you someday, if you like."

I seriously doubted that would ever happen, although I found myself wishing it would. "Thank you."

As if he knew I was about to say it was late, and it was, since I could see the glimmer of light signaling the long twilight before the day truly broke, he said quickly, "I've got more."

But we would have to get moving again soon, no matter how much I wanted to see the rest of his photographs of places that could not possibly exist.

"Perhaps tomorrow?" I took the candle, over half-burned now, from him, and blew it out. It was lighter than I thought it was. The contrast between our little pool of candlelight and the sky had fooled me. In more ways than one.

I yawned. "The goats will be awake soon."

He let out his breath. "Yeah, and hungry." He tucked the little leather case back into the bottom of his duffel bag.

As I lay back, wondering if my thoughts would let me get any sleep in the short hours left of the night, I felt a stab of envy. I had no photographs of people who loved me. So far as I knew, I had no people who loved me. Those who should have simply thought of me as a possession, to be bought and sold and put to work.

Oh, my mother tried to love me, in her own way, but she was no more capable of taking care of the child I had been than she had been of taking care of herself. She would not, could not, stand up to my father, and my father did not, did not...

* * *

The goats woke up early, as they had every morning ever since we'd arrived in Dyea how many months ago, now? Baaing and bleating and demanding to be fed. And dealt with otherwise. I wrinkled my nose. Sleeping on the boat was expedient, but we could not picket the goats on land unless we were there with them. They would draw every bear and wolf for a hundred miles in any direction. And having managed to drag them this far, none of us was willing to allow that to happen.

But they certainly did not lend a pleasant scent to the boat. I nudged at Will, who, I had noticed, was able to sleep through about anything if he was determined enough.

"I'll take care of them, Karin," Eric said.

"Why should he sleep later than the rest of us?" I asked, feeling more than a bit testy. "He certainly kept me awake late enough last night."

"What? Was he snoring again?"

I felt myself coloring, for no reason I could fathom. "No." I nudged Will again. Even if Eric was going to clean up after the goats, it did not mean Will was going to be allowed to sleep the day away.

"Come on," I told him, "if you wish to eat you need to get out of my kitchen. And go build me a fire." I pushed one more time.

He snuffled, yawned, and almost rolled himself right off the boat. I grabbed an arm. "Watch out!"

"Huh? What?" He shook my arm off, looked down where he was half hanging over the gunwale, then jumped back. "What am I –?"

He always had been the slowest of us to wake up. "You fell asleep down here last night. After your little magic lantern show."

He scowled at me. "It's daylight damned near twenty-four hours a day. Why the hell do we have to get up so early every morning?"

"Go fetch me some wood and I'll make you some coffee. The world will look better to you then."

Grumbling still, he pulled on his boots and went ashore. Before long I could see the fire on the bank, and went to join him.

* * *

We reached the end of Lake Laberge and headed down what Will's book called the Thirty-Mile River, which made no sense to me. Were we still not on the Yukon River? But, I supposed, as long as we were headed towards Dawson it did not matter.

The landscape was still beautiful, but even beauty can become monotonous after enough of it. We ran through several smaller rapids, none of which held anything near the challenge of the White Horse at Miles Canyon. Samson escaped twice and fell overboard once more. Eric went over the side and rescued him, bellowing angrily. The goat, that is, not Eric.

Eric, once he got his breath back, used his voice for cursing in Norwegian. One of the advantages of our language for the purpose is the more serious the invective the more words it takes to express it. Some of Eric's epithets had him breathless again before he could finish them

Samson's ladies, on the other hand, repaid their lord for his daring by wanting to have nothing to do with his sopping wet person.

We passed another Indian village, giving it as wide a berth as we could manage, and several places along the river piled high with wood. At one of them, a man was cutting lengths with an axe.

"Does he really expect steamboats to run this far upriver?" I asked.

"Don't know why else he'd be cutting all that wood. It's good for us, though," Will added.

"Why?"

"Because it means the river must be pretty clear from this point on for steamboats to get this far."

"No more rapids?" I asked, disappointed.

He laughed. "No more shallow ones, anyway."

* * *

And so went the days. Eric insisted on stopping more often than Will and I wanted to photograph whatever he could find to take pictures of, the scenery, the passing flotilla, the woodpiles.

As a result, we began our days early and ended them late to make up the time, but while we waited for Eric, Will and I sat and talked. And looked at his photographs.

"That's a buffalo," he told me one afternoon, showing me a photo of an enormous shaggy creature looking as if it wore a tattered old rug on its back. "Not many of those left. My dad used to go after the poachers who hunted them, until my mother told him he needed to find a safer way to make a living and he threw in with Calfee."

"Poachers?"

"It's illegal to hunt in the national park and the buffalo are almost gone. They're trying to save what's left." He put the photo back, but took his time before he pulled out the next one. "What does your dad do?" He looked at me expectantly.

He kept trying to pry more out of me, poor man. I sighed. It was only fair. "He was a timberman before the Panic. A foreman in a logging camp."

"What does he do now?"

"Whatever he can find." Which wasn't much and hadn't been ever since he'd lost his job.

Will nodded understanding. "I hope my dad's not in the same position when I get back. I want to go to college, but if they're hurting, my gold'll go to them first."

I knew all about that kind of debt. "Mine won't." I raised my chin. "They've had all they're going to get out of me."

He didn't look surprised. "I kind of thought that might be the situation."

I heard myself say, almost against my will, "The only reason I haven't been married off by now is because no one offered Father enough for me."

That did surprise him. "Is that how they do it in Norway? Your dad needs to get with the times." He put an arm around me.

I didn't shrug it off, even though I knew I should. "I don't know if that's how they do it in Norway. All I know is that if I didn't run away, I'd end up just like my mother."

"And how did she end up?"

I did tug away from him then, even though it made me feel far too alone, something I should have been used to by now, but I'd gotten comfortable with Will. Too comfortable. "Too many babies, too much work, and not enough money. I want more than that."

He nodded. Damn him for understanding too much. "And so you ran away. Is this what you thought it would be like?"

I had to smile, in spite of everything. "No."

"Better?"

Now I laughed.

"Well?" he demanded, laughing with me.

"With you and Eric? It could have been much worse."

He sobered. So did I. I hadn't let myself think about what could have happened to me had they not rescued me, starting with helping me escape from that odious Captain Trelane. He, obviously, was thinking the same thing. He reached for my hand. "Karin –"

I couldn't meet his gaze. He let his breath out. "Karin, when we get to Dawson – would you think about –."

I could feel my eyes going wide. But then, over his shoulder, I saw Eric headed down the riverbank towards us. I don't think I had ever been so glad to see anyone in all my life. "There he is. Finally."

Will turned, then looked like he wanted to murder someone, possibly Eric. Or maybe me. But he only said, "Let's get this show on the road. We've been wasting too much time as it is."

CHAPTER 22

The river had changed when we reached the settlement of Hootalinqua, yet another Indian village. This one was much bigger than the ones we'd seen before, and marked the end of the Thirty-Mile River. Now we were on the Yukon River proper, and the many rivers which added their water to the main channel had not only caused it to widen dramatically, but had turned it gray with silt. Every time I dipped my washpot into it, I had to wait and let the nasty stuff settle to the bottom before I could use it.

I had thought we were done with rapids. Will's book certainly made very light of the Five Fingers, downstream from Hootalinqua, so named because rocks in the center of the river divide the waters into five channels. Eric aimed the boat towards the one farthest to the right, after watching – and photographing – several boats ahead of us as they churned into and, in one case, crashed against one of the islands, breaking up into several pieces.

Our own passage through was an exhilarating few moments, but nothing compared to the White Horse. Almost anticlimactic.

But we had barely settled ourselves back down after Five Fingers before we heard roaring again. Eric looked at Will. Will looked back at Eric. "More?"

Eric shrugged.

"We must be almost upon them," I said.

"I don't think so," said Eric.

Will scrambled for his book, and thumbed through it, muttering.

"But they're so loud." I knew I sounded plaintive. They sounded louder than the White Horse had when we were immediately above it.

193

"Yes." Eric sounded distinctly unhappy.

The everpresent baaing of the goats changed from their usual, resigned 'are we ever going to get off this boat' bleats to a distinct note of panic.

Eric cast an eye forward, then shrugged again. The roaring got louder.

Then we came around the bend, and saw something that made the White Horse look like a mere riffle. The banks rose to almost canyon-like depth, rising sheerly from the surface of the water. The current picked up speed, even from the increased pace from the Five Fingers. We could not stop to recoinnoiter, we could not even slow down.

Will glanced up and dropped his book. "Get the oars, dammit."

But I was already heading forward with mine. We barely got to our positions before the first wave crashed over the bow. I shook the water out of my face just in time to push us away from the wall of rock looming up in front of me. The boat was rocking, swaying back and forth as it bounded through the canyon faster than even Samson could run.

We dodged boulder after boulder, shoving at them with the oars to keep the boat out of harm's way, coming close to smashing against them more times than I wanted to count.

Then Will shouted, "Watch out!"

"Will!" But he was gesticulating wildly at me as the biggest wave I've ever seen, crashing against something hidden under the churning water, threw the boat up and straight into the overhanging side of the canyon

I was lucky. The brunt of the water and the overhanging rock hit on Will's side of the boat, with a crash sufficient to knock me down but not overboard. As I scrambled to my feet I could see we weren't out of it yet. I grabbed my oar again. Will did not. He did not begin to get up.

I could not spare even a second. The boat was bucking like a wild bull. Trusting Eric was still back at the sweep, I dashed to the prow with my oar. There was no hope for it. If someone did not make sure we got through to smooth water, none of us would survive.

We did make it through to smooth water. It couldn't have been more than a few more moments before the canyon widened out, shot us down one last chute, and spewed us out into another kind of maelstrom altogether. Eric aimed us through the wrecks and floating debris towards shore. He found us a place among the various crafts ranging from intact to piles of soaking wet goods and shattered lumber.

All this I presumed he did as the next time I took notice we were tied up on shore and Eric was with me, crouched by Will's side. He had not moved, except as the motion of the boat shifted him, and his eyes were still closed.

Eric seemed to have lost all his English, and I could not understand one word in five of his babbled Norwegian, southern dialect as it was.

"Hush," I told him, my hands in Will's hair, feeling his skull for bumps, gashes, anything that might explain – there. Behind his ear, a lump was rising fast enough I could feel it changing under my fingertips. Will moaned but did not rouse.

Eric, who had, amazingly enough, obeyed my request for quiet, started babbling again. "I said, hush! Now go get his bedroll, and something to put under his head."

Eric babbled on.

Was the man beyond hope? Our partner, our friend, the man who had saved my life and my hopes more times than I wanted to admit, was lying unconscious on the boat. And all the man could do was stand there?

"Is the boat damaged?" I demanded.

That seemed to get through. "I do not know. I don't think so."

"Well, go check." I shook my head. "I can't worry about you now, too. Get out of my way."

A few moments later Will's bedroll thudded down beside me, along with a sack holding part of my supply of fabric. The bedroll was dry. The sack was not, but it was rubberized canvas, so after I unrolled the bedroll I pulled some of my precious cloth out and rolled it into a pad for Will's head. Fabric would wash, I told myself. I did not need to tell myself Will's head was worth any amount of cloth, or anything else. The fact was as certain as the rise of the sun.

Some small part of me was aware of Eric pushing us back out away from shore and downriver again, but I did not pay attention. At least the boat must not have been damaged. If the man was willing to risk his precious cameras and plates to his ability to handle the boat by himself, then I was willing to let him risk us, too.

It was not an easy task, maneuvering Will onto his bedroll and makeshift pillow, but I managed it. I would have liked to get him under shelter as well, but the only cover on offer was Eric's dark cabin, and it was not large enough for the purpose. So I draped him in mosquito netting and we stayed out on deck, and I hoped and prayed we were not about to head into yet more rapids.

I did not know what to do for him. I was no nurse. I carefully padded his head so he would not hit the bump again, and I waited, my heart in my throat, for him to wake up.

* * *

I do not know how far we floated down the blessedly calm but swift river before Will began to rouse. I do know the biggest challenge Eric faced was dodging the other boats as they bobbed in the current, some of them so aimlessly it seemed no one at all was steering them.

"Ow," said Will, his voice sounding surprisingly conversational if far too weak for my comfort.

"Will!" He was awake! I put a hand on his forehead.

"Ow!" He said it a bit more loudly this time.

I pulled back. "I'm sorry. I did not mean to hurt you."

He winced. "What happened?"

"You don't remember?"

He appeared to think about it. It appeared to cause him pain to think at all. But at last he said, "Rapids?"

"Yes," I said firmly, relieved. "You were hit by a wave. And perhaps a rock."

"Are you all right?"

There the man was, his head cracked half open, in pain, and he was asking if *I* was all right. I didn't know whether to crack his head the rest of the way or hug him in sheer gratitude. Or in sheer something else. "Yes, I'm fine."

"The Mounties were right."

What? "You would not be here right now if I was not on the boat."

Eric, who had maneuvered us down to a more uncrowded shore and come forward, said, "She is right. How are you?"

"My head feels like someone took an axe to it." Will sighed. "Thanks. I couldn't have manned both sides at once." He eyed us from his prone position, then tried to sit up. He went gray under his tan, and it frightened me, how easily I could hold him down.

"You stay here," I told him, and took his calloused hand. "Eric and I can manage for a while."

"I guess you'll have to." He put his head back on the cloth pad I had made, and closed his eyes. "For a little while, anyway."

His words were slightly slurred. For all his talkativeness, his speech had come much more slowly than usual, as if it was an effort. I had seen men injured in logging accidents, knew of one who had never been right in the head again after being hit in the base of his skull by a peavy. I did not think Will's injury was that bad – he was coherent enough if not his normal self – but we owed him. I owed him. And I, I cared for him. More than I should.

I had known I was tangling myself up when I had thrown my lot in with these two men, but I did not know how tightly those ties would bind me. The only thing I owed Eric was money, which was bad enough.

Even my winter's work, when his goats would have died but for my care, and the possessions he left behind when he abandoned us would have been lost forever without my watchfulness, did not pay him back in cash, or gold dust, or anything else of monetary value.

I reached into my pocket and fingered my gold nugget. After all these months rubbing against cloth, it was as smooth and silky as a piece of watered satin. But alone it would not pay my debts. Nor did I have enough from my winter's sewing to pay him off and still have enough to find and work a claim once we arrived in Dawson.

But all of that paled against what it would take to pay the debt of my life, which both men, but especially Will, had paid over and over. I could never get out from under that obligation. I had simply exchanged debt of one kind for another when I had run away for the Klondike.

I pulled the mosquito netting back over Will and got up. As I went forward to do my part in keeping our boat safe while we floated down the now-deceptively peaceful Yukon River, I glanced back at the man lying on the deck. I was fairly sure I knew what he wanted to take in trade for my debt. The question was, would I be willing to pay it. My heart was beginning to say yes.

* * *

Grateful is a very weak word for what I felt toward the river that afternoon as we floated along looking for a place to land for the night. I do not know what we would have done if we had come upon yet more rapids that day. Will lay, more still than I could have believed him capable of, on his bedroll on the deck, draped with netting, like some sort of prone statue.

At last, Eric and I maneuvered us into a small indentation along an island in the middle of the river, in the forlorn hope of escaping those incessant and enormous mosquitoes.

I set down my oar and went to Will. His eyes were closed, and if I had not seen his chest rising and falling, very slowly but deeply, I would have thought the worst.

"Will?" I said softly.

He did not answer.

I put my hand on his shoulder. "Will?"

Nothing. Just his breathing.

A shadow fell on both of us. "Can you not wake him?"

"No."

Eric knelt down, and put a hand on Will's other shoulder.

"Don't shake him," I said quickly.

"It is not good to let him sleep like that," Eric said, and before I could stop him he shook Will, gently but decisively.

Will moaned.

"Well, that is something." Eric shook him again. "Will, wake up."

Will's eyes opened. They did not look quite right, but his lips moved. "Why?"

We spoke simultaneously.

"You've slept long enough."

"You need to eat."

"'M not h'ngry." His eyes opened wide. "Oh, God." He lurched. I think he was trying to sit up, but all he managed was to roll to his side. His whole body heaved, though, and I barely jumped out of the way in time to avoid the contents of his gut as they came pouring out of his mouth.

He hadn't eaten since morning, and it was past suppertime. I would not have thought his stomach still held so much.

"Oh, God," he moaned again.

I looked up helplessly at Eric as the nasty yellow puddle spread.

"I will be right back." I hoped he was off to fetch rags at the very least.

"Will?"

"Wha'?"

"Look at me. Please."

He opened his eyes, blinking at the light. "Why?" His voice was weak.

"Can you see me?"

His body heaved again, but it was only a long, long breath. "Yeah."

"Does your head hurt?"

His eyes focused into a disbelieving stare. "No."

Well, if he could muster sarcasm under the circumstances he must not be that badly off. I tried not to look too relieved. "What can I do?"

"Le' me sleep." He closed his eyes again.

At that point Eric came back. I stared up at him helplessly. He was bearing rags after all, as well as water, both a cupful and a bucketful. Handing me the cup, he said, "See if he will drink," then he took the bucket and poured water on the ugly yellow mess, careful not to get any on Will, and began to wipe it all overboard with the rags.

"Will?" I softened my voice still further.

"Go 'way."

"Would you like some water?"

His eyes opened again. It was not an easy task, getting water down a man who did not wish to lift his head. I did it for him, handling his head as carefully as I would a newborn babe. He swished the water around in his mouth, and spit it out, then took a second sip and swallowed it.

His eyes were already closing again as I lowered him back down.

The rhythm of his breathing changed to that of sleep as I watched. I rearranged the mosquito bar over him, and went to join Eric where he was sluicing the last of Will's vomit over the side of the boat.

"The lump does not feel any larger," I told him.

"Good."

"What can I do?"

"There is not much to be done." He threw the last of the rags overboard, and we watched them float downstream. "Wake him and check on him every two or three hours. If we let him sleep too long at a time, he may not wake up. And pray." He did not look any more convinced at the efficacy of that last treatment than I felt about it.

Then he shook his head as if clearing it, and his expression changed to its usual lighthearted mask. "I will go care for the goats. How long until supper? We need to be off early in the morning."

I don't think he meant to sound so callous. And it wasn't as if I didn't know we were in more of a hurry now than ever. But my tone was still sharp when I told him I would have something ready by the time he was done.

CHAPTER 23

We floated around the last bend into Dawson City two days later. I should have been elated, but for me at least our long-sought destination had lost its allure. It was no less muddy and bug-ridden than any other place along the river, just a great deal more crowded. I did not care if it was the Paris of the north, as I heard some fool yell out from shore, or if it was Paris, France. I only cared about one thing.

Will was no better. He had become more and more difficult to rouse, and harder to keep awake once the onerous task had been accomplished. The bump on the back of his head had receded a little, but it was still swollen and sore. And he would not, or could not, eat. He had not vomited again after that first time, but it hadn't been for lack of trying. His face was gray under the grime and sweat.

And it was all my fault. If I had been on that side – I was shorter, the rock would have missed me altogether. But no. It was as ingrained in his nature as it was in mine to be stubborn. If I had not been on the boat, he would have not been compelled to keep me from harm when I was, and he would be whole, and healthy. I could not fault him, but oh, I wished he had not come to care for me so much.

I wished I had not come to care for him so much.

I glanced up to watch Eric negotiate with a large man in the standard uniform of canvas trousers and flannel shirt for the right to tie our boat to his, which appeared to be tied in turn to another boat. That one was tied to yet another whose owners had somehow managed to commandeer a piece of the riverbank as their own.

The entire shore was lined with craft four and five deep, strung out almost halfway across to the other bank.

Eric, having apparently concluded his negotiations successfully, firmly lashed our boat to its new mooring and came back over to me. "I will go inquire about a doctor."

"Thank you."

"You prepare him. I am sure he will need to be moved."

I nodded, and turned back to my patient. My patient. He was about to be taken off my hands, at last. I was supposed to be happy, and I *was* happy, I told myself. At last he would be under a doctor's care, he would begin to get well, he would be himself again. He *would* get well. He had not died, so he would *not* die. He would get well, we would –

And my thoughts, as they had for days now, stopped abruptly. For all I knew he would never want to see my face again, after what I had put him through. He had almost told me he loved me, I think, but that was before I had caused such a terrible thing to happen to him.

All the time my thoughts were jumbling along as they had for the last two days, I was spreading the sturdiest blanket out next to him, doubling it to add to its strength, and folding a pad for his poor head and neck. I eased him over onto it a bit at a time with all the care I could muster, which was far more than I had once believed myself capable of.

There. I had just finished tucking the padding more securely under his head when I realized his eyes were open, and looking at me. They were clear for the first time in days, not cloudy, not confused.

"We're here," I told him. "Dawson City. Eric has gone to find a doctor. We're going to get you off this boat and find someone who can help you."

"Don't."

I stared at him. "You need a doctor, Will."

"Don't." His voice was weak, but the word was clear. As was the rest. "Give up. Don't. Not because of me."

I let out my breath. But before I could tell him he was the one I was not about to give up on, Eric was climbing back over the boats from shore. And with him was a man with a black leather bag.

* * *

The doctor, for so he turned out to be, exuded authority with every breath he exhaled. He examined Will, proclaimed that he must come to his hospital, the best in Dawson City, and there he would receive treatment, which would make him "right as rain." The crowd who had followed him, which appeared to have nothing better to do, cheered at this pronouncement.

"The blanket can serve as a litter," I mentioned under the hubbub.

"No, no, we must get him on his feet."

"He cannot —"

"I am the doctor, young lady." The last word was imbued with the dubious, disdainful tone I was all too familiar with since I had begun wearing trousers, but he added another note I did not recognize until it was too late. He gestured at Eric, who shrugged his shoulders at me. They went one to each side of Will and began to lift him to his feet. As I could have told them would happen, Will promptly fainted.

"Go away. Put him down and go *away*. You will kill him. Eric, please help me."

Eric, his face grim, did as I asked. I barely heard the charlatan's bellowed protests as Eric took him away. I knelt back beside Will. I did not know what I was going to do, but I managed to get him back onto the blanket, and wiped his clammy face.

I don't know how long it was before Eric returned again. I did not notice him until he put a hand on my shoulder and said my name.

"Go away."

Another, raspy, gentle voice said, "Miss? If I may have a look?"

I glanced up to see an old man in a tattered priest's cassock. He was thin beyond gaunt, but his eyes were kind. "I am Father Judge. I know a little of medicine."

At least he did not look capable of slinging Will around as if he were a sack of potatoes. I moved to one side, and he knelt beside me.

His examination took considerably longer than the so-called doctor's did. When he rose again with the help of another stranger, he said, "If you would allow me to have him carried to the hospital, we could care for him there." He obviously saw the distrust I could not hide, because he added, "We will be as careful as we can possibly be."

What choice did I have? I nodded. He gestured, and he, the stranger, and Eric each went to one corner of the blanket. I went to the fourth, pushing yet another helpful stranger aside. He went to Father Judge's corner and took the corner of the blanket from him, instead.

It was not an easy journey over three rocking boats and up to the shore. I had barely struggled a few steps with my share of the blanket when yet another stranger, a big burly man with a thick brown beard, came up and took it gently from me. After that I walked beside Will's head, watching him the entire way.

* * *

It was some way to the priest's hospital, a plank building on the far edge of town, but Will did not waken until he was set down on one of many cots in a large room and the men went away. His eyes did open then, but only briefly, and I could not be sure how much he saw or comprehended. "You're safe," I told him. "You're going to get well now." I don't know how I knew that. Maybe it was something I saw in the priest's eyes.

I am not Catholic. My family goes to the Lutheran church, and while I attended with them by my father's decree when I lived at home, I had long been uncertain what I did believe or wanted to believe before I ever ran away. But some men inspire trust in different ways. Will did. He had from the moment I'd met him.

And, in an entirely different way, so did Father Judge. It was not that I had no choice but to trust him. I had not trusted that so-called doctor who probably would have killed Will if I had let him proceed. If I had not trusted Father Judge I would have sent him away as well. And then where would we be?

But it did not matter. I do not know why I believed him, but if Father Judge told us Will would recover, then Will would recover. And when he did, I would make sure he got home. To Montana, and that Yellowstone wonderland he loved so much.

I only backed away when the priest came to examine Will more thoroughly. He shook his head over the tender spot on the back of his head, but he was able to rouse Will again, and he nodded decisively over whatever he saw in Will's eyes. Afterwards, he gestured to Eric and me to follow him back outdoors. I left reluctantly, but I wanted to hear what he had to say.

We stood near the door of the hospital, Eric and Father Judge and I. The priest looked at us, well, at me, curiously, but he got down to business right away, for which I was grateful. "He will live. And he will recover fully, I think. It will probably take him some time, but he'll have that, God willing."

Eric let out a gusty sigh. "Good." And without another word he started down the steps to the muddy quagmire of what passed for a street.

I watched, scowling, as he disappeared into the milling crowd wandering up and down through Dawson day and night.

When I turned to go back into the hospital, I found my way blocked. "What is your relationship to my patient?" asked Father Judge.

I stared up at him. I was *not* going to be banned from Will's side. Not now. Not under any circumstances. *I* would not abandon my – companion? pseudo-husband? I took a deep breath. My friend. My more than friend.

It was a terrible time to realize I was in love with him. That I wanted him to recover so that I might return the feelings he'd begun to confess to me. Those feelings of his I had not let him express because I thought my independence more important than love.

Oh, my independence was important. And so was the gold we'd originally come for. It was more important than it had ever been, because it was the means by which I could earn his care, and our passage Outside, to the home he'd told me about, to the family who cared about him and worried about him, to the future he'd tried to finance with this harebrained scheme.

He would make it home if I had to sew twenty-four hours a day to pay for it. And he would graduate from college if it was the last thing I ever saw anyone do.

"He is my husband."

Father Judge's face softened. "Well, then, come on back in."

"Wait," I said. "I have a proposition for you."

* * *

It did not take more than four trips to haul my sewing machine, my fabrics, and my supplies to the hospital. It took me a bit longer to convince Father Judge that my sewing machine would not disturb his patients, and that the corner space he gave up next to the back door would be a good exchange for the work I could do for the hospital, but at last he gave in. We moved Will's cot so I could tend him as I worked, and I began setting things up.

It helped that they had a considerable number of items that needed mending, and a need for even more items I could make. I would have started with new clothing for the good Father himself, if he had not vetoed that in a voice too strong to have come from that gaunt personage.

Word got around quickly somehow, and many of my customers from the previous winter at Lake Bennett came by with work for me to do as well. Soon I had enough to keep me busy for as many hours as I could keep my fingers moving. I had no idea how much two steamship tickets to Seattle would cost. I did find out that the last boat for the season left in September, before freeze-up, only six weeks away. Surely Will would be well enough to travel by then.

Eric did not come back. I had not expected him to. I knew his true colors now, and he was good riddance to bad rubbish in my well-considered opinion. He was where he wanted to be, and I had no doubt he was out on the creeks somewhere, camera and tripod over his shoulder. The only saving grace was that he had taken the goats with him. Although if he had left them with me, I would have sold them and added the money to the steamship fund. Without a backward glance.

* * *

Will improved gradually. One fine day he sat up without grimacing in pain. I took a few minutes of precious time and went looking in town for something to tempt his still mostly disinterested appetite that afternoon, to celebrate. And what should I have smelled over the stench of Dawson City but the scent of lefse. I almost turned around and went back, but I could not.

Instead, I squared my shoulders and got in line.

My words, "half a dozen, please," dropped into the noise in the tent like hailstones. I had not meant them to, but Mamie's head jerked up as if yanked by a string. I braced myself.

But all she said was, "I heard you made it," with a nod, and she took my money and gave me my lefse. "I was sorry to hear about your man."

That startled me. "He's still very ill, but Father Judge says he'll mend. How did you hear?"

"Saw your other man." She flipped, spread, and rolled, her hands as deft as they ever were. "The photographer fella. Wanted to take pictures of my tent, of all things."

"Mr. Hoel is no longer part of our partnership," I said, trying not to sound hurt, as I felt every time I thought of the man.

"Funny. He sure sounded like he thought he was." Then, as the man behind me shouldered up, "How many?"

"A dozen."

I ducked out.

* * *

"These look familiar," Will said.

"They ought to be." I held one to his lips.

"I can feed myself." He reached for it, but his hand dropped back.

"You haven't done a very good job of it. Eat." I nudged it at him again, and he opened his mouth.

It gave me great satisfaction to see him chewing as if the lefse were the first thing that tasted good to him in a very long time. When he swallowed, I nudged the potato pancake at him again, and again, until he had finished it. But when I picked up another one, he laid a hand on my arm.

"Why are you still here?"

Oh, that should not have hurt, but it did. It was no one's fault but my own, however. "I do not abandon friends who need me." It came out rather more stiffly than I had intended, and my gaze dropped from watching him to my own lap.

"I didn't mean to say you would. But I thought –" He picked up another lefse.

I nodded in satisfaction. "I can work here as well as anywhere."

He gestured at the sewing machine. "Why haven't you sold that thing by now? You hate that work. Why aren't you out digging for your fortune? It's why you're here, isn't it?"

He was weak, and tired, and ill. And angry. It took me a moment to realize exactly how angry he was.

I did not know what to say at first. Then I did. "I have found my fortune already."

"Right. And you're sewing like a demon because you enjoy it."

No, I did not. But it was the only way I could watch over him and still earn our passage. "Not all fortunes are in gold."

"Oh?" He lay back, obviously exhausted simply from the small effort of eating.

But I was not done with him. I got up and went to the hospital kitchen, where the soup pot was simmering on the back of the sheet iron stove. The priest had given me permission to cook so long as I was willing for the other patients to eat from the pot as well. Since I was using as many of his provisions as I was my own, it seemed a fair trade. Cooking outdoors in Dawson was a chancy proposition at best. Food tended to leave unescorted without being constantly watched.

I filled a bowl and went back to Will. He scowled at me. "You are not my mother."

"I certainly hope not." I did not feel in the least like his mother. Or his sister. Or any of his other relations.

"You're not my nurse, either."

Instead of answering I pushed a full spoon at him. He opened his mouth. It was either that or get soup down his front. But then he took the spoon, and the bowl, which he set on his bedding, away from me, and began to feed himself, propped up on one elbow.

"Happy now?"

It was more progress than I had seen since we'd arrived here. "Yes."

"Then go away." He glared at me.

"No."

"Fine." After a few moments he shoved the – empty? yes, it was, I saw to my delight – bowl at me, and lowered himself carefully back down. "Watch me sleep, then." He closed his eyes. After a few more moments, he opened one eye, said, "Go *away*," and closed it again.

When his breathing deepened into true sleep, I took the bowl and went back to work.

CHAPTER 24

I finished as much as I could for the hospital, including a new coat for Father Judge from the fine piece of wool I had hauled all the way from Sheep Camp. He accepted it with ill grace, the first time I had seen him show anything but kindness to me, but he did accept it.

I decided to ignore the fact that I saw one of his recovered patients wearing it as he left the hospital several days later. In his own way, the priest was more stubborn than Will was.

Will himself spent most of his time behaving with his own brand of ill grace. He accepted my care only until he was able to get up and walk around by himself without getting lightheaded, and only scowled when he caught me watching him to make sure he wouldn't fall. He applied himself to getting well as if he could push the process harder if he worked at it.

I was a bit guilty of pushing him myself, I suppose. I had gone out briefly and had just stepped back into the hospital when I heard voices from our corner, calm Father Judge and – Will. *He* was not calm. He was shouting. I ran in just in time to hear, "She is *not* my wife."

I stopped dead. I had almost forgotten about my little deception. It had been harmless enough, but I should have warned Will. I knew why I hadn't. Couldn't.

"Mrs. McManis?" Father Judge had seen me.

"That's not her name," Will said flatly. "Her name is Karin Myre."

The priest looked confused, but only for a moment. Then he glanced from my stricken face to Will's furious one, and said, "I will be back in a few moments. You will settle this between you." He added, his glare at Will – at Will? I was the one who had lied to him – almost as furious as Will's own. "Keep your voices down. I will not have the peace of this hospital further disturbed." And with that he strode off.

I stood frozen, conscious of every eye in the room, although I could only see Will's.

"Come here." He sank down onto the cot. He sounded as if he had used up every bit of his meager energy stores in denying me to the priest. "Dammit, I'm not going to bite. Get over here."

I went, haltingly.

He pulled his feet up and gestured at the foot of the cot. "Sit down."

I sat.

"Why'd you lie to him?"

I swallowed. "Because he would not have let me stay by you otherwise."

One thick eyebrow went up, but he remained silent.

"You needed me."

The other eyebrow joined it.

I glanced around the room. Every conscious person in the place was watching. I turned my gaze back to him. Surely he was not asking me to –

But he was. The eyebrows came back down, but his gaze was implacable. He was not giving me a choice. "You don't owe me anything."

Oh, but I did. It wasn't only that, but I did. Still, he was giving me a way out. I would not have to tell him my true feelings in front of all these curious men. "You were hurt trying to warn me. You saved my life."

His gaze fell. My heart fell with it to my boots. Wait, I thought wildly, I meant I love you – "Well, then," he said to his blanket, "You've done more than enough. Go on. I can manage from here on in."

But *I* couldn't –

"Good luck, Karin."

Stupidly I went back to my sewing. After a while, he got up and came over to me. "That's not what I meant."

I did not glance up, but kept pumping the treadle and guiding the fabric, as if I could not do it in my sleep.

"Karin."

I took a deep breath, for courage. "Father Judge may chase me out of here, but you cannot."

He sank down on the floor, cross-legged, and looked up at me. "I appreciate everything you've done for me."

I did not want his appreciation. "You are more than welcome."

His hand came out and touched me on the shoulder. I shrugged it off. Or tried to, at any rate. I could not summon the effort to put much into it.

His other hand came to rest on my treadle foot, bringing it to a stop. "Won't you even look at me?" He sounded almost plaintive.

"Why? If it is for more of your thanks, I do not want them."

"What do you want?"

For you to tell me you love me, I didn't say, even though I wanted to more than anything. "I want to earn enough money to buy passage on a steamship away from this terrible place. It is not what I expected it to be, and if I cannot have what I want, then –"

"If you can't say what you want, how do you expect to get it?"

I folded my arms over the top of the machine and pillowed my head on them. He stood, slowly, bracing himself on me. His hand slipped from my shoulder, but only so he could put his arm around my waist. His other hand lifted to complete my imprisonment. Not that I wasn't imprisoned by my own feelings already.

"Karin?" He lifted me to my feet. I hadn't thought he'd be able to do that yet. I remembered the last time he'd lifted me. It seemed so long ago. "Let's go for a walk."

"You shouldn't be –"

"You've been babying me for far too long. I shouldn't be here –" He let the sentence hang. And, indeed, he did seem steadier on his feet than I'd have thought. I let him lead the way outdoors.

He took a deep breath and grimaced. "It's supposed to smell better out here." But he took my arm and led off, heading slowly but steadily away from town.

We didn't walk far, only around the bend in the river, where civilization, such as it was, petered off into a quagmire. We picked our way around the edge until I spotted a boulder.

"Sit down," I told him.

He sighed, and sat. His hand went up to rub the back of his head.

"You're still hurting, aren't you?"

"Not nearly as bad as I was." He let his hand drop. "I don't want to talk about that."

I wasn't sure I wanted to know what he wanted to talk about, so I held my tongue.

"Where are you going when you get back Outside?"

Now I was sure I didn't want to know. Too late.

"I don't know," I admitted.

"Not back to Seattle?"

"Not if I can help it." I took a deep breath. "I was thinking about Montana."

He stared at me, then – deflated is the best way I can think to describe it. "Montana's a big place."

I couldn't lie to him any more. "Someone once told me Helena is nice. And I would like to see those geysers."

"They're not in Helena, they're in Yellowstone."

"Oh. I suppose it would not be good to go looking for them by myself."

His eyes widened, then slowly he began to smile. In a moment it had broadened into a grin. "That's for sure. You might get lost, and as my dad could tell you, Yellowstone's a really bad place to get lost."

"I don't suppose you could recommend a guide." Now I was enjoying this as much as he was, and I knew my face showed it. Which was fine with me. I had always enjoyed our banter. I would always enjoy it.

"I'd be glad to offer my services." Then he sobered, although his gaze was still warm. "But I do charge for them."

"I suppose we ought to make our arrangement in advance. Seeing as how the last time worked out so well."

He snorted. "Right. I still don't know how much Eric owes me. Or if he even thinks he does." He paused. "I doubt I'll see any of it, anyway."

"I have to agree."

He was silent for some time after that. His hand lifted to my chin and he held it, staring intently into my eyes until I had to pull away lest he see more than I knew how to tell. At last he asked, "Why have you changed your mind?"

He deserved to know. He had been the first one to broach the subject. Why could I not do the same this time? "I'm afraid." It came out as a whisper. "No wait –"

Will hooted. "You?" Then he took my chin in his fingers again and he wouldn't let me go. "You really are. That's only the second time since I've known you."

"You don't have to sound so surprised," I told him in disgust.

But he was smiling again. "You," *he* told *me*, "have no reason to be afraid. Not of me."

"You are the most terrifying person I have ever met."

He actually laughed. "Me? Why?" He still held my chin, and he leaned down until our lips were almost touching. "I just want to protect you. Take care of you."

I squeezed my eyes shut, then opened them again. I needed to see his eyes, no matter how frightened I was of what I might see in them. "Love me?"

"Karin, you sweet fool, I've loved you forever."

He kissed me. It felt like coming home.

* * *

"So you really don't want to stay and try to make our fortune?" Will's question came some time later, as we strolled back to the hospital. It was time to pack up and leave, if only we had a place to go while we waited for the steamship.

"You are not well enough to work a claim yet, and it will be winter again soon."

"I can." He sighed. "But I think you're right. This isn't the place for us. We'll pitch the tent again for the duration."

"That makes sense." Much as I didn't want it to. But we couldn't impose on Father Judge any longer.

We strolled on, making plans, until Will came to a stop and faced me, taking my hands. "The last time I tried to bring up the subject, you dodged like I was asking you to take a bullet for me. You appear to have changed your mind, but I'd like to be sure."

I held my breath.

He cocked his head at me. "So?"

I let it out in a whoosh. "So?"

He rolled his eyes, his exasperation clear. "We *are* getting married, right? Not much point in all this otherwise."

"Such a romantic proposal," I complained, laughing.

He didn't laugh. "You didn't give me a chance to try a romantic one."

And I had lived to regret it. "You have another chance now." I squeezed both of his hands as they held mine. "I'm not refusing you."

Still so serious. "That's a yes?"

I nodded.

"What will it take to get you to say the words? Pliers?"

I took a deep breath. And here I thought I had run to the Klondike to keep *from* being married off. Well, it was my choice this time. Honestly, it had been my choice all along, I just hadn't known it. "Yes, I will marry you." I knew I was grinning, even if it was in sheer relief, because he was grinning back at me.

"Hallelujah." He leaned down and kissed me again. "Let's go find the priest."

"Right now?" The man certainly could kiss. I was still a bit befuddled.

"Yes. Before you change your mind again."

Letting go of one hand, he tugged me back towards town with the other.

He didn't seem to be worried whether the priest would marry us, even after my deception, and I can't say as I was worried about it, either. My thoughts were too full of silly repetitions of Mrs. William McManis, and Karin Marie McManis, and of my hand warm in his, to allow for much else.

So when we arrived back at the hospital, neither of us expected the hail, in a voice I had hoped never to hear again.

CHAPTER 25

"It's about the hell time."

I stopped dead. So did Will. "Lawson. What do you want?" His hand tightened on mine so much I squeaked, but he did not loosen his grip.

"What you owe me, for starters." He hadn't changed. He still looked like a tree stump and acted like he owned the world. Well, he didn't own us.

"What, the lumber? I left you your share. I don't owe you a damned thing."

Lawson took a step forward. "Not so's I could find it."

Will stiffened. "That's not my fault."

"And whose fault is it, I'd like to know? Took me three days before I could go looking for it. I've probably got boards in half the boats in Dawson."

"I gave you no more than you deserved." The disdain in Will's voice was too audible.

Lawson shrugged, but it was obvious he didn't like it. Then he looked at me, as if for the first time, and his tone changed to something altogether worse. "Still got the girl, I see. Maybe we can come to an arrangement."

I gulped. Will could defend me all he liked, but he wasn't completely healthy yet and surely not up to a fight.

Will let go of my hand, but only long enough to wrap his arm around me. It felt like an iron bar, but only I knew he was shaking slightly. Whether with rage or with weakness I had no way of knowing. "Miss Myre is no part of this."

"And here I thought she'd miss her friend." It should have been said with a sneer, like some stage villain, but he was casual, almost offhand.

"Friend?" I couldn't help it.

"Your Mrs. Thielsen." The Mrs. came out with a slight curl of his lip. "Mamie. She's working for me now. Lost her boat and needed some help. She's repaying me in trade."

In *lefse*? "Oh. You helped her set up her bakery?"

"Hardly." He laughed. It sounded so ugly. "But I told her she could, so long as it didn't interfere with her real work. You and I could come to the same kind of arrangement."

"Oh." I did not know what to say to that. Or to think. Poor Mamie, I thought. Not that – no, no one deserved –

But Will knew exactly what to say. "This is not Miss Myre's debt."

"Oh, so you do agree you owe me." He'd been gradually moving closer to us, I suddenly realized, and now he closed the last bit of distance. "Well, this is the only property you have that I want." He grabbed my wrist.

I jerked back. He hung on. Will snarled at him, and jerked back for both of us. "She's not property, you jackass."

Lawson stared at where Will and I were hanging onto each other for dear life. "Looks like she is to me." He grabbed for me again, and Will shoved me behind him.

Will was better, even I had to admit that, but he was in no condition to fight, for me or anything else. And Mr. Lawson had a glint in his eye that boded poorly for anyone crossing him. But what was the alternative? I could not, could not – I could do anything if it kept Will safe, I discovered.

"Will, don't," I heard myself say.

"Yeah, Will, don't," Lawson said mockingly.

"Karin, stay out of this."

I ran towards the hospital, just a few steps away, careful to stay out of reach of both men, neither one of whom was paying me much attention, anyway. They were dancing around each other like a pair of prizefighters. I heard the first punch hit its mark, but did not look back to see who had done the hitting and who had been hit.

Father Judge was, thank goodness, in his office, a small, cramped space at the front of the building. He glanced up, indifferently at first, then he seemed to take in my agitation. I don't know if he decided my upset overruled my sin, or if he had forgiven me for it, but he said mildly, "What is the matter now, child?"

"There's a fight, sir," I panted. "Will can't, he's not well yet, he's going to get hurt again."

He shot a glance toward the ceiling, although I suspect he was looking well beyond it, then back down at me. "Where?"

"Right out front. Please come."

He didn't question my faith in his ability to stop whatever was going on out there, but got up and strode out. I followed him, hoping against hope Will had managed a lucky punch, something, anything –

They were gone.

* * *

"Young woman," Father Judge began, turning back to me.

"They were just here. I swear they were."

One of the ubiquitous throng nodded and said, "They went that way," and pointed. Such was the haphazard layout of a town grown like Topsy practically overnight that the respectable hospital was no more than a few yards away from Second Avenue, where most of the adventuresses hawked their wares.

I headed in that direction, but I had taken no more than two steps when a bony hand landed squarely on my shoulder.

I glared up at him. "I have to go."

"Why?"

He was not going to believe anything I said right now, that was obvious. I ducked out from under his hand and ran.

I searched up and down, heedless of the stares I received. No decent woman went anywhere near that hideous row of tiny little cabins, each one with its wide paned-glass window in front. Some of the windows had shabby calico curtains pulled closed, others were wide open, with scantily-dressed women displaying their goods, I suppose one would call them, for sale. Their eyes went wide when they saw me. I could hear noises coming from some of the cribs, noises I tried very hard to ignore.

Another hand came down on my shoulder. This one was much meatier and stronger than gaunt Father Judge's was. It swung me around.

"What are you doing here?"

I didn't know whether to shriek and run, or collapse in relief. I settled for panting out, "I am looking for someone."

The Mountie gazed down at me in disapproval. He was young, probably not much older than I was, but I envied his air of authority. "You shouldn't be here."

"No, she shouldn't," said Lawson, coming up behind us. "Come on, Sally."

"Who is she to you?"

"My sister."

My mouth literally dropped open, leaving me speechless. Apparently the Mountie took this for agreement, because he nodded. "Take her away from here."

"I will." Lawson took hold of my arm. "She's a handful."

"She does appear to be."

"I'd never have brought her with me if she hadn't stowed away. But I couldn't send her back home alone all the way from Skaguay."

I finally found my voice. "I am *not* his sister!"

The Mountie's eyebrows went up.

Lawson grinned, hideously. "She keeps trying to run away. It's not the first time."

I jerked away. "He is trying to kidnap me! And what did you do with Will?"

The Mountie stared from me to Lawson and back again. "Who is Will?"

"My husband."

Now it was Lawson's turn to stare.

"That's right," said a female voice from behind me.

I wheeled. "Mrs. Thielsen!"

She smiled sadly. "No."

I drew back.

"I lied to you more than you did to me."

Before I could open my mouth, Lawson said, "Mamie, you keep your nose out of this and get back to work."

Mamie's chin went up. "I will not let you do to her what you did to me."

"It's none of your business. She's doing it to herself."

"I am not!" I was not doing anything but trying to find the man I loved, and no one, not Lawson, not the entire brigade of Northwest Mounted Police, was going to stop me.

The Mountie sighed. "Come with me, young lady."

I dug in my heels. "Not until I find Will."

"Will's missing?" Mamie asked. She sounded genuinely concerned.

"He was already hurt, and that monster," I gestured at the stolid Lawson, "picked a fight with him."

Lawson bristled. "He cheated me."

"Well, where is he?" demanded the Mountie.

"I'm not telling anyone until my debt's paid."

"We owe him no debt," I stated firmly.

Lawson glared at me. "You want him back, you pay."

I thought about the money I had saved for our steamship passage. It would do me no good without Will. Nothing would do me any good without Will.

"How much?" I took a deep breath. "I have some money. But," I added, "I am not paying you one cent until I see him and know he's all right."

Lawson was eyeing me speculatively. The Mountie had an insultingly incredulous expression on his face. I glanced over at Mamie. She nodded. Lawson glanced over at her and frowned. "Mamie, get back to work."

She smiled sweetly at him. "Not this time of day."

"Then go the hell away."

"You do not own me."

"The hell I don't."

The Mountie had apparently found his voice. "The hell you do, Mister. And you will show this young woman where her husband is."

"Not till I get what's owed me."

"Not till I see him. What are you waiting for?" I asked him.

He looked from me, to the Mountie, to Mamie. His frown deepened. "Show me your dust."

I kept it on my person at all times. I even slept with it. To do otherwise would have been foolish in the extreme. Slowly I pulled the small tightly-tied sack out of my jacket pocket.

It was not an impressive amount, but it was everything I had been able to amass in the last six weeks. Almost enough for two steamship tickets, I had hoped. Now we would be stranded here for our second winter in the north. I wanted to weep.

Lawson's hand was quicker than my eye. He was off and running before I even realized my hand was empty. I screamed. Mamie screamed. The Mountie utterly forgot himself and swore more inventively than I'd have thought he was capable of as he took off after the villain. All up and down the street, doors popped open and half-naked women and their men gaped out. I barely saw them as I ran, too.

Yet another hand came down on my shoulder. "Let go!" I tried to jerk away, but he hung on.

"Karin? What are you doing in this place?"

I stared at him. "Eric?"

He was standing in the middle of the street, fully dressed, with that damned camera over his shoulder. He had popped up like some genie. Again. But I could not have cared less what he was doing, if he was taking lewd photos or performing indecent acts with these poor women. "Let me go!"

"Not here."

"That man stole my dust, and he took Will!"

Eric's eyes went even wider than they already were. "Then come on."

I could hear the sounds of an altercation already. Thumps, thuds, cursing, a woman's scream.

A beloved voice pitched at a bellow. "Goddamn it, Lawson. You son of a bitch." And a deafening crash.

Eric was moving far too slowly. I jerked away again, and was successful this time. I could hear more cursing, this time from behind me as I tore down the street, the mud sucking at my boots, toward my betrothed.

* * *

"You're sure you're all right?" I couldn't help asking him.

"Yes, for the thousandth time, I'm fine." Will winced. "My head hurts."

My breath drew in.

"Not like that," he added in a reassuring tone.

I wasn't reassured. "Come sit down."

The exasperated Mountie had finally insisted that we all, including Lawson, Mamie, Eric, and the two soiled doves still complaining about the damage to their cribs, go with him to the shabby cabin serving as the Dawson headquarters for the Royal Northwest Mounted Police.

Lawson, who was still muttering about being ganged up on, had been slumped into a chair by the Mountie who'd half-carried him there. Will was leaning on me rather more heavily than I think he realized, but he was upright.

He'd managed to get himself loose from the ropes around his wrists before Lawson got back to him, and pitched the nasty man through the window the women were complaining about. Before Lawson could get to his feet again, Mamie had jumped in and finished the job by beaning him with a chamberpot.

I had not thanked her for that yet, even though I knew she hadn't done it for us. I didn't know everything he forced her to do to pay him for his so-called help, and I did not want to. But it was all past her now. She stood in the middle of the room, her skirt stained with the contents of that chamberpot and her head held high.

I finally managed to nudge Will into another chair. Surprisingly, he went without a struggle. I went to stand in front of Mamie, who glanced down at me in surprise.

"Thank you."

She smiled. "Go back to your husband."

"He isn't —"

"He will be, won't he?"

I nodded firmly. "As soon as it can be arranged."

"Go see to him, then."

We did not have to stay there long. Will was acting in self-defense, the Mountie told his superior, and the rope burns on Will's wrists backed him up, as did I. I was torn between staying to help Mamie in her defense and taking my man back to the hospital to see what he'd done to himself this time.

Eric came over to me. "Go."

"But Mamie?"

"She saved my partner's life. I will make sure she is treated fairly."

So he still considered us his partners. I suppose I should not have been surprised. Eric Hoel had some very odd ideas. "Thank you."

"Now go. Get Will away from here. If he gets into another kafoffle it will kill him."

I sighed. "My gold —" My bag of dust had vanished in the melee, and the Mountie had not been all that interested in helping me find it. I suspected one of the soiled doves was very happy right about now.

Eric's gaze sharpened. "Do not worry about that. Now go."

It wasn't as if I had much of a choice. I went back to Will, and we made our way, rather more slowly than he would have liked, I think, back to the hospital.

CHAPTER 26

As it turned out, much to the relief of all concerned including Father Judge, who had been the one to call for the Mountie, Will did not incur any further damage to himself by his adventures, so at least that part of our plans was not set back.

"We'll be all right," he told me. "I'll find work, and we'll be on the first boat out of here in the spring."

"I'm sorry."

"For what?"

I held out my empty hands. "Losing the dust."

He took them. "You did it to save me."

Sheepishly I smiled at him. "I should have known you wouldn't need me to."

His fingers tightened on mine. "It doesn't matter. Ready?"

No need to ask for what. "Oh, yes."

And that is how I ended up married after all, in spite of everything, and glad of it. Father Judge performed the ceremony in the canvas-roofed church next to the hospital, and Mamie, wearing a clean skirt, and Eric were witnesses. After Will had kissed me to seal our vows, Eric stepped forward.

"I would like to kiss the bride," he said, with far more solemnity than I'd thought him capable of. "And to give you your wedding gift." From the pack he had set on the first bench serving as pew he pulled two small sacks.

"Oh!" I said. I recognized the first one.

"I found it," Mamie said smugly. Found, I imagine, was not the appropriate term, but I wasn't going to quibble.

"That she did, and gave it to me for safekeeping." He handed it to me. The weight was comforting in my hands, and I smiled up at Will, then said, "Mamie, you deserve at least part of this."

But she was shaking her head. "I have been rewarded, never you mind." She turned to – admire? Eric, who was putting the other sack into Will's hands.

It was about half again as big as the one I held.

"You did not think," Eric told him, "that I was not going to compensate you both for all that you have done for me?"

"I, I –"

"I hired you, Will. We had an agreement, did we not? And while what you did was not quite what I hired you to do, you have more than earned this."

He turned to me. "And while we did not have a formal contract, Karin – Mrs. McManis," he added, his expression amusingly satisfied, "You have far more than paid me back for your passage on the *Tacoma Belle*. If it were not for the two of you, I would not have had Samson and his ladies to sell for almost ten times what I paid for them, nor had the luxury of time to take the photographs that have made my fortune, while you did the hard work."

"F-fortune?"

"Enough to travel back home in style, and provide for my family for a good long time."

"Oh." I was speechless. So was Will, apparently.

He laughed, that wonderful guffaw that I had first heard back in the hold of the *Tacoma Belle*. "Now let me take your wedding picture, and then we must hurry, or we will miss our boat."

He moved the camera into place before Will found his voice. "We?"

I found mine as the shutter snapped. "Mamie?"

She shook her head. "I'm staying here. I think I could like it, now."

I went over and hugged her. She was stiff for a moment, then hugged me back. "Thank you. And good luck."

"You, too."

As he packed the camera back up, Eric said to Will, "You did say you wished to go home,"

"Well, yes, but we don't have tickets."

"That should not be a problem."

Will hefted the sack in his hand. "No, I suppose not." He looked at me. "Got anything you want to take with you?"

"Yes," I told him, and went to pack up my sewing machine.

* * *

I will not bore you with the details of our honeymoon trip. It was long, and tedious, but not in the least strenuous, for which I was grateful. Aboard a battered little steamer called the *Hannah* we floated down the great Yukon River to the port of St. Michael, past the endless rust, brown, and gold of the autumn wilderness. It was punctuated only by the occasional Indian village or abandoned mining camp, and the enormous piles of wood tended by men scruffy by even my new standards, who waved as we went past.

I call it a honeymoon trip, but I would have preferred one much less crowded. The *Hannah* had been announced as the last ship to head Outside before the river froze up, and she was crammed full. Most of her passengers were men who had sold their outfits in Dawson to pay for their tickets, and who were headed home from their great adventure empty-handed.

Not many made their fortunes in the Klondike. Most who did arrived and staked their claims long before the great rush of 1898. And most of those who did make fortunes won and lost them without so much as a second thought, as if they were so many wooden nickels, and not enough money to fund a life of ease Outside for the rest of their lives.

Our two small sacks of dust were not a fortune by anyone's standards, but they were enough. As for me, I had made a fortune of another kind, and I was content.

In the days it took for us to float downriver, it was my pleasure to watch Will complete the recovery of his former strength and self-possession. I had known he would, but I think he had to prove to himself – and who better to prove it on than that villain Lawson? – that he could.

Or maybe it was one of the several other momentous events of our wedding day that did it. It did not matter which one, as long as it did.

* * *

The cold, sea-damp wind scudded through the dilapidated village of St. Michael, perched on the edge of the great delta of the Yukon River, as we disembarked. I shivered. Ocean air felt so much colder than the dry chill of the interior. Will smiled down at me and wrapped an arm around me. I smiled back up at him. "Any excuse?"

"Something like that." Then he glanced over at Eric, and frowned. "Where are you going? I thought we were going to see about a ship out of this place."

Eric shrugged. I knew that sheepish look well. So did Will, if the tightening of his arm meant anything at all. "You're not sailing with us, are you?"

Eric waved a hand towards the general vicinity of the water. "I thought I might take more plates first. There is a rumor of gold across the sound, at a place called Nome."

"But what about your wife?" I asked. "I thought you wrote her. If you delay too long, you'll be stuck here for another winter." I glanced around at the miserable huddle of shacks and shivered again. Compared to St. Michael, Dawson was a metropolis.

"She will understand." I supposed she would. Any woman married to Eric must have the patience of Penelope waiting for Odysseus.

"Well," said Will. "Are you telling us good-bye, then?"

Eric chuckled. "I suppose I am."

"Were you going to say anything?" I demanded. "Or were you just going to vanish again?"

The sheepish look returned to his face, and his mouth opened, then shut.

"You were. Well, not this time, you old rascal." I ducked out of Will's warm hold, and stepped forward to wrap my arms around Eric. He stood stock still for a moment, then I felt his arms come around my shoulders.

A moment later I lifted my head and stepped back, feeling a bit more unsteady than I should have. I cleared my throat and looked up at him. His face would have made me laugh if I hadn't been afraid laughing would lead to tears. A more nonplussed-looking expression I have never seen.

Will *was* laughing, drat the man. But he sobered when he took Eric's hand and shook it. "Good luck."

"Thank you."

I added, "And take care of yourself. Don't stay up here forever."

He smiled at me. "I will not."

Will said, "If you're ever in Montana, look us up."

Eric nodded. "I will."

"Well," said Will. "I guess we should see about our passage."

"Yes," Eric said. "Safe voyage."

And that was the last we ever saw of Eric Hoel. Once, years later, Will brought home a book of his photographs, and oh, the memories that book brought back. I will say this for him. For all the man was as undependable as the weather, he had a God-given talent. I am proud to have been his partner.

* * *

We found berths on the *Alaska King*, bound for Seattle. I spent the few hours of the voyage when I was not in our overcrowded cabin feeling too ill to leave my bunk trying to reason with Will against going to see my parents when we arrived. My arguments were weak, because I must admit my heart was against me as well. Not that I missed them, but now that I was safely married there was no reason not to at least let them know I was alive.

If indeed I still was when we arrived. The North Pacific was anything but pacific that late in the season, and the ship pitched and rolled and bounced around like a corked bottle in a sloshing tub. It was all I could do to keep any food at all down. Will, drat him, took to the ocean as if he was a born sailor, but at least he had the decency to do what he could for me. It was little enough. Nothing short of dry land was going to make any sort of difference, so far as I was concerned.

Yet the closer we came to Seattle the more I thought perhaps I could stand to go on a bit farther. Around the world, even. Anything would be better than facing my parents after all this time. They could not do anything to me, I kept telling myself. I was a legally married woman, and no longer their possession. No longer theirs to push about and treat as if I had no mind of my own. No longer theirs to demand every penny I earned.

Will knew I was worried. I don't think he truly understood why. But after we disembarked into the crowds of Seattle, I wished for nothing more than to take a street car straight to the train station and purchase tickets for Montana.

It was all too strange, after over a year in the North, and all too familiar, all at the same time. The city was utterly overwhelming in a way that I had forgotten completely.

"So, which way is Ballard?" Will asked.

I had to ask one more time. "Do we have to?"

"I'm trying to think about how I'd feel if I was your parents," Will said. "For all they know, you're dead."

It was the same argument we'd had for days now. I tried to swallow my heart back down out of my throat. "All right. But we're not staying, not a moment longer than necessary."

Will nodded. I don't know if he was agreeing with me or if he simply didn't know what he was getting into. "Lead the way."

The little frame house on Eriksson Street appeared exactly the same as it had the last time I'd seen it, over a year ago. The green paint seemed brighter, somehow, through the warm autumn drizzle, and I could tell my mother had already started putting the vegetable garden to bed for the winter. I hesitated one last time.

"Come on," said Will, taking a better grip on my arm. "It can't be half as bad as you're imagining."

I took a deep breath, but before we were halfway up the steps, the front door flew open.

And, as it turned out, Will was right. It wasn't anywhere close to as bad as what I had been imagining. We ended up staying for almost a week.

* * *

"Must you go?" It was only the fourth or fifth time my mother had asked me the question that morning. I don't think she realized we were serious about leaving until she saw me packing.

"Will's family is in Montana, Mama," I said patiently. It still astonished me that she cared. That Father cared beyond who he could marry me off to. Never mind that he approved of Will in spite of the fact that he wasn't Norwegian. The dust helped, but it wasn't only the gold.

It was, as Will told me with a grin, the fact that he'd been able to tie me down at all. "What he doesn't understand is the trick isn't tying you down, it's letting you loose."

That had deserved a kiss. And more. Just remembering it made me smile.

But Mama was still protesting. "He could find work here."

No, there had never been any question of where we would live. Will wanted to go home, to a place he'd told me so much about it felt like home to me, too, even if I hadn't been there yet.

"A wife goes with her husband, Mama, you know that." And thank goodness for that, I thought. "I'm not going nearly as far as you did."

She let out a sigh. "No, you are not."

"Train tickets aren't that expensive."

She brightened. "No, they are not."

I almost said, you could come see us, but better not to put that idea into her head. She would come up with it on her own soon enough.

Will stuck his head through the doorway. "Ready to go?"

I exhaled in relief. "I think so."

Mama went up to Will, standing toe to toe with him. "You will bring her back sometimes, will you not?"

"Yes, Mrs. Myre. I won't let her run away again."

Mama stepped back, then forward again to hug her son-in-law, surprising him into a laugh. I couldn't help thinking it served him right for making them love him almost as much as I did. "I suppose that will have to do."

She turned to me. "Write."

"Yes, Mama."

"And do not ever frighten us like that again."

"Yes, Mama." It was the one thing I did regret. Now.

"We're going to miss our train," Will said, and hefted my new trunk, filled with my trousseau, which had been waiting patiently for me all this time. "Your dad's waiting with the wagon."

I hugged Mama, and took a deep breath. "I love you, Mama."

That surprised a laugh out of her. "I love you, too, *skatten min*. Go, if you must."

Will was already gone. I followed him out the door. The house seemed to cling to me again as it once had, but the feeling was not the same. No longer a prison, but my childhood home.

EPILOGUE

The train pulled into the station at Cinnabar, Montana, just north of the Yellowstone National Park, on the afternoon of a chilly, damp October day. Will had wired to Helena from the station in Spokane, and changed our tickets upon discovering his parents had not left their photography shop for the winter yet.

That was the first train change, and after we left Spokane we began climbing the second mountain range since we'd left Seattle. This one was much larger and went on and on, past lakes and along rivers buried between steep slopes. Those slopes were covered with the oddest golden trees. They looked like pines except for the color but Will said they were called larches. The stations were few and far between. We crossed the Continental Divide, or so Will said, in the middle of the night.

Our second change had been after noon the next day in a small town called Livingston, out in the middle of brown rolling grassland and tree-tipped hills, with yet more snow-capped mountains ranging to the south. We'd had a wait until the westbound train came, bearing a few more passengers for the spur line. That had been a short ride, only a couple of hours, but with many short stops along the way. Now we were here, with those mountains towering over us to the east and west, at a station plunked down seemingly in the middle of nowhere.

I looked up at Will, feeling more than a bit lost.

He smiled down at me. "It's a bit different from what you're used to," he said, and gazed around looking satisfied as we stepped out onto the platform. The other passengers were shepherded off onto stagecoaches, their luggage stacked onto wheeled wooden carts. I couldn't help feeling a bit stranded. At least it wasn't raining, although the overcast sky looked as if it wanted to. I smoothed my new skirt. It still felt odd to be wearing one again, even after almost two weeks.

"Come on. Let's go find 'em." He took me by the hand.

I hung back. "What about our luggage?"

"It'll be fine there for now."

I looked dubiously at my trunk and our other bags where the men had piled them in a corner of the platform, then, butterflies swooping and diving in my stomach as they hadn't since Ballard, I trailed along with him to the steps at its end, down them, and into the station.

"That's strange," Will said, staring around at the empty waiting room. "They know we're coming. It's not like them to be late."

"Perhaps they mixed the date up?" Or perhaps they were not as forgiving as my parents had surprised me by being. Will had not run away, though. He had gone with his parents' knowledge. His father had even given his approval, but his mother had not. I wondered what we were going to do if she did not forgive him. Or if they did not approve of me.

"I'll ask if we can use the telephone –" He glanced out the window, and broke into a huge grin. "No. There they are. Come on."

Back outside, down more steps to the ground. A buggy, pulled by a pair of gray horses, stopped at the hitching rail. Suddenly I recognized the passengers from Will's photograph. A tall, lanky man with sandy hair and spectacles, and a shorter, plump woman, her bun graying from a mahogany color very familiar to me, climbed down. Their smiles reassured me, although I could see their looks of surprise before they hid them.

"Will, didn't you tell them?" I began, but the man turned to swing a child from the rear seat. A blackhaired little boy who couldn't be more than six years old. He didn't appear to want to get down. He was hanging back like me, I thought sheepishly. Frightened? Or perhaps just shy.

"You did not tell me you had a brother," I said to Will, who had stopped dead in his tracks.

Just then the boy peeked around Mrs. McManis's skirts. His eyes widened, and he darted past them.

Dust flying up behind his little boots, he pelted towards us. No, towards me, I realized suddenly. His grin, so like Will's, was a mile wide.

"Mama!"

AFTERWORD

Thank you for reading *True Gold*. I hope you enjoyed it. Reviews help other readers find books. I appreciate all reviews, whether positive or negative.

Would you like to know when my next book is available? You can sign up for my new release email list at mmjustus.com, or follow me on on Facebook at https://www.facebook.com/M.M.Justusauthor or on Twitter @mmjustus.

The character of Eric Hoel, and his goats, are based on a real photographer, Eric Hegg, and his animals. He took the photograph on the cover of this book, and created one of the best photographic records of the Klondike Gold Rush in existence. I don't know if his real companions were as tolerant of the glass plates or the goats, let alone Eric himself, as Will and Karin were of my Eric, but someone certainly must have been to allow him to do what he did.

If you're interested in reading more about the actual history behind this story, please go to the Pathfinders page on my website at mmjustus.com, where I have put together links to Mr. Hegg's work and a bibliography of books and websites about the the Klondike Gold Rush, as well as a collection of photos of locations in the story.

If you're interested in finding out more about Will's parents and their adventures, please take a look at the first Time in Yellowstone novel, *Repeating History*. For more about Will and Karin, take a look at the short story "Homesick." For more about that little boy in the epilogue, please turn the page for the first chapter in the third novel in the series, *Finding Home*. All are available in electronic and print versions from many vendors including your local bookstore.

FINDING HOME

No one ever talks about being left behind, but James McManis knows that one in spades. Not knowing quite why, he felt abandoned all his life. And when his wife died in childbirth, he clung to his son with everything he had.

But the harder James held on over the years, the more Chuck fought what his father wanted for him. Until finally one day the boy slips through his fingers and, in the aftermath of a horrific disaster, vanishes altogether. When James discovers what really happened to the son he tried so hard to protect it turns his whole world upside down.

James needs to learn more. About his son. About himself. About his past, and his future. But what if the knowledge he gains proves everything he thought real a lie?

CHAPTER 1

August 17, 1959

The boy took off at first light, before the beam from the streetlight shut off for the day. James heard the racket as the motorcycle roared down the street. He rolled over onto his back between the sheets and wearily rubbed his eyes. He'd strictly forbidden Chuck to leave the house today. As far as James was concerned, his son was grounded until doomsday. Or until James managed to talk the board of regents into letting him back into Colorado State University again, whichever came first. After the phone calls he'd made yesterday, he suspected doomsday would win that particular race.

The boy was taking his grandfather's death hard. But then so had James, and he wasn't ruining his life over it. Granted, he wasn't taking his father's death as hard as when he'd lost his mother five years ago, but he'd always had the closest bond with her, from the day they'd met, or so she'd told him. James had been five years old, and he didn't remember a time before that, before she'd loved him. He wished he didn't remember a time after she was gone.

He sighed and threw back the covers, sat up, and put his head in his hands and his feet on the cold floor. He supposed it didn't matter where the boy had gone. He wouldn't be gone long. Where else would he go? James ought to know, but he'd been busy, and he and Chuck had been like ships in the night since the boy'd gone off to college. *Since long before he went off to college.* Well, now James had to get him back there, once he came home.

If his son was to have a successful career and take over the business one day, he had to at least get his degree first.

* * *

James had showered, dressed for the office, and was halfway through breakfast when the phone rang. The housekeeper was clattering around in the kitchen, and she wouldn't answer it when he was in the house, anyway, so out he went to the hall to pick it up.

"Hello?"

"Mr. McManis?"

James sighed. He'd had more than enough of his father's lawyer yesterday, going over the will, to last him a good long time. "Pritchard. What can I do for you this morning?"

"I'm glad you changed your mind."

A niggling dread ran through him, but no, Pritchard wouldn't go against his wishes. And he'd made those clear. "About what?"

"Chuck came by to pick up the paperwork for the ashes. And the money for the trip."

The niggle churned into full-blown anger. James took a deep breath, let it out on a whoosh when it didn't do anything to calm him. "You should have called me first."

"I didn't see any need to." The idiot sounded downright smug. "The will was clear."

"He's my child. You had no right to go against my wishes on this."

"He's nearly twenty-one, James." The man treated him as if *he* were twenty. Just because that's how old James had been when they'd first met was no excuse. Besides, he'd been carrying a 3.8 grade point average and a job at the time. Acting like the adult he was. Unlike Chuck.

"Twenty going on twelve. He's got work to do here. He doesn't need to be taking off for parts unknown on a fool's errand."

"Yellowstone is hardly parts unknown."

"That's not the point. The boy-"

"He's not a boy. And he's grieving. You saw it. Give him a few days to go to the park to say good-bye. You can shove him back into college when he gets home." Pritchard paused, as if doubting he should put his oar in, but went ahead and did it anyway. "You could use the time apart, too."

James bit his tongue, even though it went against every instinct he had. No point in letting loose at the man. He was only doing his job. *Going over a parent's head on the orders of a dead man. Call it what it is.* Right then, no matter how much James had loved his adoptive father, he wanted him back so he could smack him on the head.

"Look. The park's where he grew up-"

"He grew up here," James said flatly.

"All right, the park's where he spent a good chunk of his childhood. It's where he spent time with his grandparents. Let him go say good-bye to them there. Is it really any skin off your nose if he skips town for a few days?"

No, it wasn't. Except for the principle of the thing. *You're the one who left him with them until he was old enough to go to school, and sent him up there every summer afterwards. If you didn't want him to care for them more than he does for you, you should have spent more time with him.*

"It's none of your business whether I go after him or not."

"But you won't."

James sighed. "Why do you care?"

Pritchard didn't answer his question, just made the niceties and hung up.

James went back to his now-cold breakfast, but it had lost its appeal. He ate anyway, and refilled his coffee, and went through the rest of his normal morning routine. He paid so little attention he was a bit surprised an hour later to find himself sitting in his high-rise office with its view of the front range of the Rockies through the floor-to-ceiling windows.

That was where mountains should be, he'd always thought. Close enough to be beautiful, far enough away to be safe. It was one of the things he'd loved about Denver from the day he'd arrived here for college, forty-seven years ago. He'd been eighteen, out to set the world on fire. And he supposed he had accomplished it in his own way, to judge by this office, the thriving accounting business, the house just off Broadway, the brand-new Lincoln every few years, the season tickets to the opera and the symphony. His client list was full of movers and shakers, his attendance in demand at charitable events. The only thing lacking was a graceful wife on his arm, but his beloved Catherine was irreplaceable.

All of which was a far cry from the cabin at Old Faithful, issued to his father as ranger family quarters, where he'd grown up, or the log cabin in West Yellowstone, not much bigger or in better repair, where his parents had retired. He'd been able to help them by then, but they wouldn't take the kind of help he'd wanted to give.

Nor did Chuck. All the boy wanted, James thought, was to go backward. Back to the boonies James had escaped from. For him. In spite of everything James had done to teach him better.

James sighed at his tidy, and full, to-do file. He didn't have time to go haring off to that godforsaken place. Time enough to try again when the boy came back. And he would come back. He had nowhere else to go.

The intercom buzzed. In the meantime, he had work to do.

* * *

He tried not to think about Chuck all day, and mostly succeeded. Tried not to let his anger loose at how things had gone badly, although that was a harder battle. Neither his employees nor the clients he saw that day deserved to be treated poorly, and they deserved his full attention as well.

But shoving his personal problems to the back of his mind all day proved wearing. Out of practice, James supposed, as he locked up his office and headed for home. It had been some time since he'd had to work at it so hard. A long time since he'd been glad for the workday to end, too. He liked his work. To spend his days creating order out of chaos, working with numbers that always responded with the same answers when you asked the same questions. Reliable, that's what they were, and James respected reliability. So did the clients he worked with. They depended on him to make those numbers work for them, and to be acceptable to the government as well as their bottom lines, and that's what he did.

Too bad the boy had to be a throwback to chaos. He should have arrived at the park by now. If he hadn't wrecked his cursed motorcycle on the way.

* * *

The house was quiet when he got home. Empty. Mrs. May was gone for the day, leaving his supper in the oven for him instead of waiting till he got home before she left. He grimaced. Her absence was clear commentary on the shouting match she'd not have been able to help overhearing yesterday. She was inordinately fond of the boy and took his side in everything, not that her vote counted. It was one reason James had kept her on for the last fifteen years.

Supper could wait a few more minutes. One thing he knew from yesterday's meeting with Pritchard was the arrangements for where Chuck would be staying for the three nights his father's will had provided for. The desk clerk at the Old Faithful Inn was pleasant and informative. James hung up the phone, relieved to know his worst nightmare hadn't come true today, so he wouldn't have to scour the roads between Denver and northwest Wyoming for a mangled motorcycle alongside the road with a dead body flung into the underbrush nearby.

His motorcycle was Chuck's pride and joy, and the only thing the boy had worked for with his own hands and brain, money earned from summer jobs and work after school as soon as he could drive. James had been so proud to see him ambitious about anything, he hadn't had the heart to fight him for something more sensible. Safer. His mistake. It had given the boy a sense of independence he wasn't mature enough for yet.

Catherine would have approved of it. But Catherine wasn't here. And hadn't been here since she'd died giving Chuck life. All the labor she'd gone through, labor that had killed her. *But she still would have approved.*

He was used to the peace and quiet, and it should have been soothing. It was hard to keep from thinking about what the boy was doing this evening, though. Scattering ashes. The thought was repugnant. What was wrong with a nice plot at Cherry Hills? A place he could have gone to pay his respects and leave flowers at his parents' graves, the way he'd always done for Catherine. He wasn't about to traipse off up to the park every time he felt the need.

He ate, although the meal was a bit dried out by the time he got to it. He left his dishes in the sink for Mrs. May in the morning, mixed himself a martini, and settled down in his easy chair for the evening. Tried to read, discovered he couldn't concentrate, mixed himself a second drink and turned on the television, realized after half an hour that he had no idea what he'd been watching but his glass was empty again.

Resisted making a third, and instead listened to the clock in the hall chiming hour after hour, till it was a decent time to go to bed. He was grieving, too, in his own way, he understood after a while, realizing his thoughts had gone to his parents, and to his memories. He'd taken it out on the boy, perhaps. Blaming him for something that wasn't his fault.

Let Chuck get his grief out of his system in his own way while James did the same. It wasn't as if they couldn't resolve their differences when he got back. He had to let the boy grow up sometime.

At last it was late enough to go to bed. He set his glass in the sink next to his supper dishes, and went upstairs.

* * *

He woke early again, when he heard the sound of a motorcycle on the street through the open window. It took his muzzy brain a moment to realize it couldn't be Chuck so soon, but by then he couldn't get back to sleep. He heard the milkman's bottles rattle as they landed on the back step, the newspaper thud on the front porch. When Mrs. May's car pulled into the driveway just as his alarm clock went off, he swung himself out of bed and began another day.

The newspaper sat next to his plate when he came down for breakfast.

"QUAKE JOLTS WESTERN STATES. HEBGEN DAM OPEN, VACATIONERS HURT" And further down the page, "TEMBLOR CRUMPLES MOUNTAINS IN DEATH, DESTRUCTION SWEEP" And, last and worst of all, below both of them, "PARK SCENE OF FEAR, CONFUSION Single Thought: 'Let's Get Out'" The headlines, in heavy black ink, and their articles, taking up the entire front page of the Rocky Mountain Post, stopped his breath. He didn't even realize he'd fallen into his chair until the dishes rattled from the force of his landing.

He stared at the paper, unable to touch it, unable to read any further as the words below the headlines blurred. He blinked, forcing himself to focus. The Hebgen Dam, right. His grandfather had taken him fishing at Hebgen Lake on occasion when he was a boy. It was just west of the park, less than an hour away as the raven flew from where his son was, this very moment.

244

He took a deep breath. "Mrs. May?" He was amazed at how calm his voice sounded, right then. He felt like he was standing in the middle of the earthquake himself, as if it were jolting him from the inside out.

She stuck her head through the door from the kitchen. "Yes, sir?"

"Did you see this?"

"Yes, sir."

God, she was cold. And he'd thought she loved the boy. "Please call the office for me. Tell Alice I've had an emergency and will be out of town for a few days. She'll need to reschedule my appointments through Thursday- no, through the rest of the week."

No, she wasn't cold. The relief on her face was palpable, even to him. So was the rare approval in her eyes.

"Yes, sir." She strode across the dining room towards the hall, then stopped in the doorway. "You bring him home. Safe."

James nodded, grabbed the paper, and strode to the car.

* * *

He was halfway to Laramie before it dawned on him he probably should have changed his clothing, and perhaps packed a suitcase, before he left. The suit and dress shoes he was wearing were not what he'd call appropriate for a rescue mission into a disaster zone, even though his jacket and tie were now in the back seat and his shirt sleeves were rolled up to the elbows. Well, he wasn't about to stop now. He'd manage. He and the boy would be on their way home this time tomorrow, anyway. He'd pick up a toothbrush somewhere, and hang the rest of it.

The radio was full of news of the quake. It had been felt as far away as Spokane and Salt Lake City. The Hebgen dam had ruptured, then no, it hadn't. People were being rescued by helicopter from a landslide caused by the quake outside the park. The death toll was still rising. There'd been a second landslide, this one in the park, and the phone lines were down. The town of West Yellowstone had been all but destroyed. The town of Ennis was being evacuated due to potential flooding. The roads were closed into the park, nobody allowed to enter or leave. Well, they'd see about trying to keep *him* out. The Gallatin and Madison County sheriffs both asked people to stay away from the Madison Canyon area. That was all right, he wasn't going there. The park superintendent came on the air and asked people to stay away from the park as well.. *Sorry, Mr. Garrison, I can't. My son's in there.*

The Lincoln ate up the miles. The only stops he made were for gas and, once, to grab something to eat when he realized he hadn't put anything in his stomach since the night before. He bought a perfectly wretched hamburger from a greasy spoon in Lander, wrapped it in a paper napkin, and ate it one-handed as he drove on.

The radio faded in and out, giving him too much time to worry before he could tune to another station from the next town, and the next, and the next. The last one came out of Jackson Hole late in the afternoon, and lasted until the Tetons blocked the signal at last, not far from Yellowstone's south entrance.

A steady stream of cars poured out, but not as many as he would have expected. He supposed most of the tourists were already gone and these were just the stragglers. He reached the gate only to find a line going in, too. So much for asking people to stay out. He wondered if they were all on missions like his own, or if they were just ghoulish curiosity seekers, but if there'd have been room to get by he'd have been five miles down the road by the time he finally reached the entrance kiosk.

"Good evening, sir. Welcome to Yellowstone. You should know, because of the earthquake, some of the roads are closed."

James fumbled with his wallet. "Can I get to Old Faithful?" He shoved the entrance fee at the ranger, who took it.

"Yes, but the West Entrance-"

"Thanks. I'm not here on vacation. My son is here."

"I'm sure he's fine, sir. As soon as the phone lines are back up they'll be letting people call through-"

He wouldn't have stopped in the first place if he'd had a choice. James put his foot on the gas and roared off into the deepening shadows. *No, he won't be fine,* he thought, *but only because I'm going to ground him forever after I find him myself.*

* * *

He'd never have known anything happened to look at the place so far, even if he was still a couple of hours from Old Faithful. But the park looked just as it had the last time he'd seen it, the last time he'd brought Chuck to stay with his grandparents here for the summer, five years ago. Miles and miles of monotonous endless forest, every lodgepole pine straight as a toothpick and indistinguishable from all the others. The road was the same, too, no buckles, no cracks. He was going faster than was safe, but one of the reasons he'd always bought Lincolns as soon as he could afford them was for their handling. He didn't see a single animal, which was just as well. Probably all scared back into the woods where they belonged.

Lake Yellowstone, enormous and ringed with jagged mountains, gleamed in the fading light behind him as he made the last turn toward Old Faithful and began the climb over the Continental Divide. He had to slow down now, to navigate the twists and turns. The Lincoln growled as he wrenched the wheel back and forth.

He'd made the two crossings of the divide and was on the downward slope when he saw the first crack in the pavement in the beam from his headlights. Not much to look at, a long, narrow split that caused the outer edge of the asphalt to tilt slightly. If this was the kind of damage all the panic was about-

The next crack was a bit wider, and ran diagonally off the road into the forest, its path marked with trees tilted at crazy angles. He shrugged the sight off as the car bounced over it and several more like it and kept going.

Even when he came around the last corner and saw the buildings at Old Faithful, it didn't seem that awful. A number of emergency vehicles were scattered about, but no one seemed to be doing anything. People were wandering around. Some were even seated at the benches at Old Faithful, for all the world as if it was a perfectly normal evening.

James let out a deep breath and swung the car into a surprisingly empty parking space in front of the Inn. But he'd no more than opened the door when a man in uniform - not a ranger - walked up.

"I'm sorry, sir, but you can't park here. We need to keep this area clear for emergency vehicles."

"I'm just here to pick someone up. I'll be back and gone before you know it."

"I'm sorry, sir-"

But James was out and past him before the man could finish whatever he had to say.

The tremor hit when he was halfway up the stone steps to the porte cochere at the front of the Inn. He grabbed the metal pipe railing, but the shaking was over almost before it started. Well, and that wasn't so bad, either. *What a fuss.* He headed on up, but when he reached the door, it was blocked by another man in uniform.

"I'm sorry, sir, but no one may enter the building. It's too dangerous."

Dangerous? Nothing even seemed to be damaged. "I'm looking for my son."

"The building has been evacuated. No one is in there."

James waited. When the man did not continue, he could not keep the exasperation out of his voice. "Where were they evacuated *to*?"

"Excuse us." The door swung open, and several more men strode out, their clothing covered with dust, hard hats on their heads. Their boots muddy. *Muddy?* "Get out of the way. Another rock just fell from the fireplace."

James caught a glimpse of the interior of the massive lobby, stones scattered helter skelter across the now deeply gouged wooden floor, dust still settling in great clouds, water running across the floor. *Water?* The man James had been trying to pry information out of grabbed James by the arm and pulled him back. James shook the hand off and turned on the man.

"Where were the people staying here evacuated *to*, young man!"

The fellow blinked. "Most of them went to the lodge, sir."

"Thank you," James flung over his shoulder.

"Sir, you still need to move your car-"

* * *

The people milling about were not acting like tourists after all, James realized as he strode the few hundred yards down the road to the lodge, his eyes scanning them fruitlessly for the boy. They weren't admiring the scenery or wasting their time waiting for Old Faithful to go off. He guessed they were the ones stupid enough to hang around instead of leaving like sensible people after the place blew up on them last night. Even at this hour after dark they didn't seem to have the sense to go indoors.

Although he supposed indoors probably didn't seem very safe to them right now. The glimpse of the damage he'd seen inside the Inn would have made him dubious about going indoors in this place if he had the time to think about it or care.

The lodge looked the same as ever, and there weren't any emergency vehicles in front of *it*. People, none of them Chuck - good grief, where *was* he? - coming and going as if everything were perfectly normal. Until he went inside.

Controlled pandemonium was what it looked like. Crowds milling, no blond bespectacled kids sticking up above the rest. The place looked like a disaster shelter, and, indeed, a table with a Red Cross sign was set up in a corner of the big room, next to the closed photographic shop. It looked completely incongruous, but perhaps they knew where people were.

James strode over and caught the attention of one of the three men behind the table.

"May I help you?" He looked and sounded like a clerk. It was oddly comforting.

James shook the misplaced feeling off. "I'm looking for my son."

The man pulled a box of file folders closer to him. "What is his last name?"

"McManis. M-C-M-A-N-I-S."

The man selected a folder labeled with a big black M, pulled a sheet with a list of names out of it, and scanned them. "We don't have anyone by that name listed."

It had to be a mistake. "He was staying at the Inn. Arrived last night."

"I'm sorry, sir. No one by that name has registered with us."

His irritation was beginning to feel just a bit like panic. "His first name is Chuck."

"It's all by last name, sir. He's not on the list."

James took a deep breath. "What does that mean?"

"It means he did not do as the park service and the Red Cross asked everyone who was here during the quake to do."

Of course not. "Which was?"

"To come here and give us his name and tell us what he was going to do, whether he was leaving or staying, and where he could be contacted." The man paused, obviously taking in whatever James looked like by that point. James didn't want to think about what he looked like. Or care. It was just like the boy. Heaven only knew where he'd gone by now. "For just this purpose."

"What?"

"The purpose of the registration process."

"Yes, I know." It wasn't the man's fault Chuck was so irresponsible. James managed to calm his voice. "Thank you. I'm sorry."

"What is your name, sir?"

"What? Oh. James McManis. M-C-M-" The man waved him to stop, and James did, feeling a bit foolish.

"Where will you be, sir? In case your son does show up?"

"Looking for him."

"Where should we tell him to go?"

James snorted. "Chain him to the table."

The man looked sympathetic. "I'll do my best."

"Thanks. I'll keep checking back."

"That sounds like an excellent idea."

James turned away and sighed. *Now what?* It was closing in on 10 pm, and his plan hadn't gone anywhere past finding Chuck and locking him in the car for the trip back home.

He hadn't the first clue where to look next.

Available on Amazon and from other retailers.

ABOUT THE AUTHOR

M.M. Justus's first visit to Yellowstone National Park was at age four, where it snowed on the Fourth of July. She spent most of her childhood summers in the back seat of a car, traveling with her parents to almost every national park west of the Mississippi and a great many places in between.

She holds degrees in British and American literature and history and library science, and a certificate in museum studies. In her other life, she's held jobs as far flung as hog farm bookkeeper, music school secretary, professional dilettante (aka reference librarian), and museum curator, all of which are fair fodder for her fiction.

Her other interests include quilting, gardening, meteorology, and the travel bug she inherited from her father, including multiple trips back to her favorite Grand Geyser and the rest of Yellowstone. She lives on the rainy side of the Cascade mountains in Washington state within easy reach of her other favorite national park, Mt. Rainier.

Please visit her website and blog at http://mmjustus.com, on Facebook at https://www.facebook.com/M.M.Justusauthor or on Twitter @mmjustus.

BOOKS BY M.M. JUSTUS

Much Ado in Montana

Cross-Country: Adventures Alone Across America and Back

UNEARTHLY NORTHWEST

Sojourn

TIME IN YELLOWSTONE

Repeating History
True Gold
"Homesick"
Finding Home

Carbon
River
Press

.

Made in the USA
Columbia, SC
15 November 2017